TROUBLE

TROUBLE

Michael Gilbert

1817

HARPER & ROW, PUBLISHERS, New York
Cambridge, Philadelphia, San Francisco, Washington
London, Mexico City, São Paulo, Singapore, Sydney

This is a work of fiction and all the characters in it are imaginary. A number of actual organisations and institutions are mentioned but no reference is intended to the past or present holders of office in them; and in particular, whilst it has been necessary for the purposes of the book to depict one member of the Bomb Squad as being fallible over academic niceties, no reflection of any sort is intended on that devoted body of public servants.

Library of Congress Cataloging-in-Publication Data

Gilbert, Michael Francis, 1912–
　Trouble.

　I. Title.
PR6013.I3335T7　1987　　　823'.914　　　86-46067
ISBN 0-06-015741-0

87 88 89 90 91 HC 10 9 8 7 6 5 4 3 2 1

Prologue

Cuckmere Haven – Het Zoute – Hereford

The Belgian motor fishing vessel *Petite Amie* nosed her way inshore. The steadying sail, the only canvas she carried, was set on the stubby mizzenmast aft and her ninety horsepower Gardner engine was running at quarter speed. It was two o'clock in the morning of midsummer day and the moon, nearly full, was turning the blackness into a pearly dimness which would have ravished the heart of an artist.

Tinus Meagher, owner and skipper of the *Petite Amie*, was not ravished. He was in a filthy temper, made worse for him by the fact that he had no one to work it off on. What he needed was someone who would answer back and could be shouted down. His crew, on this trip, was two youngsters, neither of them suitable as a conversational punch bag.

His nephew, Marise, mazed poor boy, would chuckle at anything he said, complimentary or insulting. Dirk, who was standing beside him in the tiny wheelhouse, was a different proposition. He had, by his own account, spent some time in the French Navy and could normally be relied on to speak his mind, but he was too conscious of his dubious position on this particular trip to do more than agree with anything that was said to him.

"An ebb tide," said Meagher. "A fockink ebb tide. Think of it, boy. I'm told to lay my boat on the two fathom mark in an *ebb* tide. Have they given it one moment of thought? Do they know that my draught is two metres? Have they troubled to carry out the simple calculation which would have informed them that two metres is *more* than one fathom? Do they suppose that *less* than one fathom is a suitable clearance on an ebb tide? Well – what do you say?"

Dirk said that Herr Wulfkind had probably given no thought to the matter at all. He added that this was typical of landsmen who tried to deal with sea matters.

"Landsman or no landsman, is it beyond him to make a

calculation which would not be too hard for a child of seven? And another thing. Has he considered that we are approaching the mouth of a river? Even a small river brings down new sand-banks to its mouth every year. And how old is our chart? I will tell you. *It is twelve years old.* Had he thought of that, do you suppose?"

Dirk said that Herr Wulfkind was probably as ignorant of charts as of everything except the sale of marble. He managed to switch the conversation by announcing that he thought he could now see the Seven Sisters.

"There, surely, a point or two to starboard."

He rattled out this expression as if to demonstrate the jargon he had picked up in his brief and inglorious career in the French Navy.

"Don't think, make sure," growled Meagher.

Dirk went out on to the after deck, treading carefully to avoid the four coffin-shaped boxes which were stacked there. He had a pair of night-glasses, but did not need to use them. He could see the line of the seven cliff faces clearly enough. He judged that they were half a mile offshore and went back to the wheelhouse to report.

The skipper received the news without enthusiasm. He had reverted to a further grievance.

"Lights," he said. "You were there when the instruction was given. We were to proceed without lights. Did the fockink boggert think I was driving a motor-bus down the main street in Brussels?"

Dirk took this for a joke and sniggered. It was a mistake.

"Why do you laugh, boy? Is it because you have no more brains in your head than Herr Wulfkind? Do you think that if we sailed without lights we should not be seen? Of course we are seen. We are seen by every ship that looks into its radar screen. Just as I look into mine and see them. They say, what is this? A ship sailing without lights. He must be up to no good. Send out a warning. So I disregard such a stupid instruction. I sail with my port and starboard lights *and* my masthead light, as an honest skipper should. All the same," he added, peering out of the starboard side-window, "I think perhaps I will turn them out now."

By this time they were closing fast on the shore. Dirk went aft again. No need for glasses. He could pick out quite clearly the white posts he had been told to look for, one at each end of the line of shingle which formed a strip of beach at the foot of the cliffs.

He took out the Navy-type prismatic compass, holding it with his thumb hitched through the ring in the way he had been taught and lifting it to his eye. Then he read off a bearing to each post in turn.

Left post 348°. Right post 12°.

He shouted, "Too far out."

Meagher shouted back. "Too far out? What sort of instruction is that? You're the navigator. Tell me *how* much too far."

The trigonometry involved in this calculation was beyond Dirk. He could only guess.

"A hundred metres. Maybe two hundred."

They were level with the beach now and could see the white froth on the river as it tumbled out to sea. Meagher swung the wheel and they came round in a shoreward circle and returned on their track. He had his eyes on the echo-sounder beside the wheel. Despite his protests he was reasonably certain that it would keep him out of trouble. The graph line on the recorder had been creeping upwards for some time, but it still showed him a clearance of six metres.

More than three fathoms. He could afford to edge in a little closer.

The boat, with the tidal current heading it and with what little wind there was dead astern, was now almost completely steady. Dirk was taking readings to each post in turn as they came in.

35°, 40°, 42°, to the right hand post.

325°, 320°, 318°, to the left hand post.

He said to himself, "That'll do." The momentum of the boat would carry them forward to the 315°/45° mark which was his objective.

He shouted, in an oddly authoritative voice, "Anchor down."

Marise jumped to the capstan and let go the anchor. The boat swung gently round, presenting its stern to the beach.

The activity which followed involved all three of them. A mushroom-shaped buoy with four rings under it, which had been hanging over the side, was lowered into the water, brought round to the stern and anchored. A plank was laid

9

from the after deck to the stern rail and, one by one, the coffin-shaped boxes were manhandled up it. Each box had attached to it a length of chain ending with a snap-link. As soon as the snap-link was attached to the ring under the buoy, the case was lowered over the sides.

"And now," said Meagher, who seemed to be recovering his normal good spirits with the end of the job in sight, "we will put on the old gentleman's night cap."

This was a bonnet-shaped piece of netting with streamers of brown and black hessian and seaweed laced through it. It had been designed to fit over the rounded top of the buoy.

"Tie it firmly," said Meagher. "The old gentleman may be restless in bed. His cap must not tumble off."

The two boys laughed.

"No time for jokes," said Meagher. He stumped back to the wheelhouse. "Home now. Bring in the anchor. And we will turn on the lights. *All* the fockink lights."

The *Petite Amie* swung round and gathered speed. In the wake that it left behind, the lump of hessian and seaweed bobbed up and down.

It seemed to be beckoning.

The Cuckmere Haven caravan camp lies off the Seaford-Eastbourne road beyond Exeat Bridge. A track, cut into the enduring chalk, runs south from it for half a mile, following the left bank of the Cuckmere stream until this reaches the pebbly beach and runs out to sea below the foot of the cliffs.

The camp was full; thirty caravans, each on its allotted pitch. Most of them were occupied by married couples or by family parties. An exception was the small and gaily painted van which the fair-haired man had brought in three days before. It had been squeezed into the only remaining space, in the bottom corner of the camp, up against the southern boundary fence. This was not a favoured position, but it suited the fair-haired man, who could walk out of the camp and along the track to the beach without passing any of the other caravanners.

People who had seen him had agreed that he looked a pleasant young man, though one or two who had happened to meet him at closer quarters, on his way to the communal water-point, or shopping in the camp store, had jibbed at the word 'young'. Seen at a distance he looked like a fair-haired brown-faced boy. But it was not a boy's face.

"It's a mysterious sort of face," said Mrs. Brumby to her husband. "A face with a lot of experience behind it."

"A film star, I suppose," said Mr. Brumby.

"Well, he could be. It's that sort of face."

To which Mr. Brumby had said, "Nonsense," this being his normal reaction to his wife's ideas. "Ten to one he's a clerk in an office, enjoying a quiet weekend by the sea. Nothing mysterious about him."

Had he been in a position to observe the fair-haired man's actions at two o'clock on that midsummer morning, Mr. Brumby might have revised his opinion. It was not that he was behaving in a particularly odd way, but all of his movements had an air of planning and purpose behind them.

He had finished a very simple meal. He was now washing and drying the dishes and stowing them away in the cupboard beside the sink. An empty corned-beef tin, the heel of a loaf, the remains of a packet of butter and two cans which had held lager beer went into a pail under the sink. Like any careful housewife doing messy work, the man had been wearing rubber gloves. He did not, however, remove them when he started on the next operation, which was a general tidying up.

The blankets, which were part of the caravan stores, were folded and placed on the bunk, which was then shut down. His own linen, a pillow-case and two towels, went into his pack with his few personal belongings. He was a scrupulous tidier. An empty matchbox from a shelf above the bed was dropped into his knapsack, with the few papers in the waste-paper basket. After that he started work with a duster. He polished every surface and edge which could possibly have held dust and some which could hardly have done so. Finally, he brushed the carpet and rolled it up. By the time this housework had been finished his watch showed three forty-five a.m.

His knapsack was the sort carried by climbers. It had two straps which went over the shoulders. The man fastened it in position over the windcheater which he had put on, took a final look round, turned out the lamp over the bed and slid back the shutter which covered the window.

Midsummer day. It would be light by four o'clock, or very soon afterwards. Through the window he could see the three grey caravans. They had arrived at eight o'clock on the previous evening. Since there had been no regular site for them

11

to occupy they had been allowed to stand in a row along the southern boundary, outside the fence; thus, incidentally, blocking his exit in that direction.

This was not the only thing about the caravans which had interested him. It was the conduct of their occupants.

Normally new arrivals would emerge as soon as their caravan was in position, to fetch water, to visit the shop, to look round for acquaintances. If there were children, they would be allowed out to play whilst supper was being cooked. If it was fine, and it had been very fine all that day, a canopy might be erected and camp-chairs and tables brought out and set up.

The occupants of the three caravans had done none of these things. In fact, although he had watched from his window, he had caught no more than an occasional glimpse of any of them. They all seemed to be men. He had heard the occasional murmur of voices. Their lights had gone out promptly at eleven o'clock.

"You might have thought Last Post and Lights Out had been blown on a bugle," said the watcher. It worried him, but there was nothing he could do about it.

The boat would have come and gone. The van would be arriving at any minute now. If the agreed timings had been observed, it would drive down the track between the two wings of the camp at precisely four fifteen a.m.

It was time to take up observation.

He opened the door and stepped out. He had already chosen his position. He would be underneath the caravan in the line which fronted the track on the nearside. From there he could see the van, both arriving and departing. When it was safely away on the road to Seaford, his own job would be finished, and he would slip off by the footpath which led up-river to Alfriston where he had garaged a car, hired in a name which was not his own.

The van was an army three-tonner with four-wheel drive and ample stowage space under its canopy. As it crossed Exeat Bridge the driver glanced down at his wrist-watch. A minute short of four fifteen. In the preliminary conferences it had been suggested that there might be some mist over the river and there were contingency plans for this, but the June air was as clear as crystal. As soon as he had swung into the track he turned out both head and side lights. The surface of the track, being chalk, was easily visible and the light was growing rapidly. In less than five minutes he had reached the edge of the shingle beach and had swung the truck round, with its back to the sea.

The driver and the man who had been sitting beside him jumped down and two other men climbed out of the back. The four of them worked quietly, but without wasting any time. One of them walked to each of the posts which stood at the end of the beach, pulled out a compass and took a bearing out to sea; 225° magnetic from one post, 135° from the other.

In the growing light the clump of seaweed bobbing about two hundred yards offshore was clearly visible. The right-hand man saw it first and signalled. The left-hand man signalled back. He had seen it too.

By this time the ramp at the back of the van had been lowered and the third man, helped by the driver, had manhandled a dinghy down it and across the narrow strip of pebbled beach. It was a stout little craft of the type used in air-sea rescue operations, equipped both with oars and an outboard motor. The men climbed in. For the outward journey there was no need to risk the noise of the motor. One of the men took the oars. The other kept his eye on the watchers by the posts. They directed him by raising their right or left arms.

The man at the oars pulled steadily. The ebb tide was helping him. As soon as it was clear that they had spotted the clump of seaweed, the two men left the posts and hurried back to the van, stripping off clothes as they went.

When the boat reached the clump of seaweed, one of the men moved forward to maintain balance, the other leaned over the stern and felt for the hooks which held the lines to the rings under the steel mushroom. One by one and very carefully he unsnapped them and refixed them to the towing hooks, two on each side of the boat. When the last of the four boxes was secure, the second man started the outboard motor.

The first part of the trip back was easy enough. The length of line attached to the boxes had been calculated to keep them off the bottom until they reached shallow water. When it became clear from the drag on the lines that the boxes were grounding, the boat was still twenty-five yards from the beach. The other two men, having stripped off their outer clothes, could now be

13

seen to be wearing skin-divers' rubber suits. They waded out through the surf until they could reach the boat and unhooked one line each. Dragging the cases ashore was a painstaking operation and it had to be done slowly, lifting them over projecting lumps of rock and taking great care not to damage them. When all four were on the beach, the driver looked at his watch. It was twenty past six. That part of the operation had overrun by ten minutes.

The beach, as they knew, was used by occasional swimmers from the camp. Weeks of observation had shown that seven o'clock was the earliest that any of them arrived. There was a margin of safety, but it was a small one. The cases were stowed in the van. The boat, lifted by all four men, was hefted up and slung on top of them. The ramp was raised and bolted. Despite the cool breeze of early morning they were all sweating.

The driver said to the two men in diving-suits, "We're behind time. Can you dress as we go?"

The men nodded. The driver started the engine and the men jumped in. They headed back up the track towards the camp.

The ambush was laid with speed, efficiency and simplicity. From his point of vantage the fair-haired man observed it with a mixture of fury and the admiration of a professional for a professional job well done.

At the last moment, when the van could be heard coming up from the sea, but was still out of sight round the final bend in the track, the three caravans started up their engines and drove out, completely filling the path which ran between the border-fences of the two caravan areas. The dawn was almost up, but the caravans, grey and unlit, were not easy to spot and the van was only twenty yards away when the driver realised that his way was barred. He stamped on his brakes and skidded to a halt. A man stood up on either side of the track. They were wearing combat jackets and were carrying Hechler and Koch MP5 machine pistols. The taller of the men said, "End of journey. All out."

The driver jerked the gear into reverse, but before the van could move a shot had slammed into the engine.

The tall man said, "Don't be stupid. The next one goes into the cab. It could be your unlucky day."

There was a short and brittle pause. Then the driver and his passenger climbed down. They had recovered from the shock and seemed to be more angry than frightened.

"Some fucker sold us up the river," said the driver.

"Mustn't jump to conclusions," said the tall man. "You lot in the back, show a leg. We haven't got all day. Some of us haven't had our breakfast yet."

The canopy at the back was thrown open and the two other men climbed down.

By this time the camp was stirring. The first people brought to the caravan doors by the sound of the shot were children. The next were their parents, trying to stop them getting out.

The fair-haired man began to realise that he had not chosen a very sensible observation post.

A carroty-haired boy, wearing a track suit that he probably slept in, had jumped down just beside him. A woman from above said, "Come back, Cedric."

Cedric took no notice. He advanced cautiously towards the fence.

"Did you hear what I said? Come back this instant."

A man's voice said, "Wassup?"

The woman said, "Someone's been shooting. Cedric's outside. He'll get shot."

"Serve him right."

Cedric said, in a loud clear voice, "There's a man under our caravan. Oh, it's all right. He's going now."

The fair-haired man had been wriggling out backwards. Now he got to his feet and started to move away quickly, but Cedric's observation had been picked up by the driver of the nearest of the blocking vans. He shouted something and the flank guards spun round.

"One of the sods was under that van. Grab him."

The nearest flank guard said, "Damn." He ran up to the fence, climbed it and started after the fair-haired man.

The fugitive had two advantages. He had reconnoitred his escape route and he knew his way about. He was starting up the cliff path behind the camp before his pursuer had reached the back fence. The path was tricky, but he went up it confidently. His pursuer was not so lucky. Half way up he put his foot into a hole and came down. By the time he was up again the fair-haired man was at the top. His pursuer thought about taking a shot at him, but before he could get his gun up the fugitive had cleared the crest. Too late now. He returned, limping, to report failure.

The tall man said, "Bloody hell. He *must* be headed off." He climbed into the rearmost of the grey caravans and started to talk urgently on the wireless.

Meanwhile, the fair-haired man was making his way across the smooth turf of the cliff-top, keeping under cover as much as possible. He moved with the speed and ease of an athlete in training, partly jog-trotting, partly at a fast walk. He wasted no time, because he did not underestimate the efforts that would be made to stop him.

In less than half an hour he was crossing the side road that ran down to Birling Gap and now he altered his course northwards towards the Eastbourne road. When he reached it, just before seven, there was already some traffic. He squatted behind the hedge to observe it. The first two vehicles to pass him were a Post Office van and a lorry with two men up front. Neither of them were what he wanted.

Next came a Vauxhall Astra, with only the one driver. This looked more promising. He stepped into the road and waved.

Mr. Crombie, who travelled in gentlemen's socks, ties and underwear, had been visiting wholesalers in Brighton and had spent the night in Seaford. He had chosen one of the big hotels on the front, but it had not proved a good choice. The drag of waves on the shingle had kept him awake. Since he had followed his usual plan of paying his bill before he went to bed, there had been nothing to keep him. He had slipped away before the hotel was awake, planning to breakfast in Eastbourne which was his next port of call. Mr. Crombie had a weakness for youngsters with fair hair. He applied his brakes and said, "What can I do for you, son?"

"I have to get to Eastbourne as quickly as possible."

"Me too," said Mr. Crombie. "Climb in. Been hiking?"

"Sort of."

The fair-haired man – by no means a boy, as Mr. Crombie observed, now that he could see him more closely – was easing the knapsack off his shoulders. The car had started up the long hill to Eastdean Down and the road ahead was empty. His passenger said, "There's one thing I ought to tell you. If we're stopped, and we might be, I'm your nephew, Charles."

"Are you, indeed?" said Mr. Crombie doubtfully.

"You picked me up off the London train in Lewes and we've been together ever since."

Mr. Crombie said, "I'm not sure – " and then stopped because he saw the gun.

"You'd better be sure," said the fair-haired man. "I don't suppose it'll be anything very much in the way of a stoppage. Could be a policeman on a motor-cycle, or at worst two of them in a patrol car. I'm a good enough shot to take out the three of you."

What had he done to deserve this? Why, oh why had he stopped?

"Let's hope," said Mr. Crombie, he tried to speak lightly, but was hampered by the sudden dryness of his mouth, "that we shan't be stopped again."

"Again?"

"There was a road block the other side of 'Friston."

"Was there, though? Then it looks as if we might get through without any more trouble."

Mr. Crombie spent the next ten minutes alternately cursing his luck and offering up prayers to a God he did not believe in.

The car, directed by his passenger, who seemed relaxed, drew up in a quiet street behind Eastbourne main-line station.

Now what? thought Mr. Crombie. His heart had started to double-beat and he felt choked.

"Have you got a card?" said the fair-haired man politely.

"A card. Yes, of course." Mr. Crombie fumbled for his wallet. "Do you mean my business card, or personal?"

"Both."

The fair-haired man examined the cards. He said, "I see you live in Roehampton. A nice quiet part of London?"

"Oh, very."

"Nothing unpleasant ever happen there?"

"Unpleasant?"

"I mean, like petrol bombs thrown through doorways or people getting beaten to death by muggers."

"No, no. Nothing like that."

"Then," said the fair-haired man, "let's hope it stays that way. Which it will do, as long as you forget that you ever gave me a lift, forget what I look like, forget all about me."

"Oh, I will," said Mr. Crombie. "I've got a terrible

17

memory." He gave what was meant to be a light laugh, but which finished as something close to a whimper.

The fair-haired man picked up his knapsack, climbed out of the car and strolled away down the pavement. Mr. Crombie sat for five minutes before he could compose himself sufficiently to drive off.

By the time he did so the fair-haired man was in one of the telephone booths in the forecourt of the station. He was relieved to see that most of the other booths were vacant. He dialled a London number. When a man's voice answered he said, "Is that 0484 0406?"

"I didn't quite get that."

"I said, are you 0484 0406?"

"No. I'm afraid you've got the wrong number."

"I'm sorry. I dialled in a great hurry."

He rang off. He reckoned that he might have to wait as much as ten minutes before Sean got to a public call box and rang him back at 0484 0406, which was the number of the box he was occupying. He came through in seven minutes.

"Something wrong, Liam?"

"Something very wrong," said the fair-haired man. He described, in a few short sentences, what had happened.

"So we were blown?"

"Evidently."

"Then I can give you some information. The blowing did *not* take place at this end."

"How can you be sure?"

"You say the opposition arrived at the camp at eight o'clock last night?"

"About then, yes."

"Our pick-up team were only told the actual place and given the local details just before they started out. That was at midnight. Of course they knew what they had to do and they'd practised the drill. But until they started out the only people at this end who knew where and when the stuff was to be landed were you and me."

"I see. So the leak was on the other side of the Channel."

"Must have been."

Liam looked at his watch. He said, "It's near eight o'clock now. If the boat was on schedule it will have started back to Belgium around two thirty. It'll take them a good six hours to

18

make Het Zoute. Seven or eight if they stop to fish. If you got straight through to Dr. Bernard he'd have plenty of time to arrange a reception committee."

"I'll do that," said Sean. "What about you?"

"I'm coming up to London. This part of Sussex isn't very healthy, and getting unhealthier every minute, I guess."

At ten o'clock Liam was sitting in the station buffet watching the people crowding through the ticket barrier for the 10.15, which was the fast train to Victoria. The changes in his appearance were simple, but decisive. The fair hair had disappeared. The excellently crafted wig which he had been wearing for the past few days was packed away in his knapsack which had, with all its contents, disappeared inside a suitcase. His hair was black and close-cropped. This, combined with a pair of plain-lens steel-rimmed glasses and a knee-length black raincoat, gave him the look of a serious young clergyman. When making these purchases he had chanced on a book of sermons in a tray outside a second-hand bookshop and had purchased it for fivepence.

As he sat turning the pages and sipping his coffee, his interest was concentrated on two men. One of them was examining the notice-board which showed the times of the trains; the other was scrutinising the magazines on sale at the station bookshop. The only odd thing about them was the length of time they spent on these harmless pursuits.

The last-minute passengers hurried on to the platform, the ticket barrier clanged shut and the 10.15 departed for London. The two men moved towards the ticket collector, had a word with him and walked away. It seemed for a moment that they might be coming into the buffet, but they turned aside and disappeared through a door marked 'Staff'.

Liam finished his coffee and strolled across to the notice-board. He saw that a slow train, stopping at nearly all stations, left at a quarter to twelve. The first stop was Hassocks. He wandered out into the town and spent some time sitting in a shelter on the front, apparently absorbed in the pronouncements of Dr. Spurgeon. He had already located a taxi rank and at eleven o'clock he approached it diffidently.

The driver of the cab at the head of the rank was young and honest. He explained to the cleric that if he wanted to go to Hassocks it would be cheaper and almost as quick to take the train. He'd have to charge for the journey out and back and that would be a fiver.

Liam thanked him and explained that he was only in England for a short time and wanted to see something of the countryside.

"It's your money," said the driver agreeably. "Hop in."

Hassocks station, when Liam reached it, was almost deserted. Two middle-aged ladies and a man who looked like a farmer were sitting on a bench on the platform talking to each other. Liam stayed in the waiting room until the last moment. When the train arrived he walked out quickly and climbed into the rear carriage.

He chose the rear carriage so that when they reached Victoria he would have to walk along the whole length of the train. This would give him time to see whether there was going to be trouble at the barrier and plan accordingly. He did not think it was very likely, but it was attention to details like this that had enabled him to survive so long in his profession.

It was six o'clock in the evening before MFV *Petite Amie* tied up at Het Zoute. They had stopped to fish on the way back and Meagher had found this a slow and difficult operation without his regular crew. His nephew had known what to do, but Navy-trained Dirk had been more of a hindrance than a help.

"Not much of a catch for a day and a night," said the Port Captain, who had been making an inspection of the vessel.

"The wind was wrong," said Meagher.

"For fishermen, the wind is always wrong," said the Port Captain. "If it picked the fish up by their tails and threw them into the hold it would still be wrong."

Meagher grunted. He had no wish to exchange pleasantries with the Port Captain. He wanted only to make his report, collect the second half of his fee and get home to supper, drink and bed.

"Some people are waiting for you," said the Port Captain. "Down at the far end of the quay. They will without doubt be glad to see you. They have been waiting here since ten o'clock this morning."

It would be Wulfkind and perhaps also that smooth shyster Monnier who seemed to control the purse-strings. Meagher had met him only once and had disliked him. Let them wait. He was the one who did the work and took the risks. They sat back in comfort and pocketed the profits. And why, in the name of goodness, had they parked at the far end of the quay? To give him the trouble of walking two hundred yards, he supposed.

He was starting out, demonstrating his displeasure by walking as slowly as possible, when the Port Captain said, "All of you. They were most insistent. They wished to speak to all of you."

Meagher was puzzled. Why should anything Wulfkind wished to say to him be said in the presence of Dirk and his nephew? It was a mystery and he disliked mysteries. For a moment he hesitated. Then he concluded that the quickest way of finding the answer was to do as he was told. He signalled to the two young men to follow him.

It was a heavy car, a six-seater Cherokee Chief. He recognised neither of the two men who climbed out as he approached. They were both thick-set men with flat expressionless faces. One had slicked-down black hair; the other was nearly bald. They were wearing well-cut Brussels-style suits which should have made them look like businessmen, but somehow managed to convey quite a different impression. Policemen, perhaps, thought Meagher. He said, with a brusqueness intended to hide his uneasiness, "I was expecting Herr Wulfkind."

"He was unable to be here himself," said the bald man. "He asked us to take you to him."

"All of us?"

"All of you."

"The boat has to be attended to. There is much to do."

A third man, who had been seated beside the driver, had now got out. A real gorilla, thought Meagher. The bald man said, without altering the polite tone of his voice in any way, "If you do not, all of you, get into the car at once, I shall be regretfully forced to throw this young sprog of yours into the sea. It's a long drop and he'll bounce twice on the rocks before he reaches the water."

The second man had the rear door of the car open. The third man had moved round behind them blocking the way they had come.

"Since you are so pressing in your invitation," said Meagher, "I suppose we had better accept it."

Bradbury Lines outside the City of Hereford looks much like any other Regimental Headquarters. It is identified by the notice-board outside as 'HQ Signals Corps'. There was a single sentry on the gateway, which was crossed by a red and white striped pole. The closed-circuit television cameras were there too, but they were not in evidence.

On a morning of that same week in June a ten-year-old black Humber four-seater saloon car drew up outside this entrance.

There was nothing remarkable about either of its occupants. Reginald Mowatt, on the back seat, with a bulging brief case beside him, was fifty-ish, stoutish and placid looking. His driver, a wizened man, with the look of someone who had spent most of his life in the open; a groom, perhaps, who now looked after a car with the devotion he had previously paid to his master's horses. The only unusual item was the .388 automatic pistol which lived in a door pocket close to the driver's right hand.

The sentry said, "You was here last week, wasn't you? Thought I reckernised the car." He lifted the pole. "You know where the office is. On the right at the far end. OK?"

The office was part of an inner citadel which seemed to be much more effectively guarded than the rest of the barracks. It lay behind a wall of breeze blocks and a cement-faced ditch which was deep enough to halt the biggest lorry and might have puzzled a light tank. The only entrance was blocked by a double line of off-set concrete posts.

Mowatt got out of the car, threaded his way between the posts and presented his card to one of the sentries on the inner gate. They were a hard-faced pair who wore the beige SAS beret and winged dagger and carried Sterling L34 submachine guns. One of them stayed beside Mowatt whilst the other went into the office, returned quickly and indicated that he should go in. Neither of them spoke.

Lieutenant Colonel Every got up to greet him. He said, "I seem to remember, Reggie, that you preferred tea to coffee, so I've ordered some. Beer would be easier on the lining of your stomach."

"My stomach's too old to enjoy beer at eleven o'clock in the morning," said Mowatt. As he spoke he was examining the

Colonel carefully. There were the lines fencing the mouth which arrive as a man grows older, but his face was still free of the V-shaped furrow between the eyes which is the hallmark of worry and strain. His right arm, he noticed, was now out of the sling which it had been in since the IRA had bombed a lecture the Colonel was giving at the Military Studies Institute.

He said, "We have to congratulate you. Really a splendid bag. Four hundred pounds of torpex explosive. They could have done a great deal of damage with that."

The Colonel made no comment until an orderly, who had brought in two mugs of tea, had left the room. Then he said, "It was a spin-off for ACID, really."

Mowatt nodded. He knew about the Atomic Co-ordinated Inspection Device, brain-child of the Bomb Disposal Unit. Its enthusiastic users maintained that it not only detected the presence of explosive through any thickness of cover, but, properly used, could register its precise quantity, temperature, make-up and even its likely source.

He said, "That's true enough. I don't imagine anyone now fancies the chances of bringing in explosives through any of the recognised points of entry. We've put what you might call an acid ring round the country. They've had to fall back on older methods."

"Older methods is right," said the Colonel. "I suppose you realise that they were copying a device used by smugglers in Napoleonic times. They used to bring kegs of brandy across and sink them close to shore, attached to floats. It wasn't always successful. Sometimes their colleagues managed to fish them out before the Revenue officers arrived. Sometimes they got caught."

"As on this occasion. Have you got anything out of them?"

"There wasn't much to get. They were minor characters hired for the trip and very well paid. They were ready enough to talk. We interrogated them separately and their stories agree, so it's on the cards that they're speaking the truth."

"Then they couldn't tell you where the stuff was going?"

"Where it was going? They didn't even know what it was. Or so they said. Their instructions were to rendezvous with another van in the New Forest. That was the end of their part of the job. They thought the second van might be going to transfer the stuff to a third one."

"They're careful people," said Mowatt.

"Very," agreed the Colonel. It seemed, for a moment, that he was not going to elaborate on this. Then he added, "You appreciate that it was considerations of this sort that decided us to stop them at the camp rather than making some attempt to follow the van."

"I'm sure you were right. You couldn't risk a slip up. Much better to pick up the bird when it was under your hand."

When Every fell silent again he said, "What is it that's bothering you, Colonel?"

"We made a bad mistake."

"Oh?"

"You know the way these people like to cover and double cover every contingency. Well, on this occasion they had a man on watch in the camp."

"Another minor character?"

The Colonel said, "Far from it. One of the two men in England I'd give a finger off my right hand to get hold of."

Mowatt thought about this. Then he said, "Another finger?"

The little finger and ring-finger of the Colonel's right hand were missing.

"Cheap at the price if we could get hold of the man who now calls himself Liam."

"Then you're sure it was him?"

"Not sure, no. But one of our men spotted him. He said it wasn't so much the face as the way he moved. You know, we had a big cover party in position in case they changed the landing-point at the last moment. We had road-blocks ready, helicopters standing by and the mainline stations blocked at Lewes, Newhaven, Seaford and Eastbourne. But we didn't catch Liam."

"Maybe he went under cover and waited until dark."

"Yes. He might have done that. Or there's another possibility. We may have put our blocks in the wrong place. They were designed to stop a van, not a man on foot. I thought about that later and we checked up on the vehicles that had gone through the road-blocks, to find out if they might have picked up someone further on. They all said no. One of them, a man called Crombie, said it a bit too emphatically. I did wonder about him. On the whole, though, I'm glad some poor country bobby didn't try to stop Liam."

Mowatt said, "Yes, I'm glad about that. He's killed too many men already."

The Colonel got up and moved across to the window, as though what he had to say could not be said sitting down.

He said, "All the same, it was a bad mistake."

"How do you make that out? Agreed that you lost a slender chance of laying a wanted man by the heels, but on balance it was a great success."

"You think so?" said the Colonel. He remained standing, staring out of the window, shifting his head slowly from left to right as though he was following the movement of someone or something outside, but Mowatt knew that he was seeing things inside his own head.

When he spoke, it was slowly, as though he was dictating an official memorandum. He said, "We know quite a lot about recent IRA operations in Belgium. The man at the top seems to be a Dr. Bernard, 'Doctor' being a courtesy title. No connection with medicine. In fact, he was a very successful criminal lawyer. Too successful, really. When he gave up his practice, after a series of brushes with the police, he acquired control of a small private bank, Bernstorf Frères, in Ghent. A lot of the money raised by IRA sympathisers in America comes to him."

"Openly?"

"Oh, certainly. Open and above board. By inter-bank transfer, I imagine. It was what happened to the money afterwards that interested us. On a recent occasion we know that most of it went to Claude Monnier, who's a Brussels lawyer. He paid it over – less a handsome commission for himself no doubt – to one of his clients, a man called Josef Wulfkind. Josef is an exporter of high-class marble for decorating houses and gardens."

"Not gnomes?"

"Not gnomes," agreed Every with one of his rare smiles. "Nothing as suburban as that. He deals in statuary and fine raw marble. He owns the only quarry of note outside Carrara, at Marche-en-Famenne. Some experts rank his stuff above the Italian. I'm told it's the metallic salts in the limestone which give it its beautiful eggshell pattern and colouring."

"Marche-en-Famenne," said Mowatt. "Rings a bell. Where did I see that name?"

"It was in the papers a lot at the end of 1944. It was the

25

furthest point the German tanks reached in their Ardennes push."

"I expect that was it."

"How much do you know about marble quarrying?"

"Practically nothing."

"It's really a process of sawing and splitting, but explosives are used, from time to time, to loosen different areas in the rock face. This gave Wulfkind a pretext for ordering a quantity from the Belgian arms firm, AMG."

"Of torpex explosive?"

"Yes."

"You must correct me if I'm wrong. I know much less about these things than you do. But I'd assumed a quarry owner would use PE 808 or something of the sort. Surely nothing as dangerous as torpex?"

"The point had not escaped us. Certainly most quarrying is done with Permitted Explosive. We could only conclude that Wulfkind spun some sort of yarn to get hold of torpex – and was *very* persuasive."

"Financially persuasive?"

"I imagine so. He had a large fund to draw on. He would have needed to pay a fat fee to Tinus Meagher, who owns a motor fishing vessel called *Petite Amie* based on Het Zoute. That is, incidentally, the port from which Wulfkind ships his own stuff, so he would be likely to be in with the local characters."

"And I don't suppose Wulfkind was doing this for love."

"No. He too, as we know, was paid very handsomely. The agreement with him was that he would be responsible for the transport of the explosive from Marche-en-Famenne, through Het Zoute, to an agreed landing place on the south coast of England."

"In legal terms, a CIF contract," said Mowatt. "Carriage, insurance and freight."

"Right. But in this case, for 'insurance' read 'assurance'. Assurance that there would be no security slip ups. That's what he got so heavily paid for and it's what gave him the biggest headache. He could trust Meagher, who had done a number of jobs for him before. And his nephew, who was half-witted anyway and was under Uncle Tinus's thumb. But this operation needed a third man. And he didn't want to bring any of the normal fishing crew into it."

26

"An MFV needs three men to run it, then?"

"No. At a pinch a man who knew his job could handle it by himself. But this wasn't so straightforward. The stuff had to be put down at a precise spot and buoyed. As an extra precaution against being spotted by an outsider the buoy was covered with scrim and seaweed. The trouble was that there's a good deal of real seaweed about on that stretch of coast. Which meant that if the pick-up was to go through fast – and time was all important – the landing party had to be able to identify the buoy quickly and accurately. So what they did was to give Meagher a compass bearing to each of two posts on the beach. You follow me?"

"You're talking to an ex-gunner," said Mowatt with dignity. "I follow you exactly. The beach party would take a back bearing from the posts."

"Right. And easy enough for them with their feet on terra firma. But not so easy for Meagher. He had to manoeuvre his boat onto the precise spot. That meant that he had to have someone with him who could handle a compass competently. And someone who could be bribed or terrorised into keeping his mouth shut afterwards. Fortunately there was a candidate for the job. A young man who, according to his own account, had been slung out of the French Navy six months before for insubordination and had been living by his wits since then, loafing round the ports and seaside resorts on the north Belgian coast, picking up a few crumbs from time to time. Meagher had heard about his murky record, which had rather amused him, and had used him once or twice to clean out his fish-hold. No one knew his real name. He called himself Dirk."

When the Colonel hesitated, Mowatt realised that he had reached the heart of his story. Everything that went before, Dr. Bernard the banker, Claude Monnier the lawyer, Josef Wulfkind the quarryman, Tinus Meagher the fisherman, had been an introduction to the person who mattered: the French boy, who went under the name of Dirk.

Mowatt, who headed B11, the Irish Section of MI5, was noted for his freaks of memory. A spasmodic computer, a colleague had once called him. He collected and stored miscellaneous items of information and could collate and reproduce them without conscious efforts. Now a number of such items were coming together.

27

Every had married a widow called Marie-Louise Arents. Her former husband had been a senior officer in the French Navy. He had died twelve or fifteen years ago, leaving her with a small pension and a ten-year-old boy, Henri. Henri had early shown a preference for being called 'Henry'. He had gone to an English preparatory school and then to Clifton. He had adopted British nationality and had been accepted at Dartmouth under the Special Entry Scheme. In spite of this he had managed to keep up friendly relations with his father's family. He was, of course, bilingual. These special talents and connections had soon attracted the attention of the shadowy men who lived near St James's Park Underground station. They saw him as ideally fitted to penetrate the growing cross-Channel organisation of the IRA. Doubly valuable because, sadly, they could expect little co-operation from their French or Belgian counterparts.

These scraps of information had come to Mowatt at different times and from different sources. They now came together on the screen and the picture they made was disturbing. He took a few seconds to phrase his next remark, then he said, "I did wonder how you had got hold of so much information about the workings of the opposition across the Channel. Am I to understand that Dirk is our man?"

Instead of answering the question directly, Every said, "You realise that our idea was to leave the opposition in ignorance of exactly what had happened to their cargo. They would have known, of course, that something had gone wrong. It might have been on the beach, or on the way to wherever the stuff was going. It might have been one of the dozens of slip ups which occur even in the best run operations."

Mowatt said, "But because Liam was on the spot and managed to escape, they would know, at once, that they'd been given away by someone with inside information."

"Very exact inside information, confined to a small circle. Liam and his controller on this side. Not the pick-up team. They would have been briefed at the last moment and knew very little anyway. On the other side of the Channel: Wulfkind, old Tinus Meagher, his nephew Marise – and Dirk."

"A small field."

"A one-man field. No one seriously suspected Meagher or his half-witted nephew. Wulfkind might have been playing a double game, but it was highly unlikely. The answer to the question you asked me just now is yes. Dirk *was* our man. His cover was good, but not unbreakable. They would have needed only a contact in French naval circles to discover that no court-martial for insubordination had taken place within the last six months. Even without such clinching information they must have recognised at once that Dirk was the weak link in their chain."

"If the news got to them quickly enough, they would have been able to pick him up when the *Petite Amie* got back to Het Zoute."

"It did reach them quickly enough and they did pick him up." Every spoke so flatly that Mowatt knew what he had to say was bad.

"They tortured him, to get what they could out of him. Then they killed him, in an unnecessarily brutal way. His body was found in a refuse dump outside Brussels. His arms and his legs had been smashed before he died."

There was a long silence that Mowatt felt disinclined to break. Every came away from the window and sat down at his desk. He said, "You realise that one of their reasons for reacting in this way was because they were frightened. They had wasted a large sum of IRA money and disrupted IRA plans. That was not going to be forgotten or forgiven. The only way they can make it good is by securing an equivalent amount of explosive. Stealing it, maybe, or even paying for it themselves. And then bringing it over, successfully, on this occasion."

"Time is against them," said Mowatt. "We know that their next big campaign is due to start in Central London this winter. Probably not later than the end of November or in December. Liam has promised them that."

"Then Liam will have his work cut out. If he is in a hurry he will have to take chances and he may make mistakes. I should be happy to see him put away, permanently."

Before, when speaking of the activities of the counter-revolutionary warfare team of the SAS which he headed, the Colonel had spoken of things that 'we' did or 'we' knew. Now he said 'I'. For some reason Mowatt found this disturbing. He was fairly certain that 'Dirk' was the Colonel's stepson, but he did not feel able to put this suspicion into words.

Part One

Assembly

1

"I don't like it, Lion," said Mr. Norrie. "I want to know what's behind it and it's your job to find out."

Anthony Leone, who had long ago got used to different English versions of his name, sighed and said, "I'll do my best, sir."

Mr. Norrie was the Stipendiary at Reynolds Road Magistrates Court, in the South Eastern District of London. Anthony was the senior Probation Officer working at the court. He had seen this assignment coming his way and was not keen on it.

"If it had been a crowd of West Indian hunkies," said Mr. Norrie, "we'd have expected trouble and been ready to deal with it. But these kids are Indians – "

"Pakistanis."

"No different. They all come from the same neck of the woods, don't they? Indians are usually peaceful folk, who do their jobs and make no trouble. When they do get into trouble their Community Relations Council can usually deal with it."

"They're very helpful," agreed Anthony.

"Another thing, the police don't like handling things like this themselves. To start with, it means bringing in an interpreter."

"Actually – not in this case. The Rahmans and the Kahns have been here a long time. These are third-generation boys. They speak better English than most of their friends."

"Then that'll make your job all the easier, won't it?" said Mr. Norrie. "Although, come to think of it, didn't someone tell me you speak their lingo yourself?"

"I'm not fluent," said Anthony. "I taught in two Pakistani schools before I took on this job. One in Abbottabad and the other, up in the north east, at Rawalpindi."

"Right," said Mr. Norrie, pleased that he had remembered this item. "It makes you just the man for the job, doesn't it?"

"I did wonder if we oughtn't to involve Sergeant Ames. After all, he is our Local Community Liaison Officer."

"Sergeant Ames," said Mr. Norrie, "is useless. He's as soft and wet as my bath sponge. Do you know that the first thing Brace had to do when he took over this Division was to tell Ames *to get his hair cut*. Think of that. A police officer being told to get his hair cut."

Anthony saw that he had lost. He said, "Well, sir, all I've got so far is Monty's story."

"Monty?"

"Sorry. Sergeant Montgomery."

"Does everyone call him Monty?"

"Most people do."

"I was never really sold on that chap. The General, I mean. Bit of a charlatan. Sorry, go on."

"He was on his way to the Observatory, where they'd had an attempted break in – the third in two months. He was using the divisional van. He was crossing Lyndoch Square and he saw this crowd. Two boys fighting and a lot of other boys watching them. Some of them were Pakistanis and others were Brits and he guessed they'd all soon be joining in if he didn't do something, so he and the driver jumped out. The two boys were rolling on the ground by this time, trying to bash each other's heads on the pavement. They hauled them to their feet, told them they were committing a breach of the peace and several other offences and bundled them into the van. Then they took them straight back to the Station and charged them."

"Good," said Mr. Norrie. "Good marks for Sergeant Montgomery."

"I quite agree. He stopped what might have been a sizeable race riot."

"One of the boys – " Mr. Norrie was inspecting the charge sheet which would be the basis of that morning's proceedings. "I call him a boy, but I see he's over eighteen – is Edward Drummer. His father must be the Abel Drummer who keeps the shop in Camlet Road."

"Lovebirds, snakes, tortoises, hamsters and tropical fish. A member of the British Legion and a past chairman of the Rotary. And an honorary member of the TA branch of the Royal Engineers. Did five years territorial service with them in the fifties."

"A solid citizen," said Mr. Norrie.

One of the things he liked about his Probation Officer was

that he produced facts, not theories. To begin with, he had been a bit suspicious of him. A foreign name. Some sort of Italian? And a schoolmaster, in India, too. But these prejudices had faded when he found that the man was prepared to work a fourteen-hour day looking after his difficult charges, finding out about them and their families and backgrounds; and above all, that he had the clarity of mind to present his results concisely. As facts, not theories. Mr. Norrie preferred facts to theories.

"The only thing I know to his discredit – if you can call it that – is that he's got a bee in his bonnet about Punjabis."

"How come?"

"It's ancient history now, but his friends all know, because he still talks about it. Particularly when he's got a couple of beers under his belt at the Social Club. Seems his father was in the Engineers, too. Did very well in the war and reached the rank of Warrant Officer. Unusual for a war-time soldier. His crowd was attached to 4th Indian Division in the North African fighting. There was a Punjabi Regiment on their left at Wadi Akarit. They reported one of the tracks clear. Well, it wasn't. Sergeant Major Drummer was blown up on a teller mine. Lost an arm and a leg and died soon after he got home. Abel would have been – let me see – about ten when that happened."

"When boys of that age get ideas in their heads, they stick," agreed Mr. Norrie. "All right. Now tell me about the Pakistani boy."

"I'll know more about the Kahns when I've had a chance to talk to their father. But I can tell you one thing. They came originally from the Sabeh Kehl mountains, on the northern frontier of Pakistan and that makes them Pathans."

"Pathans? You mean the people who live in Afghanistan?" Mr. Norrie's mind traversed fragments of history remembered from his schooldays. Kabul, Kandahar, Bobs, the Khyber Pass, soldiers being disembowelled by Pathan women. "We used to have a lot of trouble with them at one time, didn't we?"

"Like the Russians are now," said Anthony happily. "But there are plenty of Pathans outside Afghanistan. This particular lot joined the infant Pakistan State when it was created. Being Muslims, there were no difficulties about religion, you see."

"I don't see," said Mr. Norrie. "I don't know anything about their religious beliefs. What I *can* see is two tough crowds of

35

boys who'll make trouble if we don't nip it in the bud. Usually, with kids, it's half the battle if we can get the fathers on our side. So what's *their* attitude?"

"That's something I shall have to find out, sir. They were both round the Station pretty quickly, asking to see Brace. It was practically a dead heat. He decided to see them separately and asked me to sit in on it. In fact, he might as well have seen them together, because they both said exactly the same thing. It wasn't their boy's fault. The other boy started it."

"Natural reaction."

"Yes. But the odd thing was that they were both keen to stress that their boy was winning. It seems to have become a sort of challenge."

"When you talk about it in that way," said Mr. Norrie, "it sounds harmless enough. If it had been two English boys, I might have given them both a smack on the bottom and let them go. But we've got a tricky situation here. You've only got to look at a street plan to see it. The Pakis all live in that triangle north of Plumstead High Street and south of the railway."

"And keep themselves to themselves. They've got their own place of worship in Rixen Road and a meeting-hall in Bisset Street."

"They've given no trouble so far," agreed Mr. Norrie. "And it's up to us to keep it that way. I can't tell you what I'm going to do until I've heard what the police have got to say, but you'll certainly be involved. Yes. What is it?"

A policeman in uniform had put his head round the door.

"Good heavens. Is it ten o'clock already? All right. Tell Combs I'm coming."

"If I might?" said Mr. Nabbs.

He was a local solicitor and appeared in most of the cases in Mr. Norrie's court.

"Yes, Mr. Nabbs."

"The police have asked me to make an application on their behalf. It would be of great assistance to them if you would take the cases of Kahn and Drummer first. Their principal witness is Police Sergeant Montgomery. He is wanted urgently at the Royal Observatory. He was, in fact, on his way there yesterday afternoon when he was diverted to take a hand in the present matter."

"I think that's reasonable," said Mr. Norrie. "Very well, Sergeant."

Sergeant Blascoe, who had a voice which could be heard across the Thames at Wapping Old Stairs, bellowed, "Drummer and Kahn" and the two boys, who had been sitting on a bench outside the court room, silent and not looking at each other, appeared and were shepherded into the low-railed dock. Mr. Combs, the Clerk of the Court, read out the charge against both of them, which was one of assault occasioning actual bodily harm. He then invited them to plead.

The boys looked blank.

Mr. Nabbs rose swiftly to his feet. He said, "I am instructed on behalf of Drummer. In view of the fact that the assault – it might perhaps be described as a mutual assault – took place in public and that the bodily harm – " he motioned towards the dock, "is all too apparent on the faces of the contestants," Ted Drummer had a black eye and a split lip and Salim Kahn had a red and purple bruise on his cheek, "I have advised my client that he should plead guilty and I am instructed so to do."

"Is Kahn represented?"

"Apparently not, Your Worship."

A figure rose in the public benches.

"I've told him he should plead guilty, My Lord."

Mr. Norrie, undisturbed at being addressed as a High Court Judge said, "And who are you?"

"I am the boy's father."

"Very well." He turned to Salim. "You understand what your father says?"

"Yes, sir."

"And you plead guilty to this charge?"

"Yes, sir."

Mr. Norrie said, "Very well. Sergeant Montgomery."

The Sergeant entered the box and explained that he had been on his way to the Royal Observatory, on duty, when his attention had been drawn to a hold-up in the traffic at Lyndoch Square, where the High Street crossed the top end of Reynolds Road. It seemed that the hold-up had been caused by two boys fighting in the road.

"*In* the road?"

"Yes, Your Worship. Rolling together on the ground. I also

37

saw a group of boys on each pavement who appeared to be supporting the contestants."

"Shouting, do you mean?"

This question seemed to puzzle Sergeant Montgomery. He said, "No, Your Worship. I didn't hear much shouting."

"Then how did you know they were supporting them?"

How had he known? An instinct born of years of street work. Second nature, impossible to explain.

He said, "To tell you the truth, sir, I thought they looked like two packs of wolves waiting for the signal to join in."

Mr. Norrie, who knew and respected the Sergeant, accepted this flight of fancy without comment. He sat for some seconds in silence. He had taken note, almost subconsciously, of the boys' demeanour. Prisoners, particularly prisoners up for the first time, normally looked either frightened or aggressive. The two boys were exhibiting no such reactions. They were standing upright and still, like sentries on an important post, who had been trained to disregard the crowd which gaped at them and concentrate on the job in hand.

Mr. Norrie found this disquieting.

He said, "Thank you, Sergeant. If that's all, you'd better get along to the observatory."

After the Sergeant had stumped out there was a further moment of silence whilst Mr. Norrie made up his mind. He said, "I'm standing this case over for three weeks for reports. The accused can have bail. I shan't ask for sureties. But they are both to be available for my Probation Officer whenever he wishes to see them – or their friends. That's all."

2

"All right, Mr. Leeowny," said Drummer. "They were fighting in the street. And that's wrong. I have to agree with that. What I want to know is, why were they kept locked up overnight?"

Anthony said, "Perhaps the police thought they needed time to cool off."

"Surely that wasn't called for. As soon as I heard about it, I was round there and saw – what's his name? – the new boss."

"Chief Superintendent Brace."

"I can't say I cared for his manner. But I didn't want to annoy him. I simply told him I'd stand surety for any sum he liked to mention. I'm not short of money. He could have let Ted out on bail there and then, couldn't he? Wouldn't have been any difficulty, would there?"

"No. The police can give bail, in a suitable case."

"That's what I mean. A suitable case. Keeping him locked up all night made him look like a criminal."

Anthony nearly said he looked like a criminal as soon as he was charged, but he had, by now, made a fair estimate of Abel Drummer. A quick look round the room had told him a lot. The mugs with regimental crests on them, the pictures on the wall, a photograph in a place of honour on the sideboard. Drummer saw him looking at it and said, "That's a party the lads gave me when I left. Five years in the 164 TA Engineer Company."

"I'd heard you were an Army man," said Anthony. "So I expect you can appreciate that NCOs – in this case Sergeant Montgomery – sometimes have to act quickly, without any chance of consulting their superior officers. Maybe they make mistakes. But it's better to do something, even if it turns out to be the wrong thing, than to do nothing for fear of putting your foot in it. It was the Sergeant who charged the boys and told them they'd be kept overnight. Brace, of course, had to back him up. An officer has to stand by his NCOs."

This was an argument which Drummer found it hard to oppose with any conviction. He said, "Well – I didn't know it was Monty who did it. Usually he's level-headed enough."

Sensing that the steam was out of his protest, Anthony seized the chance to say, "It would be helpful if you could tell me something about your boy and his friends. They go round a good deal together, I believe."

"All boys go round together. They have gangs. Did it myself when I was young. The Lions we called ourselves." He laughed self-consciously. "I guess, with us, it was more roar than claw. Ted? Yes. And his kid brother, Robin. And there's the Connors' boy, Andy. His father works in the Arsenal. And Len Lofthouse. I don't know what his father does. And Norman Younger. Of course you'll have seen *his* name in the papers."

"Norman Younger," said Anthony slowly. "Yes, indeed. He got a trial for South London when he was only sixteen. It was some sort of record, wasn't it? Picking a player that young."

"Too young, in my view. But he'll be a great player in a year or two. Play for England, maybe."

"And this is the modern version of your Lions?"

"Young Britons they call themselves. They've got a regular headquarters. I was able to pull a few strings there. It's behind the club."

"Club?"

"The Social Club. You ought to put up for membership yourself. It's a friendly sort of place."

Anthony thought about it. There were undeniable advantages. The more local characters he knew, the better. He said, "That's very kind of you."

"Consider it done. Well, as I was saying, the boys use a shed behind the club. Before we took the place over it was a stationer's shop. Old Walkinshaw. He had his own printing press – a tuppenny halfpenny affair – in a shed behind his shop."

Anthony had once boasted that not even the local taxi drivers knew more than he did about the highways and byways of Plumstead. He said, "You mean it's down Wick Lane. That sort of passage that runs behind the shops in Berridge Street."

"Right. It's not palatial. But they've cleaned it up and put in a table and some chairs. They've even got a typewriter."

"And they meet there to discuss their policy."

Drummer looked at Anthony sharply, to see whether he was laughing at him, decided that he wasn't, and said, "That's right."

"And what is their policy?"

"Their policy is the same as my policy. And I've no objection to telling you what *that* is." Anthony noticed that his face, which was naturally red, had taken on a darker colour, as though it was being heated up by the force of what he was saying. "They think and I think too, that this is a bloody fine country. The best country in the world, by a length and a half. A lot of foreigners come here and they like it, too, or they wouldn't stay here, would they? Black or brown or yellow, I don't mind what colour they are, so long as they behave themselves. Most of them do, but some of them don't. Some of

40

them think this country is easy pickings for them. Anything that's going, they've got to have it, whether they've earned it or not. People talk about underprivileged groups. What they don't realise is that it's us, the people the country belongs to, who are underprivileged. I don't expect you to understand that, being a foreigner yourself."

"Fourth-generation English," said Anthony mildly.

"Well, whether you understand it or not, that's our policy and we're prepared to fight for it – if we have to."

"I hope it won't come to fighting. A great Englishman said, 'Jaw, jaw, is better than war, war.'"

"We're not looking for trouble," agreed Drummer. "Don't think that. But if trouble comes our way we can look after ourselves. Isn't that right, Tiger?"

He dropped one hand on to the head of the Rhodesian ridgeback that was lying beside his chair. The dog, which Anthony had been admiring ever since he had come into the room, turned its head up and smiled – at least he thought it was a smile. It certainly showed all its beautiful teeth.

"Not long ago," said Azam Kahn, "there was a lot in the papers of what they were pleased to call Paki-bashing. Yes? Not so much lately."

"There was a bit of that," said Anthony, "but it was in places like Putney and Wimbledon."

"Ah, yes. Putney and Wimbledon. A lot of stupid people live there."

If Azam cared to develop this interesting conception of the western suburbs of London, Anthony had no desire to dissuade him. He was delighted to be listening once more to the careful English of a self-educated Pathan. It brought back to him the political and philosophical discussions he had had with his houseman, when he had lived outside Rawalpindi. The people of the north were great talkers, delighting in philosophical speculation and political debate.

"One mistake people in this country make is thinking that all Pakistanis are the same. Just like you might say, 'all Europeans.'"

"That's silly," agreed Anthony. "Like saying, 'all Arabs.'"

"Pakistan – and I mean Western Pakistan – is more than four times the size of Great Britain. Naturally you get many different types. In the south, there are a lot of Hindus. Nothing much wrong with them except that they spend most of their time thinking about money. Also about caste." He dismissed them with the same disapproval as the people of Wimbledon and Putney, and presumably for the same reasons. "In the north we are tribal folk. We were Mahsuds, from the Sabeh Kehl mountains. Very wild people. My father, Ghaffar Kahn, was a havildar in the 16th Field Transport Company. They were well spoken of by General Wayfull."

"Wayfull? Oh, Wavell, yes."

"I said so. That same Wayfull, who was also Viceroy. Perhaps you would like to hear what he said."

"I should like that very much."

Azam extracted from the back of his wallet a piece of paper, creased and folded in a way which suggested that it had been taken out and put back countless times.

"This I copied from General Wayfull's own book. He was speaking of the riots in Calcutta in August of 1946. Terrible riots. Five thousand people killed, many more injured. He said, 'I saw Bucher, acting Army Commander and Sixsmith, acting Area Commander, both good and sensible men who had done very well. They described events to me and the action of the troops. So far as I could see, their judgment and action had been correct and they had used the troops at the right time and in the right way. Bucher said the Indian troops, including Transport Companies, behaved very well indeed. One was manned by Mahsuds of the Sabeh Kehl whom we are now bombing.'"

Anthony could see that he was only pretending to read. It was clear that Azam knew the passage by heart. He said, "You understand we remained true to our salt even though our own homes were being bombed. That is the sort of people we are."

"It was a difficult time for everyone."

"So difficult that my father decided we must come south. We settled between Muree and Abbottabad. You know those places?"

"Very well."

"We were happy there for some years. Then came further troubles."

"I know about them, too."

"They were terrible. Terrible and unnecessary. You must

understand that we frontier Muslims did not hate the Hindus. Why should we? When Pathans kill, they kill for family reasons, not for religion. Nor do we kill women and children. That was vile. So we decided to leave. We and our friends, the Rahmans. They thought as we did. They are an Adam-Khel Afridi family."

"Was it difficult?"

"Difficult? How? To come here? No difficulty at all. My father was a skilled motor mechanic. The Rahmans were locksmiths. Both families got category B vouchers. That was under the rules of the Department of Environment. We had been citizens of Pakistan. Now we became citizens of this country. Very simple. My father set up his garage and repair shop. East London Motors, he named it. You know it? It is where Reynolds Road runs into the High Street. A fine corner site."

And almost exactly the place where the fight took place, thought Anthony. No-man's-land, between Pakistani territory and the conservative, middle-class settlements of Maindy Road and Camlet Street. It was an uncomfortable thought. He said, "The Rahmans are your neighbours. I have seen their shop, I think. 'Abdul Rahman, Locksmith'."

"Abdul is dead now. The shop is run by his widow, Tahira, a fine woman. And Gulmar, their eldest son."

"And it would be their children," said Anthony, feeling his way cautiously, "who are the particular friends of your children."

"What you are trying to say," said Azam with a broad smile, "is, 'this is a gang', yes?"

"Yes."

"There are others, too. There is Saghir Abbas, who they call Sher, and his cousins, the Randhawars and – oh, many others. But Salim and Rahim are the leaders."

"When you and the Rahmans came here – that would have been when – 1949?"

"1950. We were the first. Others followed."

"Had you any particular reason for coming to this part of London?"

"We are loyal servants of the Crown. We came here because it is a Royal Borough."

"Plumstead – a Royal Borough? I thought that Kensington – "

43

"Certainly it is royal. Does it not contain the Royal Arsenal, the Royal Artillery Barracks, the Royal Dockyard, the Royal Observatory – "

Anthony laughed. He said, "I hadn't thought about it that way before. I agree that there's a good deal of royalty about. May I give you some advice?"

"Of course," said Azam. "That is your job, is it not?"

"Very well. You said, just now, that you were loyal servants of the Crown. One of the things that the Crown values most is peace. It used to be called the King's peace."

"That I know," said Azam. "You must not imagine that we have not studied English history. The King's peace covered all the highroads in this country. People must be able to pass along their highways unmolested. So, if anyone did wrong to another on the highway, he had committed a breach of the King's peace and the King would punish him. Right?"

"Right," said Anthony, glad that this scrap of legal history should have sunk in.

"But," said Azam, "this peace extended only as far as the cleared borders of the road. Beyond that, lay the forest. In the forest, it was each man for himself. Tell me, now. Where does the forest begin?"

Sergeant Whitaker was hobbling briskly along Royal Observatory Road. He was wearing his Number One outfit, with the SAS flash. He was on his way to what promised to be an enjoyable social occasion in the Sergeants' Mess at the Royal Artillery Barracks. His host, inviting him, had warned him that it was likely to be a damp evening; which he understood to mean that a lot of beer would be consumed. He himself held the beer-drinking record for his Squadron. Seventeen consecutive pints. The runner up, the Squadron Commander Captain Musgrave, had failed at the fifteenth. If the gunners imagined they were beer drinkers, he was prepared to show them the light.

He was hobbling because, months before, he had dislocated his ankle chasing a light-haired bugger up a steep cliff path above Cuckmere Haven and although it now caused him very little trouble, it had never really set properly.

It was at this moment that the very man he was thinking about came out of a side turning and walked away up the pavement ahead of him.

He was in no doubt about the identification. He had seen the face as the man looked back from the cliff top, apart from which he could almost have identified him from his walk alone; the springy, confident walk of an athlete in top class training.

Whitaker slightly increased his own pace, but knew that he could not keep up for long. To his relief Blondie swung across the road and went through the wrought-iron gates on the other side. Some sort of up-market shop.

He peered cautiously through the gates. His quarry had walked up the stone-flagged path, climbed the shallow steps and was now pulling the wrought-iron bell-push beside the double doors of the house. Better to wait outside and see what happened next. If only there had been a telephone box in sight, but there never was when you wanted one most.

He examined the notice board which announced, in flowing script, *Arthur Drayling and Company. Foreign Tiles, Statuary and Ironwork*. Immediately inside the gate was an attractive lady, unclad and balancing dangerously on a pillar. If she had slipped she would have fallen into the mouth of one or other of the lions who flanked her. An evil-looking boy was waiting, hopefully, for this to happen.

Whitaker had no doubt as to his duty. His projected evening must go by the board. He had to wait until Blondie came out and then try to keep up with him. Next time he stopped he might be able to get a message through and get instructions and help. There was a useful vantage point opposite the gate of Drayling's establishment. The entrance to Greenhill Secondary School was set back, and by squatting on the low wall, he could rest his ankle and remain almost out of sight.

Time passed. Half past seven when he had first caught sight of the man. Now past eight. Eight fifteen. Nearly eight thirty, when Blondie came walking back down the path.

Whitaker was relieved to discover that his quarry was now walking more slowly, with his head bent forward as though he was thinking out some problem. Fifty yards on, he seemed to make his mind up, swung left into Frances Street and slightly increased his pace. There were two men ahead of him and a man and a woman coming in the other direction, arguing noisily. Whitaker was glad they were there. Footsteps on that particular piece of pavement seemed to echo loudly. Maybe it had been built over one of the water ducts running south from the Thames.

Keeping their original distances apart they passed the long frontage of the Royal Infantry Barracks. Blondie had slowed again, allowing the pair in front of him to draw ahead.

Whitaker thought, ten to one he's making for Woolwich station and will be heading back to London. That would suit him well. If he could discover what ticket his man bought, he would make a dash for a telephone. There would be boxes outside the station. If Captain Musgrave moved with his usual speed he could set up a reception committee.

At this point the road went into a short tunnel under the railway. He could hear a train approaching. This would be helpful, particularly since the two men ahead had now turned down a side road. The noise of the train would mask the sound of his own footsteps.

It had not occurred to him that the same thought might be in his quarry's mind and that his pace had been carefully adjusted to ensure that they both entered the tunnel under the railway at the moment when the train was passing on top of it.

He had the first inkling of this when he realised that Blondie had swung round and was almost on top of him.

After that he had no time for thought. A blow with the left hand swung horizontally hit him in the bottom of the stomach. As he doubled forward, the hard edge of the right hand came up and slashed him under the nose.

The blow fractured the bone of his nose. The pain was horrible. It brought Whitaker to his knees, where he stayed for counted seconds, his eyes blinded by tears, trying to master the nausea, trying to absorb the pain, trying to think what the hell he ought to do.

An effort of will-power got him on to his feet. He staggered clear of the tunnel. There was no sign of his quarry, nor had he expected that there would be; but there was a telephone box.

A woman, who was coming out of it, took one look at him and scuttled off up the pavement. The number he had to call had been so drilled into him that he had no difficulty in remembering it. The next thing was to find some money. He managed that, too.

He recognised the voice at the other end as belonging to the Orderly Room Corporal. He said, "Put me through to the skipper. Emergency routine."

46

"Can't hear you, chum. Who is it?"

Whitaker was finding it difficult to speak. He realised that his mouth was full of blood. He spat some out and said, "It's Sergeant Whitaker, Corporal Dunn. You heard me say emergency. If you don't pull your bloody finger out, you're for the high jump."

"All right, all right. Matter of fact the skipper's still in his office. Putting you through."

Captain Musgrave listened in silence to Whitaker's recital; half narrative, half confession. Then he said, "I've got Colonel Every here in the office with me. He's been listening on an extension. He'd like a word with you."

Christ, thought Whitaker. The old man himself. Now you're for it.

But Colonel Every's voice was surprisingly mild. He said, "I suppose you didn't happen to notice whether this man – I've no doubt that he's a character we know as Liam – actually used the station. I imagine it was the Woolwich Dockyard station."

Whitaker realised that the Colonel had been following his movements on a street plan and this gave him an illogical feeling of security. He said, "I'm afraid not, sir. I wasn't really in a state to notice very much."

"Broke your nose, did he? Underarm swing. Very painful. I ran into it once by mistake in combat training. On the whole, of course, you were lucky."

"Lucky, sir?"

"If Liam had thought you'd recognised him as the man at the caravan camp, he'd have shot you, no question."

"If he didn't recognise me, why did he attack me?"

"Just playfulness. I imagine he thought you were planning to proposition him. You wouldn't have been the first to try. It's that lovely blond hair of his."

Whitaker was almost more staggered by this outrageous suggestion than he had been by the assault itself.

Colonel Every's voice sharpened. He said, "Listen to me, because this is important. Get yourself back to base without attracting any unnecessary attention. We don't want the local police in on this. Not yet, anyway. Our own medico will look after you. You know the drill. Any questions?"

"No questions, sir."

Whitaker replaced the receiver gently. He had stopped bleeding and was conscious only of the intolerable ache which centred on the bridge of his nose and spread from the point of his jaw clear up to the top of his skull.

"Playful!" he said bitterly.

3

The plate outside the surgery in Maindy Road said 'Dr. Wilfred Graham, Dr. Anthony Laborde, Dr. Jennifer Marshal' – and in smaller letters and clearly a later addition, 'Dr. K. Dalpat'.

Whilst she waited to be attended to, Sergeant Montgomery's wife, Florence, was passing the time discussing the merits of these medicos with the only other occupant of the waiting-room, Shazada Kahn. Mrs. Montgomery was forty-five. On the whole she had stood up pretty well to the delivery of five children: one born dead; two boys and two girls surviving; also to the occasional brutality of her husband. It was mainly verbal brutality, but it was cumulatively wearing and had begun to affect her health.

"The one I used to see," she said, "was Dr. Graham, but I'm afraid he's what you might call old-fashioned. When it comes to nerves he's out of his depth entirely. Or perhaps," with a smile, "he doesn't think people like me ought to have nerves."

Shazada smiled back politely. She was so apprehensive about what lay ahead that she could hardly take in anything Mrs. Montgomery was saying.

"So my husband said, why don't you change to that woman doctor? That's what women doctors are for, to look after other women, aren't they? I didn't agree with him there. No, I said, you go to a doctor because you think he can do you good. Dr. Laborde's modern. You can tell that by the way he talks. *He* understands nerves. Ah well, I suppose you'll be seeing Dr. Marshal."

48

"No. I'm on Dr. Dalpat's list."

"Of course, dear. He's from the same part as you, isn't he?"

"Not quite," said Shazada. She was used to the illusion that India was a small green patch on the map and that everyone in it knew everyone else. "Actually he's a Punjabi. He comes from Rajkot."

"And that's different, is it?"

"It's about a thousand miles south of the place we came from."

"Well, fancy that." All this was leading up to what Mrs. Montgomery really wanted to know. She said, "And what can it be that brings a young lady like you to the doctor? I'm sure you look a picture of health."

Shazada was ready. She said, "It's a cough. It comes on at night and keeps me awake."

"They've got some very good cough mixtures in the chemists. I always use Dr. Blossom's Lung Syrup. Have you tried it?"

"I don't think I've tried that one, no."

"Which one do you prefer then?"

"I'm not sure of its name. It's dark brown and rather sticky."

"And is that the only one you've tried?"

"So far, yes."

"Well there now. If your cough really is troublesome, I should have thought you'd have shopped round until you found something that did do it some good."

"Mrs. Montgomery," said the nurse, putting her head through the hatchway from the dispensary. "Dr. Laborde will see you now."

Shazada watched her departure with relief. It wasn't that she was ashamed of what she was doing. Why should she be? She was doing it for Tim really, not for herself. And anyway dozens of her friends, girls at the school she had just left and girls at work, did it as a matter of course –

"Miss Kahn. Dr. Dalpat is free now. He has the room at the end of the passage, on the left."

As the newest member of the medical firm, Dr. Dalpat had naturally been given the worst room. Its chief drawback was its smallness. There was hardly space for more than a desk and a chair and the patient was forced to sit on the same side as the doctor.

49

It would have been difficult enough to say what she had to say across the wide separation of a table. Sitting almost arm in arm made it much harder.

"Well, young lady," said Dr. Dalpat, "what can I do for you? Let me see." He shuffled some cards out of the filing cabinet under his left elbow. "Kahn. Bisset Street. Number 16. Is that right?"

"Yes."

"Your father is Azam Kahn. Yes? He keeps the garage in Lyndoch Square. A fine mechanic. I take my car there when it makes improper noises. Just as he comes to me when his body behaves in the same way."

Shazada smiled faintly.

"I see that I have patched up both of your brothers recently. Salim and Rahim. Right? They seem to spend much of their time fighting. Of course, all boys fight. But not girls. Girls fight only with their tongues. The scars that they leave are not visible. So what is it that I can do for – " he looked down at the card and then up at the girl, "the charming Shazada?"

Shazada took a deep breath. She said, "I want the pill."

"That is a very imprecise way of talking about a medicament." Dr. Dalpat grinned in a way which lifted his upper lip and showed his white teeth. "I have many dozen different sorts of pills. Pushy manufacturers send me lists of them every week. They assure me that they will deal with every conceivable human need. Now what particular ailment is it that is afflicting you?"

Shazada took another anguished breath. She said, "I want the pill for – I mean, the pill which prevents you from becoming pregnant."

"I should have thought you were rather young to be married."

"I'm – I'm not."

"You're not married?"

"No."

Dr. Dalpat looked her up and down. She was, he saw, blushing. This made her look even more attractive. He said, "You realise that the pill you mention is designed for married women. Women who might not – for perfectly understandable reasons – wish for pregnancy at a particular time. They are not intended to encourage promiscuous sex. How old are you?"

50

"Sixteen."

"The person you should be discussing this with is your mother."

"My mother is dead."

Dr. Dalpat, who had their records on his desk in front of him, was aware of this. But he was enjoying the conversation too much to cut it short.

He said, "Your father then."

"I couldn't talk to him about it."

"Why not?"

"He wouldn't understand."

"Or do you mean, perhaps, that he would understand only too well?"

Shazada had nothing to say to this. She only wanted him to stop talking and say whether she could have what she wanted.

Dr. Dalpat looked at her thoughtfully. He wondered what lucky boy was going to have this treat. It would be agreeable if he could extract one or two – well, one or two details.

He said, "I think I ought to know a little more about what your intentions are."

"I can't – "

"You have some definite plan then? Don't be ashamed to discuss it. I am a doctor. I understand such things. Some boy has gone a certain distance with you and desires to go further."

Shazada started to get up. It was going to be awkward, squeezing round the end of the desk, but she had to get out of the room.

Dr. Dalpat saw that he had gone too far. He took a form out of the drawer which was partly filled in, scribbled something on it and threw it at Shazada. He said, "Very well. If you want to go to the devil, young lady, I can't stop you."

When Mrs. Montgomery got back from the doctor's she found, not entirely to her surprise, that her husband was not home. His relief, in which he was one of three sergeants and twenty constables, nominally did an eight-hour spell each day, but this was so organised that he could expect either two afternoons or an afternoon and an evening off on alternate weeks. This free time was liable to be interfered with by his special duty at the docks, or entirely abandoned if any of the frequent crises arose which afflicted the life of a policeman.

51

And his wife, thought Mrs. Montgomery. She was not bitter about it, but thought that when he did get an evening off he might occasionally devote it to her and the children.

He had pushed off after tea without any real explanation of his plans, but since she had seen him get into Drayling's car which was parked at the end of the road, she had a fair idea that he was making for the Catford Greyhound Track.

She disliked Arthur Drayling for no more particular reason than that when, on a single occasion, he had come into their house he had spent most of his time enquiring about her disciplinary methods. Did she spank all the children when they were naughty, eh? And what did she use? A hairbrush or a slipper? When he had been a boy he had found that a hairbrush was more painful, ha, ha, particularly when trousers had been taken down. Mrs. Montgomery, who very rarely gave her children more than a cuff over the ear when she finally lost her temper, found this sort of talk distasteful.

Also she suspected that her husband was in Drayling's debt. She guessed this, because the money lost on horses and greyhounds had not come out of the housekeeping. Her husband handed over the same amount as usual every Friday and seemed to have enough of his pay left for his normal drinking and smoking, which could only mean one thing. Someone must be financing his betting and if things went wrong this could produce a difficult situation.

She had a feeling that things had been going wrong lately.

She thanked the neighbour who had been keeping an eye on the kids while she was at the doctor, put on the kettle and settled down to the one sure palliative for all life's ills, a cup of tea.

When her husband came back she could see that that afternoon, at least, had been successful. For once he was prepared to tell her something. He explained that a greyhound which he had been watching for some time had at last come good. "He was a lazy bastard," said Monty. "Never exerted himself. Never showed his true form. Unplaced in six races. We had a feeling that seven was his lucky number. Put twenty quid each on him, at twenties. Four hundred smackers. What do you say to that?"

"I'd say it was time to stop."

Her husband took this surprisingly well. He said, "And you

52

might be right at that, love. The whole game's as crooked as a corkscrew. I've got a feeling that this afternoon's effort was rigged. They'd been holding this dog back to get the odds right. Giving him something in his feed most likely."

"If it's like that you ought to keep clear of it."

"I can't knock it off just yet, but one more like this afternoon and I'll be in the clear and we'll have something to celebrate. So what did the old medico say to you this afternoon?"

"He said I mustn't worry so much."

"Good advice."

"And he gave me some pills. To make me sleep better at night."

"I'm glad about that," said her husband. "At the moment you thresh round so much you keep me awake. Or would do, if I wasn't so bloody tired."

"I had a talk with that Kahn girl. She was waiting to see the new doctor."

"The Jabi?"

"That's the one. And guess what she told me? Said she was seeing him because of a cough that was keeping her awake nights." Mrs. Montgomery chuckled. "As if I didn't know exactly what she wanted. A free handout of the pill. That's what she was after."

"Is that the one they call Shah? Sister of the boy I nicked. Rather a tasty little bint."

"They're all alike," said Mrs. Montgomery. "Black, brown or yellow. All they think about is boys."

"I wouldn't mind a helping from that particular dish myself."

"Get along with you. She wouldn't have any use for you."

"Oh, what makes you think that?"

"You're the wrong colour and the wrong age. It's some black kid just out of school who's after her, I don't mind betting."

She would have lost her bet.

Shazada and Sapper Timothy Sunley were in each other's arms with only a thin layer of straw between them and the rough planks of the stable loft. They were lying so tightly together that each could feel the other's heart beating against its rib cage.

She had first seen him in the supermarket. She had been lucky to get a job there after leaving school at the end of that summer term. He was wearing faded blue jeans and a khaki polo-necked sweater and his hair, which he had forgotten to brush, tumbled in a wave over his forehead. She had thought he looked very nice. Tim was on a week's leave. His platoon was currently mounting the guard at the Royal Arsenal. When the main part of the Arsenal moved away from London some bits had been left behind, including the Explosives Office and Laboratory and a number of Powder Magazines. These had to be guarded and platoons of the local Sapper Unit undertook this in turns.

When Tim had finished his shopping he had wheeled his trolley across to the tills. He had seemed to pick out the one where she was working. When he had smiled at her, her heart had jumped and then seemed to turn right over. After that matters had progressed rapidly.

They couldn't meet every day, but they met whenever his tour of duty allowed him away from the Arsenal. His desire for her body had been so strong and so straightforward that it had both excited and scared her. The difficulty was finding somewhere they could be together and away from inquisitive eyes.

It was Shazada who had suggested the Old Farm. This was a derelict building on the far side of the track called Picquet Way, which ran north from behind Azam Kahn's garage. She had sometimes walked up it on a Sunday, with her brothers. For a hundred yards it was a public way, serving a sportsground. After that it was barred by a steel fence and a gate and there was a notice stating that the road was private. It led only to the Proof Butts and Powder Magazines.

"Perfect," said Tim. "No difficulty for you getting through the hedge on this side. I can come straight across from the Arsenal."

"How?"

"Easy. Everyone in our section knows about it. It's a sort of private back door. We use it when we don't want to go out through the main gate. I'm sure we could find what we want in there."

What they had found was the stable. It was all that was left of a building that had been destroyed by fire and abandoned fifty years before. The grounds were overgrown with interlaced laurels, elder, thorn, holly and yew, a mingling of the original

54

garden with the invading wilderness. It formed a more effective barrier than the simple wire fence which surrounded it. They had reached the stable with scratched hands and faces. This had increased the excitement.

Well knowing the nosey habits of her family Shazada had persuaded Marlene, her best friend at the store, to alibi her. When she went out in the evening they started together to go to the pictures. Marlene left her when she was safely started up Picquet Way. She was older than Shazada and had her own opinion of Tim. What she thought was, a lot of prick and not much backbone, but she was too nice-minded to express it in such words.

Shazada had reached the stable three times without, as far as she knew, attracting attention. On each occasion Tim had become more insistent.

When she pushed him away, he let her go reluctantly.

He said, "Did you get them?"

"I took the first one yesterday. It was horrid."

"I thought they didn't taste?"

"I meant getting them was horrid. It was that new doctor. Doctor Dalpat."

Tim laughed. "The boys call him Doctor Cowpat – did you know? So he was horrible?"

"Yes."

"You mean he messed you about?"

"He didn't touch me. It was the way he looked at me and the things he said. I think he wanted me to tell him all about you."

"But you didn't."

"Of course not."

Tim relaxed. He said, "I tell you what. I could get one or two of the boys in my section to help me and we could follow him when he comes out one evening and duff him up to teach him manners."

"No. It'd only make trouble. Our family's in bad with the police as it is – did you know?" But Tim wasn't interested in her family. Shazada had all his attention.

"Did he say how long?"

"No. But I asked the chemist. He said a fortnight."

"A fortnight. I can't wait that long."

"You're rather jumping to conclusions, aren't you?"

"Am I?"

"I never promised you anything."

"But you will, won't you?"

"I'll think about it."

He slid his arm round her waist, under her jersey and rucked it up. He could feel her body, warm and soft along the length of his arm. For a moment he wondered: if he insisted would she put up much of a fight? He had just enough sense not to try. He could wait a fortnight, just about, but no longer. It was keeping him awake at night.

He said, "You don't think there's anything wrong in it, do you?"

"I don't know."

"In your religion a man's allowed four regular wives and any number of part-timers. It's to make up for not being allowed to drink. Or that's what I was told."

"I expect you've been told a lot of funny things about us. Most of them lies, probably."

"Like you say your prayers six times a day."

"Our family gave most of that up when we came to England. But they go to midday service on Fridays. That's just for the men. I'm glad I don't have to go. It's a long sermon, really."

"What about?"

Shazada said, seriously, "It seems to be mostly about what happens if you break the law. Not your law, our law. The law of Islam."

"What does happen?"

"After you've been buried, two angels visit you and ask you questions about how you've behaved. If your answers are all right, they carry you off to paradise. If you can't answer, they torture you by making the earth press down on you."

"But you don't believe it, do you?"

"When I was young I did."

"It's all nonsense. Like the devil and hell-fire and things like that."

"Are you sure that they are nonsense?"

For a moment Tim looked worried. Then he said, "Of course they are. No one believes in them nowadays."

Picquet Way was not a thoroughfare and was only really used when the sportsground was open. On this occasion, as before, Shazada succeeded in reaching the end of it without being seen. As she slipped through the back entrance and into the yard of East London Motors she met her younger brother, Rahim.

He said, "Hullo Shah. Where have you been?"

"To the cinema, with Marlene. Not that it's any business of yours."

"Good film?"

Shazada was trying desperately to remember what was on at the local cinema when an interruption occurred. At the back of the yard their father had allowed the boys to build a sort of shack and had supplied some of the wooden planks which walled and roofed it. Salim emerged from it and said, "Hurry up, Ray. Late as usual. Where have you been?"

"Nowhere special. What's up?"

"Mr. Lee-owny's coming to see us."

"What does he want?"

"I expect he wants to tell us all to behave ourselves. Me particularly."

"That's not a bad idea," said Shazada shortly. She was fond of her elder brother and did not like the idea of him being in trouble.

4

That morning Anthony Leone had said to his wife, Sandra, who was the only person with whom he discussed his protégés, "I saw the Drummer boys and their friends yesterday evening."

"Those yobs."

"Wrong. They're not yobs. I assure you they'd be horrified if anyone called them a name like that. They take themselves very seriously, let me tell you."

"As long as someone does."

"A big part of my job is going to be preventing either side taking themselves too seriously. However, let me get everything in proper order."

"Sorry," said Sandra. She realised that she was being used as a scribbling pad and went on with her dusting and polishing.

"I visited them in their headquarters. It's a building behind the Social Club. Quite a solid brick structure. Very neat and business-like inside with a desk and an old typewriter and shelves of books and maps on the wall."

"Maps?"

"Street maps, with coloured pins stuck into them. Enemy. Own Troops. Just as though they were planning a campaign. When I asked them about it they said it was a game. Mock warfare. They've got all the jargon. Front lines and reserves, supporting arms and pivots of manoeuvre."

"Dangerous game," said his wife.

"It depends on the players. Well, the big five were all there. Ted Drummer, he's unquestionably the leader and Robin, his brother. Less character, but more brains than Ted, I should guess. They call him 'Boy'."

"Ages?"

"Nineteen and sixteen. Number three is Andy Connors, who's seventeen. Planning to join up as soon as the army'll have him. His father's a sergeant in the RE Section at the Royal Arsenal. Next there's Len Lofthouse. Called the 'Lump'. He's a hefty lad; the muscleman of the group. Casual labourer, works in coal yards and cement and aggregate dumps – when he can get a job, which isn't often. And last, but by no means least, Norman Younger."

"The boy football wonder."

"And a bit conscious of it."

"For heaven's sake," said Sandra, suspending her polishing, "how can you expect a kid who's not yet seventeen and sees his picture every week in the local press – and sometimes in the national papers as well – not to think he's something special?"

"OK. Down with the media," said Anthony. "Bad medicine for the young."

"Have the Drummer boys got jobs?"

"Ted helps his father in the shop. He's a bit self-conscious about that. I mean, if they were selling something macho like guns or sports kits it'd be different. But canaries and goldfish!"

"I see his point. And Robin?"

"Just left Plumstead Secondary. Should really have stayed on another year. I had a word with Mr. Locke, the head. He's convinced Robin could have had a place at university, but he wouldn't stay on and Locke wasn't going to keep him against his will. Probably a correct decision."

"Unemployed?"

"No. He's got a job and a good one, with the Clipstone Sand and Gravel Company. It's on the river, north of Cooling. Robin got it through a friend at school, whose father works there. He goes there every morning on his motorbike. Twenty-six miles. His best time so far is thirty-four minutes."

"He'll be a dead Young Briton if he doesn't watch it."

"He does most of it on the A2. He says he can average eighty on one stretch."

Sandra said, "Well, they don't sound a bad bunch, really."

Anthony considered this as carefully as he considered all his wife's opinions. "Individually," he said, "there's nothing wrong with them. A bit of brains and a bit of brawn. It was the gang spirit, combined with the maps on the wall, that I didn't like. They were a damned sight too military. When I asked Drummer Senior about them he told me that their policy was – 'Put Britain First'."

"And what's wrong with that?"

"Nothing. As long as the corollary isn't – 'Keep the Others in their Place.' And there's another thing. A sort of personal rivalry between Ted and Salim."

"In the old days," said Sandra, "when two tribes had a difference of opinion, they let their headmen fight it out in single combat and agreed to abide by the result. It's a pity we can't do the same thing now."

"Prime Minister against Prime Minister?"

"Why not?"

"Some of them are women nowadays."

"So what? Women fight just as hard as men. And twice as dirty."

Anthony tried to visualise the heads of England and France in bare-fisted combat. He said, "Well, it's a lovely idea."

He had arranged to visit the opposition that evening. This had to take place after hours as three of the boys, he knew, had jobs. When he got to the yard behind the Kahn garage and workshop he found that their meeting place was an altogether more ramshackle affair than the headquarters of the Young Britons. It had been knocked together out of planks and sheets of plywood. The sloping roof had once been part of an outsize packing-case. He could still see the words 'East London Motors' stencilled across it. It reminded him of constructions he had seen in the slums of Abbottabad. There, whole families had lived in them.

This interior was arranged more like a living-room than an army headquarters; a decrepit sofa, a newish armchair, a card-table and three collapsible canvas chairs of the type used by army officers as camp equipment. There were five boys present, two of whom, Salim and Rahim Kahn, he had met already. Salim introduced the other three to him with adult formality. Javed Rahman, Rameez Rahman the brother of Javed, and Saghir Abbas a friend of both families. Later, as the discussion became more relaxed, he identified them as Jay, Ram and Sher.

Anthony opened on the same line he had pursued on the previous evening. He said that they were all of them old enough to behave sensibly. Salim had not been in any trouble before. Nor, as far as he knew, had the other boys – had they?

Four heads were shaken.

Very well then. He couldn't promise anything, but he thought it most likely that the magistrate would bind Salim over or give him a conditional discharge. But if there was any further trouble, then the police would be bound to take a very serious view of it after this warning. Did they understand that?

Four pairs of eyes were fixed on Salim.

At this point in his previous interview, Ted Drummer had said, predictably, that they were none of them looking for trouble, and if other people left them alone, they would leave other people alone. He expected Salim to use much the same formula. Instead, after a pause, he said, very respectfully, "We have been told that you lived at Rawalpindi, sir. Is that true?"

"Yes. Why?"

"Then you will have acquired some knowledge of our people."

"Of the Afridis? Yes, a little."

"With us a feud is a serious matter. An affair of honour."

"And who, precisely, do you imagine you have a feud with?"

"Perhaps a feud is too serious a word. But I have a quarrel with Edward Drummer which will have to be settled. He has been spreading untruths about me."

"Oh. What has he been saying?"

Salim looked at Saghir, who nodded.

"He said, when other boys were present, Jay and Sher were there too, that if the police had not intervened he would have given me such a beating as would have taught me manners. I did not object – " Salim showed his teeth for a moment in a tight smile, "to him saying that he was *trying* to teach me manners. What was incorrect was saying that he was succeeding."

"Oh come. That's not a serious matter. Anyone who takes part in a fight which gets stopped may think he is winning."

Five heads were shaken in violent dissent.

Salim said, "We know, and he knows, that I was winning. He has not been taught to fight in the same way that I have. Unfortunately my foot slipped and we fell to the ground together. That was when my face was bruised. Not by him, you understand, but by the fall. It made no difference. If the policeman had not been there, the fight would have ended in his destruction."

"I think," said Rameez, "that if the policeman had not been there his friends would have joined in to save his skin."

"Ram's right," said Rahim. "They all knew that he was being defeated."

"And if that had happened," said Anthony, "I suppose you would all have joined in."

"Of course," said Saghir. "And many of our friends who had heard the words used."

Now we're coming to it, thought Anthony. He said, "Tell me. What *was* it all about?"

Salim said, "The clock in the square was striking five as we came past. Ted Drummer shouted across the street – "

"Loudly, so that all could hear," said Rameez.

"The hour of prayer. Get out your mats, monkeys."

Oh dear, said Anthony to himself.

"That was not only insulting, it was stupid. Our family and the Rahman family have, in fact, given up the five-fold ritual of public worship. We confine ourselves to the first prayer and the last, which we observe in the privacy of our homes. It was not an easy decision, you understand. But our fathers considered the matter together and decided that since we were settled now permanently in England it would be sensible to modify the strict demand and that was how we should be brought up."

61

"I agree," said Anthony, "that what Ted Drummer said was stupid and tactless. Would it not have been better to ignore it altogether?"

"If I had been permitted to continue the fight to its appointed end, I should have been satisfied."

Anthony found it difficult to know what to say. His years in India had taught him that his religion meant a great deal more to a Muslim than Christianity did to the average Englishman. He had witnessed some of the unspeakably terrible results of this. He said, choosing his words and speaking slowly, "You are of the frontier Muslims. In the troubles which followed partition you took no part in the massacres. You were not fanatical, as were the Sikhs. In fact, your father told me that it was because his father disapproved of the violence that he brought his family to England. That is your tradition. A tradition of tolerance."

Salim said, with a tiny smile at the corner of his mouth which gave him a curiously adult look, "We do not plan to massacre Ted Drummer and his friends. But an insult has been given, heard by all here. It must be answered appropriately."

As Anthony said later that evening to his wife, "I was just about gravelled. There was such a serious logic in what Salim said."

"So what did you do?"

"I pushed off feeling ineffective. As I was leaving something rather odd happened. I ran into their father, Azam Kahn, being talked to by a man, who slid off as soon as he saw me coming, but not before I'd got a good look at his face."

"The press, I suppose."

"That's what he told Azam."

"But he wasn't?"

"Do you remember, when Elfe was staying with us in Rawalpindi, in connection with the trouble which was being stirred up among the Sikhs, he pointed a man out to me one day? I don't think he was one of the rabble-rousers, but Elfe seemed to think he was important."

"I remember him saying something about it. Why?"

"Well, that was the man I saw talking to Azam."

Sandra refrained from saying, are you sure? She knew that one of the faculties her husband was proud of – and a very useful one in his present job – was a memory for faces. About other things he made mistakes. About faces rarely.

She said, "Elfe told us his name. An uncommon one."

"He did. And I've forgotten it. I hoped you'd remember it."

Sandra shook her head slowly.

Next morning at breakfast she put down the coffee pot she was holding and said, "Firn. Spelt with an 'i'."

"That's right," said Anthony. "Olaf Firn. Good. With a name like that he shouldn't be too difficult to locate."

"He might have had some perfectly legitimate reason for talking to Azam. Maybe he has got a job on one of the national papers. Since the Brixton business they get excited about any racial trouble. Last month there were paragraphs and paragraphs about that white boy who spat in a black teacher's eye."

"You could be right. But if there's something else behind it, I've a feeling I ought to find out what it is."

This was a sound resolution, but like many sound resolutions, not easy to put into practice. Anthony's first call was at the public library, where he spent an hour with books of reference. Telephone directories, street directories, lists of lawyers, doctors, accountants, estate agents, dentists and veterinary surgeons. Drawing a blank with these he contacted a friend in the Post Office, knowing that they had more extensive nominal lists than any other government department. The friend was helpful, but warned Anthony that the references he had access to were confined to the south east postal district, from Southwark in the north west to Eltham in the south east. This district they covered in detail, street by street, but they produced no Firn.

Anthony knew that, if he was to go any further, he would need official help. He spoke to the magistrate's clerk who arranged for him to have a word with Mr. Norrie as soon as court rose for that day. This would serve a double purpose, since it was time he made an interim report. The summons came at one o'clock and he found the magistrate in a good temper. He had contrived to dispose of the court's business by lunchtime. It was an unusual thing to happen and it left him free to devote the afternoon to his hobby: the perusal, arrangement and classification of a vast stamp collection. King George the Fifth had had a larger one, but apart from his royal rival he believed that there were few collections in private hands to match his own.

He listened with half his attention to what Anthony had to

tell him and said, "If you think it's important you could ask Elfe about it, I suppose."

"I thought about that, sir. But he's rather a senior man. Head of the Special Branch. And besides, he may not like the idea of me following up something he said to me in confidence. I'd prefer to handle it a bit more discreetly."

Norrie said, "What I could do is have a word with Chief Superintendent Tancred at District. He's a good chap and I know him well enough to talk to him unofficially. He'd have access to the computerised records at Central and could put in an enquiry without having to explain what it was all about."

Anthony thanked him. Both he and Sandra had liked Elfe, but he was a formidable person.

He decided to spend the afternoon watching South London, whose second team had a midweek game. After all, he told his conscience, this would be partly business. He would be able to watch Norman Younger in action and form some impression of the character of that hopeful English international.

5

Arthur Drayling ranked in the general view, including his own, as one of the leading citizens of Plumstead. His shop or, as he sometimes called it, his studio, was also his private house. It stood in an acre and a half of garden and was fronted by a colonnade in the Italian style. Photographs of the beautiful things it contained, statues, baths and fountains, porticoes, wrought-iron gates and railings, appeared regularly in *Country Life* and *The Connoisseur*. It was a business which he had built up, with hard work and real artistic taste, over the forty years since he had left Oxford with an unimpressive degree, a small patrimony and a liking for instructive travel.

He was a heavily-built man. The bald dome of his head, sun-burned by the regular trips which he still took to Mediterranean countries, was surrounded by a fringe of curly auburn hair.

The reputation he had earned and the money he had made should have been the recipe for a relaxed and happy existence. If it was, it was curious that on that particular evening he seemed unable to sit still. He was in the main living-room of his house. It faced the back part of the garden, which sloped slightly downhill, with a view across Woolwich Common.

For no apparent reason he jumped up and paced across the room. This had as many gods and goddesses in it as any heathen pantheon. His objective seemed to be to admire for the hundredth time the young athlete in the corner. He stroked a hand over the smooth contours. It was a fine reproduction of an original by Donatello and he had refused many offers for it.

To his surprise he found that his hand was sweating. The weather was warm, but surely not as warm as all that? Probably he had allowed the room to get stuffy. He looked at his watch. Six o'clock. The club would be open. He would walk round for a drink.

He felt better as soon as he was out of the house. It was one of the incomparable evenings that early October sometimes brings, when the sun goes down in red splendour and there is a tiny, but invigorating, foretaste of winter in the air. When he reached the point where Perry Road turned right, along the north west wall of the Infantry Barracks, he stood for a moment listening to a train which was clattering along the line between the Arsenal and the Dockyard stations.

He was beginning to throw off the feelings which threatened him whenever he thought of the evening, when that vile boy had turned up, unannounced and horribly self-possessed, out of the autumn dusk. It was not so much the threat to his material welfare; it was the destruction of his peace of mind. Intolerable persecution. Unthinkable submission. He started to walk briskly as though by moving fast he could put the thought of it behind him. The exercise was doing him good. He was beginning to recover some of his poise. He strode along the pavement, crossed Berridge Street at the end and headed for the club.

He was too preoccupied to notice the man who turned the corner into Perry Road some seconds after he did and kept a careful distance behind him.

He found reassurance in his welcome at the club. The

65

ex-corporal of marines, who acted as caretaker, said, "Good evening, sir. You'll find quite a crowd here already. They were all talking about that piece in the paper about you." This was the first article in a daily series being run by the *Woolwich Herald* on notable local businessmen. No question that he was one of the most important businessmen in Woolwich and certainly the most important man in the club that evening. Not, he reflected, that the group present that evening amounted to much in the way of competition.

Little Mr. Nabbs, the solicitor; Crispin Locke, headmaster of the local secondary school, tall, thin and pedantic; Abel Drummer; Bernard Seligman, the grocer and a number of minor characters, hardly worth a glance. He accepted a drink from Seligman, who was holding forth on the unfair competition of supermarkets with decent old-fashioned provision merchants; 'provision merchant' being a description he preferred to 'grocer'.

"They buy in bulk and they undercut our prices," he said. "But I can tell you one thing. They have ten times more loss from shop-lifting than we do. Youngsters – boys and girls – go in there regularly, get behind one of the racks where they can't be seen and stuff things into their pockets or somewhere down their clothes. Then they come out with one or two small items, pay for them and walk off scot-free with the rest."

"Why don't they do it in your shop?" said Nabbs.

"Because it's arranged so that I and my assistants can watch every inch of it."

"I thought you were going to say that the sort of families who come to your shop are naturally more honest than the sort of ones who use supermarkets."

"Give 'em the chance; they're all dishonest," said Seligman gloomily. "And we know why. Schools don't teach them honesty nowadays."

"I thought it would come round to the schools soon," said Locke. "And I resent it. Tell me, how can schools teach children honesty when their parents live dishonestly?"

"Oh, come off it," said Drummer. "We're not a nation of crooks. Not yet."

"Maybe not crooks. Short changers, tax dodgers, people who travel first class with second-class tickets."

"I don't know if the present generation are more dishonest," said Nabbs. "But they're certainly cleverer. An articled clerk who joined me a year ago is already teaching me the law."

This produced a laugh. Nabbs was not a profound lawyer.

"Naturally every generation in a civilised community is cleverer than the last," said Locke. "It's the law of cumulative progress. You can't stop it. Twenty-five years ago no child would have understood computers. Now they take to them like ducks to water."

"There's one consolation," said Seligman. "In another twenty-five years *their* children will be sneering at them for not understanding the latest microchips. What do you say, Arthur?"

Called on to sum up arguments which he had heard many times before, Drayling put down his drink and pronounced, in his most judicial tones, "The thing which schools nowadays fail to teach is discipline. Financial discipline. Children who get everything free can't be expected to grasp the first rule of life. Which is, as I've often said before, that if you want something you've got to be prepared to pay for it."

"Talking of which," said Nabbs, "I'm bringing up at our committee meeting next week the question of whether those boys who use the shed behind the club house oughtn't to be asked to pay some rent."

"I'd support that," said Seligman.

"What if they can't afford to pay?" said Locke.

"I expect their fathers can help them out."

This was said with a side glance at Drummer, who ignored it and moved away.

Later Drayling joined him at a table in the corner. By this time most of the men had gone into the next room to watch a needle game of snooker and barrack the players. He said, "Don't worry about Nabbs. If he pushes his proposal through the committee you can count on me to contribute any rent they see fit to extort."

"That's very kind of you," said Drummer. "But I couldn't expect you – "

"Don't say any more about it. I'd like to do it. It'd be a privilege to support boys like yours. I heard what happened. It's right, isn't it, that the Paki said something insulting about this country and your boy knocked him down?"

"That's right," said Drummer.

He had repeated this version of it so often that he'd come to believe in it himself.

"He ought to have got a medal. Not been run up in front of old Norrie. Anyway, let me get you another drink."

It was half an hour and two drinks later when he left the club. It was dark now and the light mist which came up from the river on autumn evenings was beginning to veil the street lighting. He was glad that his route to the Arsenal station was along the public and well-used Berridge Street. There had been one or two stories of mugging in the papers. If it did happen, people said, the best thing to do was hand over your wallet and not make a fuss, but at that moment he had more money on him than he would have cared to part with. The entertainment he was after had to be paid for in cash. Quite a lot of cash.

At the Arsenal station he bought a ticket to Waterloo. There was not much traffic at that time of night and he found an empty carriage. No one followed him on to the platform and no one got on to the train after he did.

The man who had been following him was now seated in a car outside the station. The driver, a top-class rally driver, was confident that he could keep up with the train. In fact they missed it at Dockyard, owing to a jam in Woolwich Church Street, but made good use of a long clear stretch in Woolwich Road and were ahead of it at Maze Hill and again at Deptford. By this time it was fairly clear that their man was making for Central London. Unfortunately there were three termini on that particular line: London Bridge, Waterloo and Charing Cross. At London Bridge, with its maze of entrances and exits, they had to take a chance and it was a relief to see their man coming down the steps from Waterloo West and moving off down the road.

"Underground now, Max," said the driver. His passenger, who was the older of the two, a thickly-built man with weight-putter's shoulders and a shovel-shaped inquisitive nose, grunted and got out. Like a lot of big men he was lazy and preferred driving to walking. Luckily Drayling was not moving fast. As predicted, he was making for the Underground station in York Road. Since he bought his ticket at the machine, Max could only do the same and follow him down the long escalator and get into the train two carriages behind him. He had a lot of experience and he knew, from half a dozen tiny indications, that his quarry was, for the moment, easy and unsuspicious.

It would be different when he got closer to wherever it was he was going.

Drayling got out at Charing Cross station, passed the frontage of St Martins-in-the-Fields and strolled up the Charing Cross Road. He was walking more slowly now and stopped once or twice to look into booksellers' windows, as if interested in the titles shown there.

Max crossed to the other pavement and got well ahead of him. It was usually better to follow a suspicious man from in front. Also he wanted a chance to talk on the bat-phone which lived inconspicuously inside his coat. The car, if it had followed their agreed plan, should be in Soho Square by now. He found an empty doorway and stepped inside.

"Jonty. Max here. Are you on site?"

"Been here three minutes. Where've you been? Stopped off for a drink somewhere I suppose."

Max ignored this. He said, "The bod is coming up Charing Cross Road now. He's beginning to look fidgety, so I can't get too close. When he reaches Cambridge Circus, I'll tell you which way he turns. OK?"

Jonty, who had done his early service at West End Central, knew Soho. He said, "Dean Street, Greek Street, or maybe Barnard Street or Lord Scrope Street. I can watch the far end of any of them, as soon as we know which one it is."

"Right. He's at the Circus now. I'll have to shift."

When Drayling, after a number of hesitations and looks behind him, reached the corner of Barnard Street, he saw the bulky man, who had been hurrying along the pavement ahead of him, turn off down a side street. There were two girls coming towards him, holding arms and giggling. He let them go past him before he turned into Barnard Street. He was telling himself that it was absurd to be so cautious. No one was in the least interested in him.

The lighting in Barnard Street was not good and the doorway he wanted, Number 54, was midway between two of the old-fashioned lamp posts. He dived into it as quickly as possible.

"Did you get him?" said Max.

69

"I think so. The doorway in the building two up from the lamp post."

"Snap. Can you park the car and come down on foot?"

They met outside Number 54. It was a tall building of age-darkened brick which might have been put up at any time in the last 150 years. The houses on either side had suffered in the blitz and had been rebuilt, but only up to third-storey height, so that they looked like young friends supporting a taller and frailer man between them. All three buildings seemed to be full of offices. There was a frame inside the doorway of Number 54 which held cards. The ground floor and the three floors above it were occupied by two firms of wholesale fruit importers, a tailor and cutter, a vendor of canteen ware and a commission agent.

Max went out into the street and peered up.

"Only lights showing," he said, "on the top floor."

They had noticed that there was a space in the frame for the top floor, but no card.

Jonty, who was two inches shorter than Max and a few pounds lighter, a welter-weight compared to a heavyweight, said, "Suppose I'd better go up and have a squint, eh?"

"Better have a story ready if he bumps you. What are you doing? Buying a new suit or laying a few bets?"

"If I hear him, I'll come down fast. Then we put on the old drunk and fighting act. Right?"

They were a resourceful pair of goons who often operated together. The routine referred to had caused a useful diversion on more than one difficult occasion. This time it was not needed. A few minutes later Jonty reappeared and said, "There's a card on the door. Just tacked on. Looks new. Says, 'The Photographic Supplies Company'. I could see a light under the door and could hear men's voices. That's where the old bugger's holed up, for sure. What now?"

"I been thinking," said Max. "What we'd better do is, I'll stop here. You take the car, quick as you can, to West End Central. There'll be someone there you know who'll help. Ask him for the form."

Jonty said, "It was four years ago. But if my old oppo, Bill Bailey, is still there, he'd give us what we want. He knows every filthy rat's nest and whore's nest in this stinking square mile."

Like many policemen he had a puritan streak in him. Some

70

of the episodes during his posting in Soho had turned his stomach. Fortunately Sergeant Bailey was still at West End Central and was available. He welcomed his old friend boisterously and suggested a move to the Eagle and Child. Its private bar had, by long use, become a clubroom for local police officers.

"OK. But mussen be too long," said Jonty, "or I'll get stick from Max."

"Doesn't take long to drink a pint of wallop, boy."

"You've twisted my arm."

As soon as they were settled Sergeant Bailey said, "All right. What can I do for our political arm? What's the job?"

"Straight surveillance," said Jonty. He explained where they had got to.

"Number 54," said Bailey thoughtfully. "Yerrs. We've been wonderin' a bit about that. The new people on the top floor. Call themselves photographers."

"Photographic Supplies."

"Pornographic Supplies, more likely."

"What gives you that idea?"

"You haven't been round the back, have you? No. Well it's an old house and it's got one of those real old-fashioned fire escapes. You know the sort I mean? You can jack up the bottom section. Then it's out of reach of anyone down below. It always used to be kept that way at night, but since the top floor tenants have been there it seems it's been left down."

"Don't the other tenants object?"

"Maybe they haven't spotted it. They're mostly locked up and away by six o'clock. And it isn't too easy to see the back of the house, but there's an old boy has a studio in the block in Lord Scrope Street. He's a commercial artist and works late. He mentioned once he'd spotted boys going up the escape."

"Boys?"

"Twelve-year olds. That sort of age. He thought they might be sneak-thieves trying to break into the offices. That's why he reported it."

"But you don't think they were?"

"If you ask me," said Sergeant Bailey, "I'd say as like as not they were filthy little brats who'd sell their bums for a fiver."

Jonty thought about this. He knew enough about Soho not to be surprised, but his upper lip curled.

He said, "That's the scene now, is it?"

"PE's the name of the game. Paedophiliac Exchange. We raided a place the other day. They had a collection of photographs of boys in their nothings."

"Boys, not girls?"

"Boys mostly. Photographs and a collection of films. Some of the things they got up to – well – "

"Has the owner of this one got a name?"

"In our records he's a Mr. Lamb. Initials B.A."

"Baa Lamb. That's sweet."

"Oh, he's a sweet person."

"And you think that Number 54 is a new PE."

"Could be. Looks as if it might be the place they take the photographs and do the filming. We've got a friend in the tobacconist's opposite."

By 'friend' Jonty understood that he meant someone who would give the police occasional help without doing anything particularly active.

"He told us he thought he'd seen film equipment going in recently. We'll find out when we raid it."

"When will that be?"

"When we find time," said Bailey wearily. "Fast as you rake out one nest the rats set up another."

Jonty finished his drink, thanked Bailey and drove back to Barnard Street where he found Max propping up a lamp post.

"The bod came out ten minutes ago," he said, "and pissed off. Seeing as how you'd left me on my tod," he sniffed, "and taken yourself off for a drink – am I right? – I couldn't do much about him. Anyway I guess he was heading for home. What did you get?"

Jonty told him what he'd got. He said, "So what do we do now?"

"Report," said Max.

6

Two days later when Anthony got back after a frustrating afternoon spent trying to locate a certain Simon Leibovitz – one of his charges who had absconded for the second time from home without leaving an address – his wife said, "There's a man been to see you. He came about an hour ago, waited for a bit and then pushed off and said he'd look in later. Name of Robinson."

"Robinson?" Anthony made a mental check of the people on his conscience, but Robinson rang no bells. "What sort of man?"

"A policeman, I guess. From the way he barged in here as though the place belonged to him."

"Then I hope he gives me time to finish my supper before he barges in again. It's been one of those days." Over his supper he told her about it. It was always a relief to do this.

His visitor arrived with the coffee. Anthony thought that his wife's instinct had been correct. The man was thin and slight, neatly dressed, but not too neatly. He had a scarred and pitted face and a clipped moustache. If he was a policeman, he was a fairly senior one. He refused the offer of a cup of coffee and Sandra, gathering that the conversation would be official, withdrew to the kitchen to do the washing-up.

She guessed that she would hear all about it later.

As soon as the door was shut, his visitor said, "You've been making enquiries about a man called Firn. Why?"

"Before I answer any questions," said Anthony, "I'd like to know a little more about you. You introduced yourself to my wife as Mr. Robinson."

"Well?"

"Well, we'd get on a lot more easily if you told me your real name. And rank. Chief Superintendent? Commander?"

His visitor's face, which had been registering disapproval, thawed very slightly.

"Chief Superintendent Bearstead."

"Then you must be – let me think – second in command to Elfe at Special Branch."

"You know Commander Elfe?"

"Jack Elfe stayed in my house for a few days when he came out to Rawalpindi four years ago. It was he who pointed Firn out to me."

"I see," said Bearstead. He had relaxed at the mention of Elfe's name, but now seemed to be climbing back on to his official horse. "That explains how you knew the man's name, but it doesn't explain why you're making personal enquiries about him."

"Let's be clear about that. They're not personal."

"No?"

"I'm making them as part of my duty to the court, which is to find out everything I can about two lots of boys – their friends, their visitors and their background. And I made this particular enquiry through Mr. Norrie, the Metropolitan Magistrate, and he passed it on through Chief Superintendent Tancred, at District. And now will you have that drink I offered you? I usually take a glass of whisky as a night cap."

If he says yes, thought Anthony, we might get somewhere. If he says no, we're stuck.

"Thank you," said Bearstead. "With plenty of water in it." He swirled the drink round in the glass. He seemed to be giving himself time to think. Then he said, "When you were in Pakistan I imagine you were doing the same sort of job as you are here."

"Actually, no. I was a teacher."

A drop in temperature.

Bearstead said, "Oh, a schoolmaster."

"Why is it," said Anthony, "that whenever anyone admits that he has taught in a school he is automatically distrusted and disliked?"

Bearstead thought about this, downed some of the whisky and, to Anthony's relief, smiled. "I suppose," he said, "it's because most of us suffered from them when we were young. All right, I'll come to the point. But first, I'll have to have your word that nothing I say goes any further. No further at all. Not one inch. Not to your wife, not to that magistrate, not to Tancred at District."

Anthony said, "That's asking for two lots of trouble. Domestic and professional. I could agree about my wife – reluctantly. But if what you're going to tell me affects the boys – which I imagine it does – then I've got to tell Norrie. I report to him. That's part of my duty."

"I'm sorry," said Bearstead flatly. "It happens that you're in a position to help us. I wouldn't be exaggerating if I said in a unique position. And unless I have your word, I can't go any further."

Anthony hesitated. It was not only curiosity. It was also that, for no very definite reason, he was beginning to like and trust this thin, sun-dried man. In his job he met policemen of all sizes and qualities, some of them nice and reliable, some nasty and unreliable; all of them pulled in opposite directions by the conflict of power with responsibility. He felt prepared, on five minutes acquaintanceship, to put Bearstead into the top echelon.

He said, "Couldn't we compromise on this? I'll promise that I'll only say anything to Norrie *after* I've cleared it with you and got your consent."

Bearstead said, "If we didn't need you so badly, I wouldn't even agree to that. But we do, so I will." He paused and took the sort of deep breath a man takes before he dives into cold water. "How much do you know about the activities of terrorists?"

"Only what I read in the press."

"They get their share of media coverage," said Bearstead drily. "At the moment, then, there are four main groups. I'm not putting them in order of importance or efficiency. There's the PLO in the Middle East. They're a fragmented organisation now, not a single unit, which means they've lost a lot of their sharp edge. There's the Brigata Rossa in Italy, there's the Red Army Faction in Germany, who took over from the Baader-Meinhoff lot when its leaders were liquidated – or liquidated themselves – and last, but by no means least, there's the IRA. There are smaller groups, like the ETA Basque Independence movement, the Armenians in Turkey and the Moluccan Freedom Fighters in Holland. I don't say they're not dangerous, but they don't present the same problem to us, as they confine themselves mostly to their own patch. The other four are international. They'll hijack a plane flying from Paris to Morocco, murder a diplomat in Ankara or a policeman in Liverpool and sometimes it's difficult to see what they hope to gain by it."

"Might it be to persuade the people who supply them with money that they're earning their keep?"

"Could be. Or there might be nothing that you or I would consider a sensible reason. They're fanatics. Which means that they're not too worried about being caught or killed on the job. And they all suffer from the same built-in weakness. Their organisations are loose enough to be penetrated and all of them have been. Sometimes it might be only marginal penetration, like knowing where their funds come from and who passes messages and so on. But it means that if they've got an important job to do – what they call targeted action – they like to get outside help. Which brings in one of two or three real professionals who'll work for anyone who pays them. People like Willi Voss and Carlos Sanchez. Or Zohair Akache, who was killed by the SAS at Mogadishu. Before he joined the PLO Zohair had been working for the Baader Meinhoff group and before that for the ETA. They are chameleons. They adopt the names and nationalities of the group they are helping. The one we are now interested in calls himself Liam and has probably cultivated a sweet Irish accent. Actually, so far as we know he's a Lithuanian. Russian-trained, like the others."

"And Firn?"

"Olaf Firn is their paymaster."

"You mean that if one of the groups wants an important job done they get hold of Firn and say, 'Here's the cash. Please arrange for someone to do it.'"

"That's exactly what I mean."

"Then – surely – if you know this, all you've got to do is keep your eye on Firn and he'll lead you to these professional killers."

Bearstead smiled sourly. He said, "Tell me, Mr. Leone, how do you imagine Firn would set about hiring a professional killer? Perhaps you see him meeting him in a back street pub with a shopping bag full of used one pound notes?"

"All right," said Anthony. "Pax. It was a stupid thing to say. I'm sure that if you could have followed him you would have done."

"Olaf Firn is an accountant, with an office in Cheapside. He runs it under another name, of course. I believe he's very well thought of as a tax adviser. And you could bug his telephone and fan his mail every day in the year and learn nothing except how to outsmart the Inland Revenue. He operates accounts, for himself and his clients, in Luxembourg, Zurich, Lichtenstein, Abu Dhabi, Bombay and, for all we know, in Timbuktu and the Pearl Islands. He travels a lot, mostly in Europe and America, but also in the Middle East and India. He's on Christian-name terms with some of the top finance men in those countries and attends high-powered conferences as an adviser on arbitrage and liquidity. You see a flat-footed policeman sitting in the corner, at one of these conferences, taking notes perhaps?"

"You've made your point."

"If we're to deal with Firn and with the men he employs and pays – they too have accounts in half a dozen countries – there's only one possible way. We have to be ahead of them, not plodding behind them. We have to know, or guess, what they're going to do *and be there first.*"

Bearstead finished his drink. Anthony leaned across and refilled his glass. He did it smoothly, to avoid breaking in on the flow of words. He had rarely heard anything which interested him more completely and he wanted, above all, to know how he might possibly be involved.

Bearstead said, "Recently an SAS man happened to recognise Liam. It seems Liam was visiting the premises of one of your leading local characters: Arthur Drayling. You know him?"

"The garden man? Yes, I've met him."

"I'll leave out the details of how the SAS man happened to recognise him, because they don't affect what I have to say, but you can take it from me that it was an outrageous fluke. The sort of thing a betting man would rank as a hundred to one chance. You follow me? Right. Now let's look at you and Firn. The fact that you recognised him depended on you being at Azam Kahn's place at that particular moment *and* on having talked to Commander Elfe when you were in Pakistan. What would you call that? Another hundred to one chance?"

"Certainly. Also on my wife having remembered his name. I'm good at faces; bad at names. I'd totally forgotten it."

"And when you combine a pair of hundred to one chances?"

"I'm not a great mathematician, but I imagine you multiply

them together and call it ten thousand to one. Would that be right?"

"Something of the sort. Makes you believe in providence, doesn't it? But there was more to it than that. There was you."

"Me?"

"Providence has slipped us one more card. You're ideally placed to see how things develop. Much better placed than anyone we could bring in. And far less likely to arouse suspicion. It's your official job to keep in contact with those two lots of boys, isn't it? And you say you know Drayling."

"Not well. Though I may get to know him better if I'm elected to our Social Club. What exactly do you want me to do?"

Bearstead thought for some time about this. Anthony, who knew how such people worked, suspected that he was framing a directive, which he would later put into writing, to protect himself if his initiative was questioned.

He said, "Let me put it like this, Mr. Leone. By chance we know that Olaf Firn and Liam are interested in this part of south east London. They have an operation under way. Firn may, for once, be playing a more active part than usual. What we would very much like to know is the connection, if it exists, between Drayling and these warring groups of boys. All we're asking you to do is to keep your eyes open. We're not asking you to do anything heroic."

"Thank you," said Anthony.

"I'll give you a number to ring. It's manned twenty-four hours a day. And if you pick up anything – any tiny scrap of information, however far fetched or trivial, which might help us – let us have it at once."

"Then the way to look at it," said Anthony, "is that you've got two points. Join two points together and you get a straight line. Extend that line in either direction and it may lead you to where you want to go. Am I right?"

"I can see that you were once a schoolmaster," said Bearstead. But the smile which accompanied the words was surprisingly friendly.

7

It had been on the Wednesday that Max and Jonty, knock-about artists and members of the Special Branch of the Metropolitan Police, had made their first visit to Barnard Street. Friday evening found them comfortably established in the first-floor sitting-room over the top of the friendly tobacconist.

The lights from all the lower-floor windows in Number 54 had long been turned out. The last to go had been the Commission Agent who had hurried away at half past eight.

"Off to spend his ill-gottens on a champagne supper," said Max. He and Jonty were making inroads into a crate of bottled beer supplied by their host. At ten o'clock the light from the top-storey window was still showing. To start with it had been visible between two carelessly drawn curtains. Just before ten o'clock it had blazed out suddenly, at many times its original power, and had then, as suddenly, been cut off, seemingly by some sort of blind or shutter drawn down behind the curtains.

Only the smallest chink of light was now visible.

"Looks like it's time to move," said Jonty, gulping down the last of the beer in his glass.

They thanked their host. Their offer to pay for the beer was refused. Max was carrying an old-fashioned carpet-bag which clinked as they walked out into the street and crossed it. When they had climbed to the top floor of Number 54 they stood for quite a while in the darkness of the stair-head, listening. They could hear voices. It seemed that the Photographic Supplies Company was still doing business, but the well-fitting door masked the sound. It was not even possible to make out how many people were talking.

"Two locks," said Jonty. "Better tackle the big fellow first."

The mortice lock was holding the door so tightly against the jamb that there was, as things stood, no chance of slipping the Yale lock.

Max took two rings of keys out of his bag, a dozen on each ring. He examined them carefully in the light of Jonty's torch. They were odd-looking keys, long in the shank but with fewer wards than the normal key and these with their edges filed down smooth. Max tried out a number of them, taking care not to press too hard when he met resistance. Once he felt that the key was going to hold, but at the last moment it slipped.

"Nearly had her there," said Jonty softly. "Try the other lot."

At the twentieth effort, when he had worked through most of the keys on the second ring, Max felt the gate of the lock lift and move. Unhurriedly he pressed home. This time the key went all the way with a sweet click. Once the mortice lock was open the door gave back a fraction in its frame and Max was able to insert a piece of stiff talc and ease back the tongue of the Yale lock. The door swung open a few inches, then checked. They could see the bright steel links of the chain which held it.

"Wadder yer know," said Jonty. "Two locks *and* a chain. A secretive little creature, Mr. Baa Lamb." He opened the bag, which Max had deposited carefully on the floor to prevent it clinking, and with equal care extracted a pair of metal shears. They had long handles and stubby blades. Whilst Max held the door ajar he inserted the shears, homing the blades on either side of the chain. Then he exerted the considerable strength of his arms and wrists, the shears closed, and the chain fell into two parts.

Jonty eased the door open.

They were looking down an unlighted hallway. There were two doors on either side of it and a door at the end. Light was filtering out from under the bottom of the far door. They could hear more clearly now. Most of the talking seemed to be done by one man with a high-pitched voice.

"Baa Lamb bleating," murmured Max.

They moved forward up the hall, which was uncarpeted, and paused outside the end door. They were close enough now to make out words. The voice said, "I think we'll have this one with your hand on your hip, Leslie."

Max turned the handle cautiously and slid the door open wide enough for both of them to peer in.

The voice, it was clear, belonged to the man who was standing, with his back to them, alongside a lamp which was focused on a small stage at the other side of the room. On the stage was standing a boy. He was wearing a school cap on the back of his head, a look of horrified surprise on his face and nothing else at all.

The man registered the look on the boy's face and swung round. Max felt for the switch, turned on the overhead light and both men moved in.

There was a moment of complete silence; a tableau formed by four motionless figures.

Then Max said, "Get your clothes on, you shocking little nit and beat it. If you aren't clear in three minutes you'll get a boot up your beautiful bottom."

The boy scuttled out.

The man, who seemed to be recovering a little from the first shock, said, "What are you doing? You've no right to be here. These are private premises. Perfectly private."

The words were bold, but there was a quaver behind them.

Jonty said, "Mr. Lamb, I suppose. Mr. Baa Lamb."

The white tufts of hair round a bald head gave the name an unpleasing sort of appropriateness.

"You've no right to question me. Who are you? Are you policemen?"

"Policemen? Certainly not. We're Bimbo and Bombo, the world-famous knock-about artists. Our act has been applauded by the crowned heads of Yurrup. And now that we've been properly introduced, I'll let you into a secret. We're experts at duffing people up. And unless you do what you're told and behave yourself like a proper little lambkin, you're going to get duffed up like you've never been duffed up before. Right, Bimbo?"

"Right, Bombo."

The two men advanced on Lamb, who retreated until the back of his legs hit the edge of the stage and he sat down suddenly.

The two men towered over him.

"T-tell me what you want and I'll see if I can help."

The last remnants of bravado were draining out of his voice.

"That's nice. First thing, suppose you show us round."

"Show us the geography," suggested Max with a horrific smirk.

"That's right. The gee-ography."

81

Lamb got back on to his feet. It was difficult, with the men standing almost on top of him, but he managed it, by sliding to one side.

"This is the studio."

"The Stoodio. Make a note of that, Bimbo."

"Dooly noted, Bombo."

"There are four other rooms." Lamb was out in the hall by now. "The two on the left are my private quarters. Do you want to see them?"

"Do we want to see them, Bimbo?"

"Later, perhaps."

"These other two – I suppose you might call them studios as well."

"Two more stoodios. Quite a stoodious place."

Both men laughed heartily. Lamb contributed a wan smile.

The first room was almost unfurnished. There was a trestle table with some electrical gear on it and in the corner, a lot of film equipment, some of it still crated. Jonty noticed that the makers' names had been filed off the equipment and that the crates had no marks on them. Max was examining the only decorative piece in the room: a large mirror in a metal frame, set into the right-hand wall. There was a switch beside it. When he pressed it the mirror tilted fractionally. It had become a pane of transparent blue glass.

"Interesting," said Jonty.

"Educational," agreed Max, who had walked over to look at it.

Through the glass they could see the second room. This was furnished as a simple bedroom. An iron bed, with a mattress and two folded blankets, a chair beside it, a chest of drawers and a hanging-cupboard.

Max said, "This is where the action takes place?"

"We haven't really got round to using it yet."

"Mustn't hurry him," said Jonty. "Important educational work. I think we've seen all we need here. Now we can get on with our real business." He smiled.

"Right," said Max. He had picked up off the table a length of flex with a three-pin plug on one end of it. The other ends of the flex were bare. "This might be useful." As he swung it round in his hand he, too, was smiling.

"Made for the job," agreed Jonty.

"Considerate having apparatus like this laid out, all ready for us."

"Thoughtful."

"W-what are you talking about?" said Lamb. A little of his courage had come back while he was showing his unwelcome guests round. Now it was ebbing again. The smiles were upsetting him more than the words.

"Back to the studio, Bimbo?"

"More room there. Come along, Lamb."

"Lamb to the slaughter."

"I wouldn't say slaughter. Not necessarily slaughter. It all depends how co-operative our Lamb is going to be."

They moved out into the hall. The front door was still ajar. Max shut it. He said, "Well, look at this. There's a bolt, too."

He shot the bolt. "Some people never learn, do they? If you want to keep undesirable characters out, one bolt is worth two locks and a chain."

"I'll remember it in future," said Lamb, trying out a smile.

"Come on," said Jonty. "Stop frigging about. We haven't got all night."

Lamb was herded back into the studio. Max placed a chair on the stage and jerked his thumb at it.

"You want me to sit down?"

"You're a good guesser."

Lamb perched on the chair. He was blinking in the strong light focused on him.

"Something I forgot," said Max. "You wouldn't by any chance have such a thing as a portable radio? A transistor. Something like that."

"There's one in my bedroom. Would you like me to fetch it?"

"My friend here can do that."

Whilst Jonty was away, Max examined the wainscoting beside the stage, where he discovered a power-point which was being used for a small electric fire. He disconnected the fire and moved it away. Lamb watched him, tried to say something, but was unable to find words.

Jonty came back carrying a small and battered transistor. "It's not much of a set," he said, "but it'll have to do."

"W-what do you want it for?"

Jonty looked surprised. "To make a noise, of course. The louder the better."

83

Max had fitted the plug on the end of the piece of flex into the socket. Now, using a small knife, he was baring the insulation on the wires at the other end.

Lamb said, desperately, "Can't you tell me what you want?"

"What we've done," said Max, "is, we've considered your case very carefully and decided on the appropriate treatment." He spoke like a family doctor. "What we'll do, is, wire your balls to this flex and turn the power on."

"You – you can't."

"He thinks we can't. Why should he think that, Bimbo?"

"Very strange. Of course we can. We're experts. Done it dozens of times."

"Who was the last person we did it to? That old Chinaman, wasn't it?"

"Right. And boy, did he scream. Now you know why we need a bit of music. Ready, Bombo?"

"Ready."

Jonty swung round on Mr. Lamb and said, without any trace of his former geniality, "Take your trousers off. Or have 'em took."

Lamb said, "Anything you want I'll do. Really I will. I'm not at all strong. It's my heart. If you do that," – he looked at the gleaming copper wires that Max was holding– "you'll kill me."

Max said, "We wouldn't want that, of course."

"Why won't you say what you want?"

"I'll tell you." It was the family doctor speaking again. "What we've found, by experience, is that *after* a subject has had the treatment he doesn't prevaricate."

"He's more willing to co-operate," explained Jonty carefully.

"I'm willing now. Really I am."

"Well – just for once – perhaps. We'll do it your way."

Jonty shook his head. Clearly he was a traditionalist who disapproved of changing well-established routines.

"I don't like it," he said. "It's irregular. But we don't want him corpsing on us."

Max disconnected the plug and started to wind up the wire. He said, "All right. Question time. Do you remember a character who came here two nights ago? Tall man with reddish hair and a bald patch?"

"Yes, I remember him."

"Had he got a name?"

"He called himself Mr. Taylor. People who come here sometimes don't like to use their real names."

"What had you got on him?"

When Lamb hesitated, Max started uncoiling the wire. This was enough.

"We had a photograph. One that was taken, without him knowing about it, at our last place. That was in Frith Street."

"Through one of those mirror doo-hickies?"

"Yes."

"Let's have a look at it."

No hesitation this time. Lamb trotted across to the corner where there was a piece of furniture which had already aroused Jonty's curiosity. It was a metal chest, of the size of two large filing cabinets laid flat. The lid was designed to open upwards and there was a single keyhole in the green painted front. The general effect was as though a fair-sized safe had been laid over on its back.

Lamb squatted in front of it. The hand which held the key was shaking so much that he had some difficulty getting it into the hole.

"Give it to me," said Jonty. "I'll do it."

"If you tried to open it," said Lamb, with an apologetic smile, "you wouldn't find anything inside when you'd got it open."

"Box of tricks, is it?" said Jonty. "I've heard of 'em, but never seen one." He squatted down beside Lamb to observe his manoeuvres.

The key, once Lamb had got it inserted, could only go in a certain way because of a steel pointer, attached to the shank, parallel with the flattened end of the key. Now that he was close to the box Jonty could see that there was a clock face of numbers round the keyhole. As the pointer moved against the numbers on the clock it was a simple matter to gauge, without possibility of error, exactly how far the key turned on each occasion.

First anti-clockwise to ten o'clock. Then, clockwise, to four o'clock; clockwise again to six o'clock, then up to twelve o'clock.

Lamb took the key out, put it back in his pocket and opened the lid. He needed both hands to do it. The lid, like the rest of the box, was made of steel and lined with what looked like

85

asbestos. The interior had no shelves or subdivisions of any sort. It was full of numbered cardboard folders standing on end. Lamb consulted his pocket-book and selected one of the folders. It was divided into sections, each of which held a single photograph.

Lamb pulled out one of the photographs, gave it to Jonty, pushed the folder back and began the careful ritual of relocking the box.

Jonty, his face expressionless, handed the photograph to Max, who looked at it for a long moment before putting it away in his inside pocket.

He said, "Leslie didn't have his hand on his hip that time, did he?"

8

"I'm not sure that Abel is going to like this," said Sandra Leone.

She was reading a copy of the local paper that had appeared that Saturday morning. For some time now it had been running a daily piece on local notabilities, which had started with a stately and appreciative article on Arthur Drayling, his artistry and his national reputation, but the author was, by now, finding himself a bit short of suitably eminent subjects. Today the spotlight was turned on Abel Drummer and the writer, lacking reportable facts, had fallen back on wit and imagination.

Under the heading 'Birdman of Thameside' he had described the livestock in which the Drummer emporium dealt and had indulged a fancy that, spending his working-day among small animals, birds and reptiles, the proprietor would unconsciously assimilate some of the characteristics of each. Might not his speaking voice gradually acquire the squeak of his mice, the hiss of his grass-snakes and the twitter of his budgerigars?

It was a fairly harmless piece of leg-pulling, but Anthony

agreed with his wife that it was unlikely to appeal to Abel. He was thinking about it as he set out for the court building to pick up some reports that were waiting for him. Maindy Road was normally a quiet thoroughfare, but as he turned into it he noticed a small crowd beginning to collect at the far end and he realised that something unusual was happening. On both sides of the road, people had stopped walking and were bunching together, not doing anything, just staring and chattering.

As he approached he saw that the centre of attraction was a man, kneeling beside a dog. The man was Abel Drummer. The dog was his Rhodesian ridgeback, Tiger and Tiger was sprawled on the pavement in the abandoned attitude of death. Anthony could see, as he got nearer, the dark blood which disfigured the handsome black and tan head.

Hit and run? If a car had hit a dog it could hardly have got away down the street without being seen and certainly its number would have been noted. Someone was muttering. Anthony edged closer.

"Bloody Pakis. Hit the dog. Killed it."

"Hit it with a hammer," said a man who seemed to have been closest to the incident.

"Do you know who it was?" said Anthony. A horrible suspicion was growing in his mind.

"All bloody Pakis look the same to me," said the man. "Why don't we kick the lot out? Send the bastards back where they belong."

He had spoken loud enough to be heard and there was a murmur of sympathy from the people round him. The soft sound of the woodwind and the strings before the brass opened its throat.

Abel Drummer looked up and recognised Anthony.

"Your friends," he said bitterly. "Your brown friends."

Anthony knew what he had to do, but had little heart for it. He slid out of the group and made his way up Reynolds Road to the premises of East London Motors. He found all five of the boys in the shed behind the garage. He thought they looked serious, but neither guilty nor frightened. They did not seem surprised to see him. They might almost have been expecting him.

"You know what I've come about," said Anthony. He was angry and made no attempt to conceal his anger.

"That dog," said Salim.

87

"Yes. Mr. Drummer's dog. I thought you understood when I told you that you had to keep clear of trouble. Not stir up more, for God's sake."

"But Mr. Lee-owny – "

"If you're looking for a spell inside, all I can say is you're setting about it in the right way, although you might have thought of a better way of doing it than murdering a fine dog like that."

"Mr. Lee-owny. Please listen. All we did was protect ourselves. That dog was out to kill *us*."

"I don't believe it."

"It's true. He came straight across the road and made a jump at Sher. Didn't he?"

Four heads nodded.

"And Sher just happened to have a hammer with him?"

"That's right. He'd just bought it. It was for some work he was going to do here."

Saghir nodded and pointed to two or three boards which were lying in the corner. He seemed to be the most shaken of the five.

"And you're telling me that this dog – a trained dog – left his master and came across the road for no reason at all and attacked you."

"That's what happened."

"And you'd done nothing to provoke him?"

"Well – "

"Let's have it."

"It wasn't the dog we provoked," said Rahim, speaking for the first time. "Not exactly. It was Mr. Drummer."

"How did you provoke him?"

"We all whistled. You know, sort of made bird noises."

"It was that thing we read in the paper this morning. About him being a birdman. It was only a joke."

"A joke!" said Anthony bitterly. "That's your idea of a joke. I hope you've all had a good laugh." He looked round at five faces which had become suddenly apprehensive. The anger in Anthony's voice disturbed them. "Because of all the stupid bloody jokes I've ever heard of, this gets top marks as the stupidest bloody joke of the whole bloody year."

"I can assure you," said Superintendent Brace, "that you have my full sympathy."

The Superintendent was a thick-set man with a firm chin and light blue eyes. Single-minded determination and adherence to the rule book had brought him from police recruit to his present rank. The only sign of the passage of twenty strenuous years was a scattering of white in his hair.

He said, "He was a fine dog. Did you see which of the boys hit him?"

"It was difficult. I was on the other side of the road and there was this bunch of them, you see. Four or five. I know who they were. They've been fighting with my boy and his lot ever since – well, you know about that."

"You mean the incident involving your older boy and Salim Kahn. Was it Salim who hit the dog?"

Abel Drummer hesitated. He would clearly have liked to say that it was Salim, but he had already admitted that he was uncertain. He said, "It was one of them. They hang round together. Your Probation Officer knows their names. I expect he's already talked to them."

"I'll have a word with Mr. Leone." The way in which Brace said this did not indicate any particular regard for his Probation Officer. "As soon as we find out which one it was, he'll be charged; with creating a disturbance and damage to property. Your property."

When Brace had heard of the incident late on Saturday, he had had a word with Mr. Nabbs, who advised the police in such matters. To start with, Mr. Nabbs had seemed to experience some difficulty in deciding exactly what offence had been committed, but had settled for what seemed to be two possible ones – "And, of course, if our investigations show that they were all in it, the charge will be conspiracy to commit those offences."

"If you can make an example of them," said Abel, "it will reassure people that they can walk their own streets without having to submit to foreign hooliganism."

Brace said, "Quite so." There was one point which had to be settled. He said, "Can you tell me why your dog should have crossed the street?"

"Well, the boys were whistling."

"Whistling? To your dog?"

"I suppose so. That's what it sounded like. Anyway, he went over to see what they wanted. I expect when he arrived they

89

were scared. Tiger was a big dog. He could look pretty fierce when he was roused."

"And you think the whistling annoyed him?"

"It must have done. It annoyed me, I know."

Brace had been making a careful note. He said, "The boys attracted the dog across the road by whistling, then panicked and hit him. That's right is it?"

"That's right."

"Then you can leave it to me, Mr. Drummer. They won't get away with this." He paused, and added, "You understand that I'm not being influenced by the fact that the boys were Pakistanis. I'd take the same action if they'd been any colour: white, brown or yellow. I want that to be clear."

"Of course," said Abel. "I understand that."

At the same time, on that Monday morning, Mr. Norrie had visitors. Normally he liked to spend the time between the end of his breakfast and the opening of the court in studying the charge sheet and the reports from policemen, doctors and other interested parties that came with them. He also liked to discuss them with Anthony, whose views on his own and on other people's cases, he often found helpful.

He allowed himself to be interrupted on this occasion because he knew both of the interrupters and had a feeling that they would not have come unless they had something important to say. Mrs. Roundhays, widow of Simon Roundhays, twice Mayor of the Borough. Colonel Ramilies, retired from the Army and running a kennels near the Common.

"Won't waste your time," said Mrs. Roundhays. "Just thought you ought to know. Was walking back down Maindy Road on Saturday morning. I'd met the Colonel in the High Street when we were both doing our shopping. I'd two bags. Both a bit heavy. Mistake to do your shopping only once a week. He kindly offered to carry one of them." She smiled at Colonel Ramilies, who smiled back. The Colonel was a widower. Norrie thought, it might be a good thing if they hitched up and then decided, no, they were both perfectly happy on their own. The thought had distracted him for a moment from what Mrs. Roundhays was saying. Her delivery was telegraphic and needed close attention.

"You were saying that you saw Mr. Drummer – "

"Saw him and heard him. Set the dog on the boys."

"He set the dog on them? You're sure?"

Mrs. Roundhays looked at him blankly. Then she said, "What do you mean, am I sure? Do you think I'm imagining it?"

"No, of course not. I'd already heard about it from my Probation Officer. He seemed to think it was the dog that took the initiative."

"Wasn't the dog. Was Drummer."

"If I might," said Colonel Ramilies. "As you know I've had a good deal of experience in training dogs. In fact, two years ago, when they were short-handed, I helped the police. I had some of their dogs in my kennels for a time. Alsatians. Not, in my view, the best dogs for the job. They're too highly strung. They can be trained, of course, but if I had my way I'd use Airedales. Placid Yorkshire tykes. However, as I was saying, any dog can be trained and Mr. Drummer's ridgeback had been."

"By you?"

"Yes. I had him for three months when he was young. Do you know much about training dogs, Mr. Norrie?"

"Practically nothing."

"There are four basic commands. 'Stand', 'Go', 'Hold' and 'Tackle'. When they're told to hold someone their objective is his arm, particularly if he's got some sort of weapon in his hand. 'Tackle' is more serious. It *doesn't* mean go for his throat. It means, knock the man down and stand over him. They get up what speed they can and launch their full weight at the subject's chest. Nine times out of ten it sends him sprawling."

"And which command was given on this occasion?"

"I wasn't near enough to hear. But I can tell you this. Unless *some* command had been given, the boys on the other side of the road could have whistled until they were blue in the face before he'd have moved from his master's side."

"They weren't really whistling, either," said Mrs. Roundhays. "Not in the way you'd whistle to call a dog. More like chirruping."

"Chirruping?"

"Making bird noises."

"I see," said Mr. Norrie. "Yes. That explains a lot. If anything further comes of this incident, you'll probably be called on to give evidence. I've got your addresses. I'd better have your telephone numbers as well. Thank you for coming along."

When they had gone he telephoned Reynolds Road Police Station and asked for Superintendent Brace.

"All that I can properly say at this moment," said Norrie, "is that if Drummer presses charges and the matter comes to court, Mrs. Roundhays and Colonel Ramilies will both want to speak. I can't tell you what decision I should come to without hearing the story from the other side."

"I suppose so," said Brace. He had met the Colonel and had little doubt that his evidence would be conclusive; the more so if supported by someone of the standing of Mrs. Roundhays. Witnesses in magistrates' courts were still ranked in order of their rateable value. He said, "I imagine the boys will say it was an unprovoked attack."

"That's what they've told Leone."

"Does he know who hit the dog?"

"Yes. It was Saghir Abbas. The one they call Sher."

"He'll admit it?"

"So I understand. Leone has seen the ironmonger in the High Street – Bates, I think was the name – who sold him the hammer about five minutes before the incident occurred. And he tells me it's right that there was some carpentry work he had to do."

Brace said, "I see." He approved of Drummer and disliked the boys, but he was experienced enough to discount this. The evidence was now all the other way and Norrie would be bound to throw out any charge that Drummer could bring. In fact, a charge might be brought against him. Though he doubted if it would. He had not been at Reynolds Road long enough to form a firm opinion of Norrie. Other members of the force he had discussed him with had said that he was better than some they'd met; which was fairly high praise. He said, "This man, Leone. Is he reliable?"

"I've found him so. Has there been some difficulty – ?"

"Not what you'd call a difficulty, no. But one of my men happened to spot Bearstead, the Deputy Head of the Special Branch, coming out of his house. When I was talking to Leone I asked him about it. If it was police business, I thought I ought to know about it."

"Was it?"

"He wouldn't tell me. Said that it was confidential and he'd given his word to Bearstead not to pass it on."

"Well, if he'd given his word he was right to keep it. A good mark, not a bad one, don't you think?"

"I suppose so."

But you don't like Leone for it, thought Norrie, which was a pity. Because if trouble came, things would only go smoothly if all parts of the machine meshed together; the judicial, the executive and the advisory.

And trouble was coming. He could feel it, as a sailor, without looking at a barometer, could feel a coming storm by the ringing in his ears and the prickling of his skin.

9

When the news arrived from Belgium, a meeting was convened with all the speed that a major threat to security warranted. Five departments were concerned.

The Metropolitan Police were represented by the Assistant Commissioner (Crime) Maurice Haydn-Smith and Commander Salwyn the head of C 13, the Anti-terrorist Squad. The Ministry of Defence sent Major General Usher, a retired gunner officer, currently their principal adviser on security matters. Lieutenant Colonel Every drove up from SAS headquarters at Hereford, stopping to pick up Reginald Mowatt of MI5 from his house near Henley. It took him some miles out of his way, but he welcomed the opportunity of a preliminary briefing.

"I notice we're meeting at the headquarters of Special Branch," he said. "Unusual?"

"A sort of geographical compromise, I imagine," said Mowatt. "The MOD wouldn't want to come to Scotland Yard or Petty France and Scotland Yard wouldn't fancy going to

Whitehall, so they agreed on Great Peter Street. Anyway, Elfe will be in charge."

"Is a Deputy Assistant Commissioner senior to a Major General?"

"I doubt whether the matter has ever been tested," said Mowatt with a smile. "But if Elfe was there he'd run the meeting whether he was sitting at the top of the table or not."

Every nodded. He was looking out of the window as the valley of the Thames unrolled past them. It was late autumn and the trees had all turned golden brown and yellow; getting old and tired, like the two of them in the car. The difference was that the trees would be fresh and green again when the winter was past. He had a feeling that it was going to be a difficult winter and wondered which of them would survive it. Mowatt was right about Elfe; a majestic, almost a mystical figure. He had been head of the Special Branch for more than fifteen years. He had twice tried to retire and two very different Prime Ministers had begged him to stay.

Mowatt said, "What do you think, Ludo? Will this meeting get us the sort of help we need?"

"I doubt it," said Every. He sounded bitter. "It will split along the old, old lines. Regular against irregular. The army doesn't love us any more than the Met loves the Special Branch."

"Not all the Met. Don't forget that when C13 was formed it was staffed largely by the Special Branch. There's still a very close relationship. If it came to the point I believe Salwyn would side with Elfe and Bearstead."

"Why should it come to a point? If by coming to a point you mean some sort of split. Why the hell can't they work together for once?"

"They might," said Mowatt. "If they were worried enough."

"Then for God's sake, let's worry them."

"Well, gentlemen," said Elfe, "you've all read this report. I don't need to underline what it means."

The table, Mowatt noted, had been arranged with the propriety of a diplomatic lunch party. There was a chair with arms at each end, one for Elfe and one for General Usher. The two policemen, Haydn-Smith and Salwyn, had upright chairs on one side, facing Mowatt, Every and Elfe's head of operations, Chief Superintendent Bearstead. Remembering what Mowatt had said, Every was interested to observe that, with a choice of two chairs, Commander Salwyn had taken the one on Haydn-Smith's left, thus forming – whether intentionally or not it was difficult to say – a solid Special Branch block at Elfe's end of the table.

The paragraph from the Belgian newspaper *Aurore* had been photographed and clipped to a sheet of paper with an English translation tacked on to it. It was date-lined three days earlier from Liège and was headed 'The Elusive Bomb'.

A message received from our representative at Spa has produced an unusual and intriguing problem, a problem which enquiries so far have made no progress in solving. South of Liège and north west of the River Ourthe lies the large area of heathland which has, for many years now, been used in part as an artillery range for the Army and in part a bombing range for the Air Force. It is intersected by a few country roads, which are used by farmers who naturally observe the restrictions as to access and timing imposed on them by the authorities –

"If it's anything like Larkhill," muttered General Usher when he came to this point, "they go anywhere they bloody well fancy at any hour of the day or night and claim massive compensation if they run into trouble. They ought to be turned off altogether."

– It appears that yesterday the Air Force had set up an exercise which involved the dropping of a single stick of bombs, by four different planes, along a marked and surveyed line at precise intervals. The bombs were thousand-pound anti-personnel bombs with GLD fuses –

A note, in ink, in the margin said, 'Ground Level Detonation'.

The first three planes dropped their bombs accurately, with no great difficulty. By the time the fourth was airborne the early-morning mist had thickened somewhat and it is thought that this may have caused the pilot to miss the opening marker and deviate from the set line, with the result that his first bomb landed about four hundred yards north of its target. The pilot then realised his error, swung back on the proper course and dropped the remaining bombs at the correct points. There was no cause for alarm since there was an ample safety corridor on each side of the range and in any event, this particular bomb failed, for some reason, to explode. A party went out that afternoon to recover it. This was where the mystery started. It had disappeared. The pilot was able to indicate the point at which it had been dropped with considerable accuracy, since he had noted that it was close to the junction of two country tracks and, in fact, it was this that had shown him, immediately after he had dropped the bomb, that he was off his course. The surface at that point is broken by a number of fissures and ravines and is covered with long grass and heather: circumstances which make searching difficult. Wing Commander Lennaert said, "We shall persist in our efforts until we have located and recovered the bomb. One point which demands investigation is why it failed to explode."

Each man, when he had finished reading, laid the paper quietly down on the table in front of him. No one was in much doubt as to what had occurred.

Mowatt said, "Not difficult to answer the Wing Commander's question, is it? A bomb doesn't explode if the detonator has been removed."

"At least two men involved then," said the General. "The pilot and the man who loaded the bomb. A proper investigation should pin it to them easily enough."

"I imagine that the organisers will have thought of that, sir. The money they'll have paid them will blunt any bed of nails they're going to be thrown on to."

"What you're suggesting," said Haydn-Smith, "is that the whole thing was rigged. The IRA, or their local friends, knew where this particular bomb was going to be dropped, had transport and some sort of hoist handy, picked it up and carried it off."

"I'm afraid that's what I do think," said Mowatt. "I presume that as long as it was in store, this explosive was too well guarded for them to steal it. So they helped themselves to it by this somewhat unorthodox route."

"Ingenious," said the General.

"There's one thing I don't understand," said Haydn-Smith. "Of course, I know very little about bombs. I did my active service in the Navy. When the bomb failed to explode, wouldn't it have buried itself so deep that no one could possibly have hauled it out? I was reading the other day about them digging out one of the bombs dropped in the blitz. It had buried itself twenty foot down."

"Certainly," said Salwyn. "It was designed to knock down buildings and would have a delayed-action fuse. These were anti-personnel bombs, designed to go off when they hit the ground."

"All the same," said Haydn-Smith sharply, "it seems obvious to me that it would have gone down a good way, whether it exploded or not." He didn't like having things explained to him by someone junior to him in the force.

Mowatt had his eye on the General. He hoped that he was going to trot out a personal recollection. Mowatt had heard it twice before, but if he could edge the General into telling it once more, it would put him in a good temper for the rest of the meeting. He said, "I don't suppose any of us could answer *that* question, sir."

"As a matter of fact, gentlemen," said the General, "I can. I was a very young and very junior gunner officer in 1944 and the first action I saw was outside Cassino. We took over a gun position under Monte Trocchio from the New Zealanders. Some days before we arrived, it seems that the US Air Force had dropped a thousand pounder almost on to the New Zealand position. Fortunately it had failed to explode and there it was, sticking up in the ground. At least two thirds of it was showing, I remember."

"I imagine the New Zealanders raised a stink about *that*," said Every, who also knew the story.

"I'm afraid you underestimate their sense of humour. What they did was to surround it with a neat square of white cord and stick up a notice: 'Monument to the American Air Force'."

Everyone laughed. The atmosphere seemed a bit easier.

"It had to be removed, of course. Couldn't have inter-allied friction. I seem to remember that the RAOC came along with a hoist and carted it off in a three-ton lorry. No problem."

Haydn-Smith said, "What sort of explosive would a thousand pound bomb contain? And how much of it?"

"In this case we know it was torpex," said Every. "I've had a word with Lennaert. He's not nearly as happy about the incident as the newspaper report suggests. The answer to your second question is that nowadays roughly forty per cent of the bomb weight is in the explosive."

"Four hundred pounds of extremely powerful incendiary explosive, gentlemen," said Elfe. "Designed, I have no doubt, to fuel the IRA Christmas campaign in London. I take it you agree with me that it is worth any and every effort, however extreme, to keep it out of the country."

No one said anything. There was no need for them to speak. All of them round that table had experienced the power of explosives; had seen arms and legs blown off, had heard children screaming mindlessly, had smelled the mixture of blood and smoke and terror and pain.

"The object of this meeting," said Elfe, after he had allowed the silence to become uncomfortable, "is to co-ordinate our efforts. I'll begin, if I may, by asking Colonel Every to tell us about the last attempt to bring explosives into this country – happily prevented."

Speaking briskly and without reference to notes, Colonel Every described the Belgian end of the operation and the incidents of midsummer day at Cuckmere Haven.

"I'd like to emphasise one point," he said. "We had, as you know, on this occasion been tipped off as to the time and place of landing and we were able to be waiting ready for them. But even if we had not been, there is no certainty that the landing would have succeeded. The progress of the *Petite Amie* had been regularly logged on the radar screens of other boats. As soon as she turned inshore and doused her lights this was reported as suspicious to the coastguard stations at Birling Gap and Newhaven. You probably know that the coastguard services have recently been considerably augmented and re-equipped."

"One of the few sensible things the government has spent its money on," growled the Major General. "Sorry, Colonel, I interrupted you. I take it it's your opinion that now the coastguard has been forewarned there's not much chance of a simple coastal landing."

"That's what I think," said Every. "I also think that the IRA

98

dislike repeating efforts, particularly when they have failed. This time it will be something quite different. I'm sure of that."

"Something crafty," agreed Salwyn, "with a back-up scheme if it fails."

Ignoring Salwyn and directing his question pointedly at Elfe, Haydn-Smith said, "And it's your idea, Jack, that it has got something to do with the Woolwich-Plumstead district. I'd like to hear about that."

"Say your piece, Bruno."

Bearstead was ready. He repeated, in rather more formal language, what he had already said to Anthony Leone. He was listened to in silence. Not hostile exactly, but analytical.

"Then all it seems to turn on," said Haydn-Smith, "is that both Firn and the man called Liam have been spotted in the same district."

"And that Liam knocked out one of your heroes," said the General. "I thought you taught them how to fight, Ludo."

"We do our best," said Every, keeping his temper. "Everyone has an off day. Personally I thought the really interesting visitor was not Liam, but Firn. He's a money man. A back-office character. He doesn't often play an active part in these matters."

"If I might say so," said Mowatt, "I entirely agree. And I think it demonstrates the awkward position they've got themselves into as a result of the failure of their Cuckmere landing. *Everyone* who was concerned with that operation, right down the chain, Doctor Bernard, lawyer Monnier, Wulfkind, Firn and Liam are on trial. The IRA put down a lot of money and didn't get what they paid for. They don't like that. This time the explosive has *got* to get through – "

"Or they'll be hobbling round without kneecaps," said Salwyn.

No one smiled.

Haydn-Smith said, "Can we get back to this chap that Liam seems to be in contact with?"

"Arthur Drayling," said Bearstead. "A well-known importer of marble and statuary. Recently we happened to find out something rather interesting about him. He is totally and completely under Liam's thumb."

Heads jerked up.

"You'd better explain that, Bruno," said Elfe.

99

Bearstead said, "Two of my men followed him last week and found him paying an evening visit to a PE establishment in Barnard Street."

"You mean some sort of gym?" said the General.

"Not physical education, General. Paedophiliac Exchange. You may have heard of them."

"Read something in the papers about it. Pictures of small boys, isn't it?"

"Some go in for pictures. Some are more active. And some of them film the action."

"Revolting," said the General. "Why aren't they exterminated?"

Haydn-Smith said stiffly, "We do our best. But it isn't easy. If we know an address, we raid it, but we rarely find any pictures or films. They're kept in a self-destruct cabinet. There's always someone on the premises. One turn of the key and the whole lot are ashes. Once that has happened, we can only prefer a charge if one or more of the boys concerned is prepared to give evidence. Occasionally they are. Not very often. Then we can at least confiscate all the apparatus. Some of it's expensive stuff, too. But even that doesn't seem to stop them from opening up somewhere else."

"There's a lot of money behind them," said Mowatt. "Some of it almost certainly originates in Russia."

Everyone thought about this. Bearstead said, "Our men were fortunate. They paid a surprise visit to the Barnard Street establishment and managed to persuade the proprietor to open his box of tricks for them. He produced a photograph of Drayling. I've brought it to show you."

Every and Mowatt had seen it already and were interested in the different reactions; the simple disgust of the General; the disgust combined with professional curiosity of Haydn-Smith and Salwyn; the massive impassivity of Elfe.

"My men also extracted a description of the only other person a copy of this particular photograph had been given to. And it did sound very like the man who calls himself Liam."

"If we're right about where the money comes from," said Mowatt, "you realise that Liam would have privileged access to the records of a place like that."

Elfe said, "If Liam has that photograph, he's got Drayling in his pocket. He wouldn't even have to threaten to publish it. Just

100

arrange for a copy to be handed round at the club. Drayling would be finished."

"Agreed, Jack," said Haydn-Smith. "Liam could make Drayling jump through any hoop he held up. *But which hoop does he want him to jump through?* That's the real point, isn't it?"

"It's what we've been trying to work out," said Mowatt. "And I can't pretend that we've got the final answer. One thing we did notice though. The bombing range is about ten miles north of Marche-en-Famenne, which is where Wulfkind has his marble quarry."

"And Drayling is one of Wulfkind's regular customers," said Every. "We know that in the last year he's bought a number of statues, quantities of painted tiles and slab marble, iron-work railings and gates, either directly from Wulfkind, or through him as agent for other firms in Belgium."

"Then we seem to be getting somewhere," said Salwyn more happily. If anything went wrong, he knew that most of the trouble was going to come his way.

Every, who knew Salwyn well and liked him, said, "There's one snag, Jimmy. Perhaps you're thinking on the lines that the torpex might be hidden in the next consignment from Marche-en-Famenne? But bear in mind that it's all heavy stuff. It would have to be unloaded by crane. If it was landed at any of the Thameside docks – the Royals, or one of the very few private docks still operating – it would be inside a customs ring-fence and well guarded by the PLA police. And even though it had been cleared by Customs at Gravesend it wouldn't be allowed out until the Metropolitan police had passed one of their ACID detectors over it – which would show up the explosive, however cleverly it had been buried inside a hollow slab of marble or the latest copy of the Venus de Milo or the Wrestling Athletes."

"That seems common sense," said Haydn-Smith. "If they tried to land it at one of the docks they'd be asking for trouble."

"All right," said Salwyn. "Rule out the docks if you like. There are plenty of wharfs and jetties, aren't there?"

"In Gallions Reach," said Every, "which is the part of the river we're particularly interested in, I've already noted eleven wharfs on the north bank and eight on the south. Those are the main ones. There could be a number of smaller ones which aren't on the map at all."

Salwyn was beginning to look unhappy again.

"Let's get back to Drayling," said the General. "He seems to be the only firm lead that we've got. If we found that he had some connection with one particular wharf, wouldn't that narrow the field?"

"If we could discover that," said Mowatt, "I agree it'd be a long step forward. But he's a businessman with a finger in a lot of pies. The best way of checking all his contacts would be to tap his telephone."

He said this hopefully; but not very hopefully.

"Not a chance, Reggie," said Elfe. "They're getting very jumpy about that. If I could make out an exceptional case I could go to the Home Secretary personally, but what could I tell him about Drayling? That he once had a visit from a known terrorist?"

"You could go a little further than that, sir," said Bearstead. "To start with, Liam stayed there for an hour. It can't be supposed that he was buying dwarfs for his garden, so what was he talking about? Added to that, we now know that Drayling is under Liam's thumb and has to do what he's told. That practically makes him a terrorist himself."

"If you took that line with the Home Secretary," said Haydn-Smith, "mightn't you have to explain just how you got hold of that photograph? I imagine your men had to be fairly rough with the PE proprietor."

"On the contrary," said Bearstead, "they never laid a finger on him."

"So they say."

"When our men tell their own officers something," said Elfe, and his voice sounded like the clashing of icebergs, "we believe them. I don't know about your men, but our men don't lie to us."

The General said, "Come, come, gentlemen. I don't think this is getting us anywhere. If Elfe tells us that we won't get permission to tap telephones – and I take it that prohibition would go for intercepting mail as well – " Elfe nodded. For the moment he was too angry to speak. " – then we have to think of something else. Would it be possible to have his house watched?"

"It'd be a difficult place to watch," said Bearstead. "It's got more than an acre of garden. Main roads on the north and west

102

sides, the Artillery Barracks on the east and a stretch of Woolwich Common to the south. To watch it permanently you'd need a team of six on duty, in three reliefs. Say eighteen men."

"Which puts the idea out of court," said Haydn-Smith flatly. He, too, was still angry.

Bearstead said, "On the other hand it wouldn't be too difficult to have him followed when he goes out. That would only need one man on watch with a radio link to bring in any help he needed when Drayling was on the move."

"As long as we don't start getting complaints of harassment," said Haydn-Smith.

"Our men are fairly skilful at watching," said Bearstead.

And don't clump round in heavy boots like regular policemen, thought Every. Go on. Why don't you say it? Let's have a real fight.

The General intervened once more. He said, "Let's leave Drayling for the moment. What about those Pakistani boys? The ones Firn visited. How do they come into it?"

"Actually, there are two lots of boys," said Bearstead, "the Pakistanis, who congregate at a garage at the end of Plumstead High Street, and a crowd of middle-class white boys – a sort of junior National Front – who have a headquarters behind the Social Club in Camlet Road. They seem to be heading for gang war."

"But apart from the fact that Firn paid a visit to the Pakistani lot there's no reason to suppose that either of them have got any connection with our problem?"

"No real reason," agreed Bearstead, "just a hunch that they fit into the picture somewhere."

"I don't think we should neglect any lead, however unpromising," said Elfe.

"That's what I felt. And that's why I made my number with the local Probation Officer. A man called Leone."

"You considered him reliable?" asked Haydn-Smith.

"Entirely reliable, in my opinion," said Elfe flatly.

No one seemed anxious to challenge this.

Bearstead said, "I've asked him to keep one of his eyes on the boys and the other on Drayling. If we can establish *any* sort of link between them we might be able to see our way a bit more clearly."

"You're grasping at straws," said Haydn-Smith.

"Perhaps you've some better idea?" said Elfe.

"Might I make a suggestion?" said Mowatt. He, no more than the General, wanted to see the meeting degenerate into a boxing match between the police and the Special Branch. "This seems to me to be a case in which a division of labour might help. The conclusion we've reached is that the explosive will be leaving Belgium in some sort of small cargo vessel or coaster, aiming to land it somewhere in the Thames."

"Not a conclusion," said Haydn-Smith. "A guess."

"All right," said Mowatt patiently. "A guess. If it is correct, the first snag will be Customs clearance at Gravesend. But it's not a serious one. The water guard at Gravesend are mainly concerned with seeing that dutiable goods pay duty. They sometimes carry out searches and checks, but not often and particularly not if they know the ship concerned. Moreover, and this I think is the main point, Gravesend don't yet use the ACID detector. That is handled by the Metropolitan police, at the docks. They have trained special officers to operate it. If the cargo is landed at a dock, it will have no chance of getting through undetected. Which means that if the IRA are bringing it into the river they are almost certainly planning to land it at some wharf or jetty. And whisking it away by road the moment they've got it ashore."

Mowatt had been allowed to have his say, partly because no one else had any positive contribution to make, but also because he had perfected a smooth civil-service method of presenting his points.

"The problem," he continued, "really boils down to dis-covering which of a great number of possible landing points is the one they plan to use. We can then have a suitable reception party organised."

The General said, "Another way of dealing with it would be to equip the Customs people at Gravesend with this detector."

"I should be very much opposed to that," said Every, with unexpected firmness. "The men we're dealing with are danger-ous and quite ruthless. The last thing we want is a shoot-out in Gravesend Customs House. If there's going to be a battle, I'd prefer to stage it in open country at the landward end of a wharf. Preferably an isolated one."

"Something in that," said the General. And to Mowatt, "I interrupted you again. You were going to make a suggestion."

"It's a very simple one, sir. It seems to me that there are two sides to our search area. The river itself and the river banks. So far as the river is concerned we could leave it to Colonel Every to make a physical inspection of the possible landing places. The Thames Division would be a great help there. They probably know a lot about them already. Then perhaps Chief Superintendent Bearstead could tackle the landward side. That would mean making discreet enquiries about the firms that own and operate the wharfs. Most of them are no doubt entirely respectable. One or two of them, perhaps, less so. It will mean a lot of slow and detailed police work and no one could expect quick results. In both cases – " he turned deferentially towards Haydn-Smith, "they would, of course, need to be backed by your authority."

"I'm perfectly prepared," said Haydn-Smith, "to co-operate in any plan which has the remotest chance of success. I still think you're clutching at straws, but the method you suggest is, perhaps, the best way of clutching at these particular straws. I'll have a word with the people concerned."

"Thank you very much, sir."

Mowatt congratulated himself on having read the Assistant Commissioner's mind. The more the matter was dressed up as routine police work the more it would appeal to him.

"Superintendent Groener is the head of the Thames Division. South of the river is 'R' District. That's Commander Tancred. The north bank's a little more difficult. It's 'K' District as far as the Beam River. That's Commander Rowlands. But if you want to go east of the Beam River, you'll have to contact the Essex Constabulary."

"That covers the area nicely," said Bearstead. "And we're most grateful."

When the meeting had dispersed, Every and Mowatt made for the nearest pub and a badly needed drink.

"It finished all right," said Mowatt, "but there were one or two moments – "

"Why has Haydn-Smith got his knife into Salwyn?"

"I think they're both under pressure and that brings out the worst in both of them. And Haydn-Smith is the sort of leader who doesn't welcome explanations and corrections from one of his own subordinates. It's human nature, really."

"It's bloody childishness," said Every. He had none of Mowatt's tolerance of human foibles.

10

Even had Mowatt been allowed to set the sort of watch on Arthur Drayling which he had wanted, it is by no means certain that the next visit which Liam paid to him would have been detected.

The letter had arrived in Drayling's office with a great number of others. His morning post was normally heavy. It was in a crumpled buff envelope and contained one of Drayling's own invoices, a number of which Liam had thoughtfully abstracted on his previous visit. Into it he had typed an imaginative quotation for a garden gate – 'Wrought iron, five bars, decorated with rosettes and lilies – £185 delivered.' Then, across the bottom, he had scrawled in ink – 'Sorry. Your price too high. Could offer reduction of 15% with ten weeks for settlement.'

From this Drayling had understood that Liam proposed to visit him at ten o'clock on the evening of November 15th, which was this day. In fact, in less than an hour's time. The thought was disturbing, because Liam had become a figure in his dreams. He had been bound by the wrists to a ring and Liam had been beating him. The blows had hurt and he had woken up sobbing. He had not cried since he was a child. He had lain awake turning over in his mind half a dozen ways of extracting himself from the pit of shame into which he had tumbled, but none of them had stood up to examination.

Since the letter had arrived by first post on the 13th it had given him plenty of time, had he wished, to inform the police and arrange an ambush. The boy was a terrorist. He had admitted as much. Indeed, he had seemed to glory in it. Certainly the authorities would welcome the chance to take him. But when he thought about this, he remembered the last few minutes of their talk on the previous occasion.

Liam had been sprawled in one chair with a foot up on another, smoking a cheap French cigarette, flicking off the ash on to the beautiful Savvonerie carpet. Everything he had done, everything he had said, had been designed to humiliate him.

"Whenever you get a message from me – " (he had already outlined the simple code he proposed to use) "you will be in this room, on time and alone. And you will leave the terrace window unlocked. Understood?"

Drayling had nodded.

"If you understand, say yes."

"Yes."

"It might, of course, occur to you to arrange a reception committee. Police or soldiers. I will give you two reasons for not doing this. First, whatever arrangements you may have made I should contrive, then or later, to have a bullet put through your fat stomach. The doctors might save you, eventually. But I rather think the shock would kill you. A modern jacketed bullet makes a terrible mess of a man's guts. A second reason, which you may think even more cogent, is that friends of mine will disseminate a certain photograph. You understand?"

"Yes."

When Drayling thought of the insolent boy, lounging in his chair, confident in his mastery, he started to shake. Partly it was wounded pride and frustration. Partly it was a feeling that he found difficult to diagnose.

The part of Woolwich Common which lay on the south of Drayling's garden was closed to the public every evening at seven o'clock. Liam had been there since six. Towards seven, when the old park keeper waddled in to lock the gates, he had melted into the darkness of the bushes. After that he had sat for nearly three hours, with the disciplined patience that was part of his armoury, watching and listening.

At ten to ten he had eased his way over the wall of Drayling's garden. The stretch of lawn which lay behind it looked bare and harmless, but instead of crossing it directly he moved round it, keeping in the shadows until he had reached the terrace. As the clock on the Observatory Tower started to sound the hour of ten he rapped sharply on the lighted window. Drayling hurried across and swung open the unlocked French window.

"You're very prompt," he said. "Come in, come in."

"Come out, come out," said Liam. When Drayling hesitated, he said, "All right, go along and get a nice warm coat, you old softie. Only, no tricks."

"I don't need a coat," said Drayling stiffly. "I just wondered why you wanted to sit out here, instead of indoors."

"Rule number one. Never talk indoors if you can talk outside." Liam sat down on the wooden bench and patted the seat beside him. Exactly as he would have done, thought Drayling, if he'd been inviting a dog to jump up.

"Now," said Liam, "I've got some instructions for you, so listen carefully. Are you listening carefully?"

"Yes." He tried to sound natural, but sitting so close to Liam was disturbing him.

"First, I want to know about those two lots of kids who spend their time scrapping with each other."

"I don't know much about the Pakistanis. Except that two of them are sons of Azam Kahn who keeps the garage at the end of Plumstead High Street. I suppose the others are friends of theirs."

"What about the white kids?"

"The leaders are Ted and Robin Drummer. The only one of the others I know about is Norman Younger."

"The boy football wonder."

"Yes. Oh, and Andy Connors. His father's in the Army. There may be one or two others who go around with them. They call themselves the Young Britons and they've got a sort of headquarters behind our Social Club in Camlet Road."

Liam was sitting very still, seeming to docket this information. Then he said, "The two Drummer boys. What do they do besides picking fights with the Pakis?"

"Ted works in his father's pet shop. Budgerigars, goldfish and things like that. Robin's got a job at the Clipstone Sand and Gravel Works, at Cooling."

"And how come you know so much about them?"

"Their father, Abel Drummer, happens to be a friend of mine."

"Let's hear about him, then."

"What sort of things do you want to know? He's an average type of patriotic Englishman; a member of the British Legion. He belonged for some years to the local TA Engineer Regiment. Is that the sort of thing you wanted?"

"Keep going. You're painting quite a portrait."

For the first time in their acquaintance Drayling seemed to detect a note of approval in his visitor's voice.

He said, "I believe his father was a sapper and was badly wounded in North Africa on account of some mess-up with a Punjabi Regiment."

"Which accounts, no doubt, for his hostility to the Pakistani crowd."

"There's more to it than that. One of the boys killed his dog."

"Tell me about that."

Again Liam listened in silence, a silence which continued after Drayling had finished. Then he said, "I'd like to meet Abel. Have a quiet talk with him. If you asked him up here, would he come?"

"He'd come like a shot. Do I tell him what you want to talk about?"

"Goldfish."

"Goldfish?"

"That's right. Tell him you've got a friend who might be able to supply him with a consignment of Carassius Auratus Leoninus Indicus. Indian Lion-heads. Only found in some of the streams and pools of Northern Pakistan. Much rarer and more valuable than the Japanese type. They'd have to be flown over, but it'd be worth it. He could ask fifty pounds apiece for them from keen aquarists. Have you got all that?"

"I'm to tell him that you can get him some Indian Lion-heads – "

"Wrong. You're to give him the full name. Get a bit of paper and a pencil. All right. Ready? Carassius Auratus Leoninus Indicus."

In the faint light which filtered out from the drawing room, and using his knee as a pad, Drayling scribbled desperately with Liam looking over his shoulder.

"Double 's' in Carassius."

"Oh, sorry." It was like being back at school.

"Now that we're friends, Arthur, I'll tell you something that someone ought to have told you before. You're soft. Soft as suet pudding. Soft and wet as a sponge. That's right, isn't it?"

"I suppose it is."

"Don't start supposing. Is it true or not?"

"Yes."

109

"It's not really your fault. The trouble is, you've had it all your own way. You've got to the top too easily. When I asked you if Abel would come up here, you said, 'He'd come like a shot', meaning he'd be flattered to be asked. Because you're the big wheel round here. Right?"

"I suppose – I mean, yes."

"Then all the others must be pretty small wheels."

Drayling thought of the company at the club; Nabbs and Locke and Seligman and the others.

"Mind you," said Liam without waiting for an answer, "I suppose like all of us when you were young you had to take the rough with the smooth. Were you bullied at school?"

"I went to a progressive school. They didn't believe in bullying."

"Pity," said Liam. "Being bullied would have done you a lot of good." He got up. "I've been bullying you, see? And you're all the better for it, aren't you? I'll write to you in the same way, telling you the date and time I want Drummer on parade here. And one other thing, Arthur. If he wants to know something about me, you can tell him that all you know about me is that I'm a clockmaker by profession."

Before Drayling could say anything, Liam had jumped down the three steps on to the path. He made his way, straight across the lawn this time, and over the wall at the far side, slipping over it like a shadow, and disappearing into the shadows beyond.

Drayling sat staring after him. He became aware suddenly of the chill of the November evening and he was shivering as he got back into the warmth and comfort of his beautiful drawing room.

11

"What are you worried about?" said Sandra.

"Who said I was worried?"

"If you aren't worried, why have you started talking in your sleep?"

"Good God!" said Anthony. "Have I really? What did I say?"

"I was too discreet to listen. Every time you started talking I kicked you."

"I wondered what that bruise was on my thigh." Anthony drank the last of his breakfast coffee and said, "Of course you're right. I am worried."

"About what?"

"About those boys."

"They're all right now. They've been bound over haven't they? Nothing dramatic about that."

"One of the conditions of the binding over order was that they were to remain on probation to me for a further six months."

"Which only means you've got to keep an eye on them for Norrie for six months."

"Not only for Norrie."

"Who for, then?"

"Oh, I forgot. I'm not allowed to tell you."

Sandra eyed her husband tolerantly. She said, "It's for that man Bearstead, isn't it?"

"All right. I didn't tell you; you guessed it. And I can't tell you anything more."

Sandra turned up her nose, as far as a small nose can be turned up and said, "I don't want to pry into your precious secrets."

"Liar."

Sandra grinned at him in the way that had turned his heart over five years before and said, "All right. I'm a liar. Naturally I want to know all about it. But I'm not going to plague you to tell me."

"I only wish Brace was as reasonable as you are," said Anthony gloomily. "I'm in his bad books all right. And it's a nuisance, because it makes my job just that bit harder. I don't want to fight with him. As a matter of fact I think he's got a lot on his plate right now. The Special Branch have been ferreting round in his manor and there's nothing he can do about it. Orders from higher up."

"You talk about ferreting. What do you mean? Who are they? What are they doing?"

"According to Monty, who met them down at Scotland

Dock, they're a couple of real toughs. More like villains than most villains he'd met, Monty said. They've been hanging round the riverside pubs, chatting people up, and pretty free with their drinks. They seem to be interested in firms that use or operate wharfs."

"Wharfs, not docks."

"That's right. It's wharfage firms they're interested in. Brace is getting very edgy. He's beginning to wonder what it's all about. And if it's something serious, oughtn't he to know?"

"That's his bed of nails," said Sandra. She didn't like Chief Superintendent Brace. "It needn't worry you. It's nothing to do with the boys. The chances are, now they've been bound over, they'll behave themselves."

"I'm not sure. Remember, it's only the two leaders who've been bound over. If they keep clear of mischief themselves there's nothing to stop the others stirring things up."

Sandra sighed. She said, "For goodness sake, why should *anyone* want to stir things up? It doesn't get them anywhere. Me, I'm for a quiet life."

At about this time the Kahn boys and their friends were considering the same problems from a different angle. Javed Rahman said, "I heard something yesterday which you will find amusing, perhaps."

"Then let us laugh at it, Jay," said Salim.

"Ted Drummer has been taking lessons in boxing."

This was received in thoughtful silence.

"Where?" said Salim.

"And why?" added Rahim.

"Why he is doing it is obvious," said Sher. "He hopes, if he can continue the lessons for several years, that he might have some chance of being able to stand up to Salim in fair fight, for a few seconds, without getting his head knocked off."

The words 'fair fight' seemed to register with Salim. He said, thoughtfully, "Where is he getting these lessons?"

"At Tubby Pinnock's gym. Where you used to go in the old days."

At the age of sixteen Salim had been a very promising boxer, a prospect for the professional ring. He had only given it up when his father had objected, with some reason, to the company it was forcing him to keep. He said, "Isn't your father a friend of Pinnock's, Sher?"

112

"If you mean that he owes my father a good deal of money and finds it difficult to pay him, yes, that has made him very friendly indeed."

The others laughed, but Salim seemed to be pursuing a private train of thought. He said, "That would have been the work your father did for him when he was building the annexe to the gym. The one with the smaller ring in it."

"I expect so. I think there was some other work as well. It's quite a lot of money. Nearly a thousand pounds. He keeps promising to pay. He says, when his ship comes home."

"Then that means if your father asked him a special favour, he'd be likely to say yes."

"I should think so. What have you in your mind?"

Salim explained what he had in mind. The others listened attentively. They knew that they were treading on dangerous ground and would have to move very carefully.

"Ted goes in the evenings," said Javed. "Perhaps he is a little bashful about the progress he is making."

"Then one of us must be on watch, to pick the right moment. And the others must be near a telephone, so that he can get hold of them."

What Javed had said was quite true. It had needed a great deal of resolution on Ted Drummer's part to present himself at the Pinnock gym. He had done so because he had realised the unpalatable truth. The Pakistani boy was a better fighter than he was. Not just better; much better. It had been the chance of the slip that had put them rolling on the ground and enabled him to mask his inferiority. This was galling. He had been brought up in the creed that white men were superior to coloured men, black, brown or yellow. Not only cleverer, but braver and more skilful. He knew that Salim had, at one time, taken lessons in boxing at that gym. All right. This had given him a temporary advantage. So, what he had to do was have a few lessons himself and the advantage would be cancelled. Then his natural superiority as a white boy would assert itself. Incidentally he also realised that he had taken very little exercise since he had left school and that standing about all day behind the counter of a shop was a poor way of keeping fit.

On the first occasion, he had gone to the gym in the afternoon. Two young professionals had been sparring in the small ring in the annexe. In the main gym half a dozen youths were

113

exercising silently; throwing the heavy medicine ball to each other, skipping and assaulting one of the punch bags which hung from the girders.

Ted had changed, rather self-consciously, into his old school gym kit, had been equipped with a pair of large padded practice gloves and set to hitting a bouncing punch ball. On that occasion he had done no boxing.

On other occasions he had come later, when the gym was emptier, and had a few simple lessons in the art of self-defence. Pinnock, who could see that he was never going to be much use, had dealt kindly with him.

On this particular evening he was later than usual and the only other person there was a three-quarter-witted youth, known to all as 'Bim', who helped around the place and cleaned up when the customers had gone. Ted hurried into the changing-room and got into his gym kit.

When he came out, the five Pakistani boys were sitting on the bench by the door.

Pinnock said, "I'm told as how you'd 'ad a difference of opinion with one of these boys. The best way of settling something like that is in the ring. Yes?"

Ted saw that Salim was taking off the raincoat he had arrived in. Under it he was wearing boxing kit which looked a lot more professional than his own. He realised, with a cold feeling, that he was in a trap and that there was no easy way out of it.

"Orright?" said Pinnock.

"Oh, all right, yes."

"Then suppose you get weaving. And if anyone comes in, Bim, you tell 'em it's a private match and they can wait till it's over. See."

Bim said, "OK." He said it unhappily. He would have liked to have seen it.

They moved into the annexe. Pinnock had two pairs of gloves laid out. Ted noticed that they were thinner and felt much harder than the practice gloves he had used before.

Could he refuse? Could he simply walk out? They could hardly keep him there by force. The idea had only to be thought of to be rejected. It would have been an impossible lowering of the standards he had been brought up to believe in. Better a one-sided fight, than to creep away with his tail between his legs.

114

Three minutes later he was wishing he had quit and run. He had never been hurt so much in his life. Salim, who could hit him wherever he liked, had started on his body; heavy punches which landed on his chest and his arms; none of them heavy enough to give him an excuse for falling down, but all of them painful.

When Salim saw that one of the blows he had landed on the muscles of Ted's arm had hurt him badly, he concentrated on this spot measuring out repeated punishment. In desperation, Ted swung round, presenting his right shoulder and leaving his body open. Salim, instead of hitting him in the body, as he could have done, concentrated on his right arm. After a minute of this treatment Ted was so weakened that he could hardly keep his hands up. Salim backed him into the corner of the ring and having pinned him there turned his attention to his face.

To start with, they were flicks with the half open glove more than actual blows. One of them made Ted's nose bleed. He could feel the blood running into his mouth and down his chin. When he put one hand up to wipe it away on the back of the glove Salim hit him, hard and deliberately, first in one eye, then in the other. Half blinded, he went down on his knees and stayed there.

"You will now admit, perhaps," said Salim, who seemed scarcely to be out of breath, "that I am a better fighter than you."

Ted said nothing.

"Then perhaps you would prefer to continue the contest?"

Ted kept his mouth wedged. He was not going to crawl to a native.

"That's right," said Salim. "That's good. The stiff upper lip of the Sahib. We appreciate that. Let us go."

The five boys filed out. None of the others had spoken. They had not even laughed. They were a jury. They had found him guilty. Guilty of being a poor fighter. That was all.

Bim helped him to his feet. He said, "Cor, I wish I could've seen that. He's useful that Kahn boy. Better clean you up a bit, hadn't we?"

"You look after him, Bim," said Pinnock. "We're locking up now. No more for this evening." He didn't sound entirely comfortable about what had happened.

By the time Ted got home his nose had stopped bleeding and

the only visible damage was his eyes, but he was sore and aching all over; desperately sore in body and in mind, a soreness which was not improved by his father who soon got out of him what had happened.

"The bastards," he said, "the cunning low-down bloody brown shits. They've fixed us, don't you see?"

"I don't see anything," said Ted and this was almost literally true. Both eyes were beginning to swell up.

"They've fixed us properly. If they'd set on you in the street we could have thrown the book at them. Assault, public disturbance, the lot. Can't do that now. If we tried to bring the thing to court, guess what the beak'd say: good boys. That's the way to settle your differences. In the good old British manner, with gloves on, in the ring. The Kahn boy'd get a pat on the back. Example to youth."

"All right," said Ted. He was tired of his father. "It was clever. No need to go on saying it."

"It's not what I'm saying. The question is, what *you're* going to say when people see your face."

"Tell 'em I ran into a lamp post," said Ted and went out, slamming the door behind him.

"It's difficult to find out exactly what happened," said Anthony to Mr. Norrie. "But Ted Drummer is going about looking as if he exchanged his eyes for blacked-out headlights."

"What does he say about it?"

"Nothing."

"Has he complained?"

"No."

"What about his father?"

"I managed to have a word with him. It's fairly obvious that he knows what happened and that it's something to do with the Kahn boys. And that he's absolutely livid about it."

"Then why haven't we had an official complaint?"

"That's what I'm trying to find out," said Anthony patiently.

Mr. Norrie considered the matter, turning over the papers on his desk without looking at them. He said, "I can smell trouble. If the Kahns ambushed Ted and beat him up and Ted has decided to take the law into his own hands, we're going to have exactly the sort of trouble we were trying to avoid."

"I'm sorry," said Anthony.

116

"I'm not blaming you. You're not a nurse-maid. You can't keep a twenty-four-hour watch on those two gangs of hooligans. It's just that it's a bad moment. Brace has been telling me about those two louts from Special Branch who are poking their noses into things up and down the south bank of the river. He's had one complaint from Lethbridge, the big paint manufacturer, who owns Ponds Wharf. And another from Croft at the Albion Wharf – that's the sugar people. Both highly respectable firms. They want to know what the police are playing at and if they've got any questions to ask, why don't they send an officer to see them? The PLA police are getting edgy, too. They say that crime in the Port of London is their pigeon. And in the normal way of course they're right. They don't see any reason for Special Branch men – if these prize characters really are Special Branch – to be sneaking round behind their backs questioning crane-men and wharfingers."

"What does Brace say?"

"All he can say is that it's orders from higher up. Which doesn't please them at all. Lethbridge said, 'All right. If that's all you can tell me, I'll go higher up myself and see if I can find out the truth.' He'll do it, too. He's got some political pull."

"And that," said Anthony to Sandra that evening, "is just one more ingredient in what looks like a first-class mess."

"If they're clever," said Ted, "there's no reason we shouldn't be just as clever ourselves."

He had given his allies a modified account of what had happened. In his version it had been a sudden assault, more than a planned fight. Five to one, as he put it, and if he had succeeded in getting the better of Salim, no doubt the others would have carried on the good work.

"Wish I'd been there," said Len-the-Lump, flexing his considerable muscles. "I'd have given them something to take home."

"So what's the plan?" said Andy Connors.

"It'd better be good," said Norman Younger. "I mean – I'll join in anything you say, only I've been promised a first team place next Saturday, so I wouldn't want to be in any bad trouble."

"There'll be no trouble," said Ted. "We're planning this as a military operation. First thing we've got to know is whether the police visit the garage at night. Our own shop has an arrangement with the man on the beat. He looks in at midnight and four a.m. If there's anything like that we could still do it, but it would need very accurate timing."

The others were looking worried. Even Robin, who normally supported his brother, said, "Risky, innit?"

"Certainly it could be risky, but we're not going to take any risks. That's why we're giving it a dry run. We'll watch the place from midnight till five. That gives us an hour each. Any objections?"

"Yes," said Len. "If the old Bill do come along and find you hanging about in the street they'll run you in on suss. Loitering with intent is what they call it."

"No one's going to hang about in the street. Hand us down that map, Boy. The only way into the yard is on the north, from the Blaydon Road side. What we've got to do is get into the sportsground and lie up along the hedge – there – " He marked the map with a chinagraph pencil. "Norm, you've got furthest to come. You'd better take first watch. Then Andy. Boy and I can get out together. We'll do 02-00 to 04-00. Len, 04-00 to 05-00. OK?"

The war staff considered the plan. There were one or two administrative details to be fixed, but in general the idea seemed to be tactically sound.

"Then, if we find there is no police inspection, we go in two nights later. Meet at the same place in the sportsground at 01-00 hours. We don't want axes and hammers. Too noisy. Wrenches and levers should do the job. And wear your oldest sneakers."

"And gloves," said Norman. "Don't want to leave finger-prints all over the place."

The telephone pulled Azam Kahn out of his bed at three o'clock in the morning. It was the police.

"Better come down at once, sir."

"There is some trouble then?"

"There's a fire. At your garage. No panic, it's nearly out."

Azam was there inside five minutes. He ran all the way from his house, down Blaydon Road, and arrived out of breath and deeply worried. He had a lot of inflammable stuff in his garage and workshop.

There were two police cars, a fire engine and tender and a thin sprinkling of spectators. Azam was relieved to find that the fire seemed to be confined to the shanty which his sons had built at the far end of the yard. This was a blackened, damp, smoking ruin.

"Can't be certain till we go through it properly," said the police sergeant. "Can you tell us what was in the shed?"

"A few sticks of furniture. My sons and their friends used it as a meeting place."

"It looks as if the people who got in broke up the furniture, made a sort of bonfire out of it, and set it on fire. Must have done it quietly, too."

"That's right," said one of the spectators. Azam recognised him as the owner of the newspaper shop which fronted on the garage on the Plumstead High Street side. "Never heard a sound. It was the fire which woke me up. I had the brigade here quick. Didn't want it to spread."

"Quite right, Mr. Foulkes," said Azam. "You did quite right."

"If it had spread to the garage," said the firebrigade officer, "we'd have had a real blaze to deal with." He sounded faintly disappointed.

"Nothing much more to do now," said the police sergeant. "We'll be round in the morning to make a proper examination. I suppose you've got no idea who might have done a thing like this?"

"None at all," said Azam firmly.

He said the same thing to his two sons who came down to examine the damage.

"We don't want this blown up," he said. "Let the newspapers get hold of it and you don't know where it'll stop."

Salim looked thoughtfully at the heap of charred wood. A few thin wisps of smoke were coming out of it and coiling up into the November air.

Azam said, "It wouldn't cost a lot to build you another one. And a better one. I'd do that for you."

"I'll have a word with the others," said Salim. "I think, perhaps, we'll move our headquarters. We're too exposed here."

The council of war was held in the front room of Salim's house that evening. Much to her surprise Shazada was invited

to attend. Normally she was excluded from their deliberations.

Salim explained. "Why we wanted you here, Shah, was
because we thought we might move to that stable."

Shazada started to say, "What stable – ?" and then realised
that it was pointless. The boys were all grinning.

"The one where you've been having it off with young
Sunley," said Saghir.

"You're disgusting."

"Pipe down, Sher," said Salim in his commanding officer's
voice. "All we want to know, Shah, is whether this place is easy
to get at, do other people come there, that sort of thing."

"I shan't tell you anything." She launched a withering look
in the direction of Saghir and swept out of the room.

"It's all right," said Salim. "Don't worry, I'll get it all out of
her later, when she's on her own." He had no doubt about his
ability to do this. Shazada, treated reasonably, would do
anything her elder brother asked.

That evening she took him on a conducted tour.

"It's perfectly safe," she said. "No one ever comes up this
lane, unless they're using the sportsground. It doesn't lead
anywhere."

They had reached the steel gate and chain-link fence with its
'Keep Out' and 'War Office Property' signs.

"Now we have to crawl for a bit."

On her hands and knees she showed him the hole, no bigger
than the entrance to a fox's earth, which went under the
overgrown hedge on the right of the track. After they were
through the hedge it was a little easier, but the summer crop of
nettles had not entirely died and there were thorns.

She must be in love with him, thought Salim, if she does this
very often. When they had climbed through a ground-floor
window and up into the stable he looked appreciatively at the
solid brick and wood structure. It had survived the passage of
the years well.

"Just the job," he said. "Even if they found out where we'd
gone to they wouldn't burn this down in a hurry. Sit down for a
moment, Shah, and tell me about Tim."

"Tell you *what* about him?"

"Keep calm. I'm not asking about your love life. That's your
affair. I wanted to know about Tim's job."

"Oh. Well, if you mean about the army, he's in Number Three Platoon of 'C' Company of the 134th Regiment of Royal Engineers. Their headquarters is at Erith."

"Then what is he doing here?"

"He explained that. When the Arsenal moved out of London they didn't take everything with them. There are six explosive sheds out there on the marshes. They've still got stocks there. Some of it's last war stuff. They have to be guarded. The platoons take it in turns, three months at a time. Number Three Platoon is on duty until Christmas."

Salim sat on a bale of straw, swinging his legs and thinking. Shazada had found before that she could follow his thoughts with an uncanny accuracy which is more usually associated with twins.

Salim said, "Tell me about this guard duty. How's it carried out?"

"The guard is five men and a sergeant. They have a – I don't know the proper name."

"A guard-hut?"

"That's right. It's in the Arsenal grounds, near the old Gun Yard, on the river. The sentry crosses the canal by a private bridge and goes out, past the Black Sheds – that's where three of the explosive dumps are – then along to the Proof Butts, where there are three more and round in a circle and back again. Tim says it's creepy, that bit is. The night birds make noises and there are things that move about, in the rushes."

"Then he does the round on his own?"

"Yes."

"What does he do when he gets to one of these – what did you call them? – explosive stores?"

"Nothing much. What he has to do is see that the padlock is still on the door and if he saw anyone hanging about he'd have to – well – whatever sentries do."

"Challenge them."

"That's right. Challenge them."

"If he thought someone had been messing about with the padlock, I suppose he'd unlock it and look inside to see if anything had been stolen."

"I don't think he could do anything like that. He hasn't got a key and anyway he wouldn't know if anything had been stolen, because he's never seen inside one of the sheds."

"Suppose they had to get in?"

"The sergeant's got a key, I suppose."

"Where does he keep it?"

"I don't know. He's never told me things like that."

Salim thought about this, whilst Shazada watched him anxiously. Then he said, "When Tim was going his rounds, has he ever actually run into anyone – an intruder, I mean?"

"Not so far. It isn't an easy place to get into."

"That's what I was thinking. So when Tim comes to see you, how does he get out?"

"They've got some private way they use when they don't want to go out through the main gate. He's never told me what it was."

"There must be some way behind this building. We got in at the front, so it couldn't be too difficult to get out at the back. The snag is you'd still be outside the perimeter fence, wouldn't you?"

"I suppose so. Tim could tell you."

"Would he?"

"What?"

"If you asked him particularly, would he come along some time and have a word with me? Privately, I mean. Not with all the boys."

"If I asked him, I expect he would."

"Then see if you can fix it. Best would be to meet here."

"Lim."

"Yes."

"I know what you're planning to do, but don't do it. Please don't do it."

Salim looked at his sister for a long moment. It was quite dark in the stable by this time and he could just see her face as a pale blur of whiteness.

He said, "Darling Shah, if you know what I'm planning to do, you're wiser than me. Because I'm not at all sure yet what I'm planning to do."

12

"When I first came here," said Superintendent Groener, "this stretch of the river really was the Port of London. Full of cargo boats heading up for the Surrey Docks on the south bank or the India and Millwall Docks on the other side. All shut now, except for the Royals and they'll go soon. Nowadays it's a leisure-orientated highway."

The Superintendent had a North Country voice with the faintest burr in it. Agreeable to listen to, Every found.

"I expect you get all sorts," he said.

"We certainly do, Colonel. Pleasure steamers, yachts, private boats of all types and sizes."

"But you still get an occasional – I don't know the right word – I should call it a tramp steamer."

"Coasters. Yes, a few of them, but not above the Royals. Small craft, two hundred up to twelve hundred tons. The Princess Line uses the King George V Dock. One or two foreign lines like the Elskamp and the Lorraine prefer the Old Gun Dock and the Scotland. Cheaper dues and they're handier for their customers in East London, you see. But I gather it isn't docks you've got your eye on right now?"

"We don't think that our friends would risk landing this particular cargo at an official dock. They're well guarded and it would be properly scrutinised before it was allowed out. What we had in mind was a wharf or pier."

"Got plenty of those," said Groener cheerfully. "You can have a look at them as we go. More'n a hundred, I guess, between here and Gravesend."

They were seated in the forward cabin of one of the new Thames Division boats. Every had been admiring her smart black and white paint and chequered sides and now he felt the drive of her twin 220 horsepower turbo engines as they headed out into London Pool.

He said, "What can you get out of her?"

"Twenty-seven knots. Maybe thirty, if we were pushed. But anything we might have to chase is slower than we are. And we've got enough radio equipment to cut it off, or call for reinforcements if we need them. That's our mainset radio, netted to the Information Room at the Yard. The other's the marine radio. We can talk to ships on that, through Channel 14 – that's Woolwich – or Channel 12 – Gravesend. We can pick up any ship between here and Southend on one or other of those frequencies."

He looked proudly at the bank of shining instruments in front of him. Like a child, but with an unchildlike toy, thought Every. Loud hailer and siren. Flashing lights and warbler. It was a police car on water. An extension of the land arm of the Metropolitan Police.

"I'll try to define the problem for you," he said. "What I visualise is a coaster coming up river. She'll have entered her manifest at Gravesend and passed Customs. If she's a regular visitor she may not have been searched. In fact, we're indicating that that's the way we prefer it."

"Let them come up here and put their heads into it, right, Colonel?"

"Absolutely right. Ostensibly, they'll be heading for the Royals, or maybe one of those private docks you mentioned."

"Then our search area will be Blackwall Point to Barking Creek. There's nothing much beyond that except the Ford Motor works on the north bank and Erith Marshes on the south. In this stretch, you won't have to deal with more than fifty wharfs."

"I suppose that's an improvement," said Every.

They were swinging round the corner where Greenwich Reach ended and Blackwall Reach began. It was calm November weather and the river was dozing in the sun. Small, brightly painted public houses; riverside parks with children playing in them; a sunken barge which formed a gallery for a row of solemn sea-birds.

Superintendent Groener was speaking to him, pointing out the sights on his beloved river and Every was listening to Groener, but he was thinking, at the same time, about something quite different.

"That's Lovells Wharf. They deal with sugar, and the next one's a scrap-metal wharf. Morden Wharf and Delta Wharf.

They're non-operational. Bow Creek. Instones Wharf's in there, but you can only get in at high tide. You can just see – over that old lock gate – Greenland Dock and South Dock. Part of the Surrey group. Both closed up now and used for water activities. Canoeing, skiing and that sort of thing."

Was it going to be possible, thought Every, just for once, to get ahead of the opposition? To forestall the man who called himself Liam? He would be engaged in landing illegal explosives and that would put him outside the law. A type of vermin, really. No one could blame the farmer for pulling the trigger. As he thought about it, he felt the anger mounting inside him and he distrusted it.

He was a professional. Just as Liam was a professional. Professionals might kill each other, but they did not get angry about it. His first instructor, old Major Vinelott, who had killed a great many people in his time, had said to them, 'Think of yourselves as surgeons. You combat terrorism, as surgeons cut out diseased organisms. If they allowed sentiment to affect them, the hand that held the knife would be unsteady and the results disastrous. So I say to you, put aside personal feelings. Put aside passion. Do the work you are trained for. Cleanly if you can and efficiently, but above all dispassionately.'

"Coming up to Blackwall Point now," said Groener. "So better keep your eyes skinned. That opening on the left is Bow Creek. Take you straight up to Canning Town station, but it's a high-tide entrance and you might not get out again. If I had to pick a south bank landing place it'd be about here."

"Why just here?"

"I'll bring the boat over and you can see. Once you were on shore you'd be on your own. No houses or factories. Just the wharf and a quarter of a mile of track running across the marshes till you hit Woolwich Road."

"Ideal for us as well. Easy to block a single track. Whose wharfs are they?"

"The first one, just below the Point, is Universal Wharf. Don't know much about it, but we can put an enquiry through. The next one is Breakspeare. Run by a transport firm called Blaikmores. Nothing against them. Then Suffolk Wharf, said to belong to one of the co-operatives. After that Angersteins and the two Charlton Wharfs. Then Durham Wharf – that's a firm of glass bottle manufacturers. British Ropes, Silicate, Thames,

Warspite, St Marys and St Andrews, Mastpond, Tuffs Wharf and The New Ferry."

As they closed on the built-up area round the Royal Dockyard, the wharfs were coming thick and close together. Every wasn't bothering to write names down. He knew he could get them out of *Gaze's List*. He was more interested in assessing their possibilities as clandestine landing places. The first three, as Groener had said, possessed clear advantages.

"Not much on the north bank until you get to Harland and Wolff. You'll have heard of them. Then the Silvertown Rubber Company. Tennis balls and golf balls, among other things. The next lot are all Tate and Lyle, until you get to Standard Telephones and Cable. This is Gallions Reach. You can see the Barrier ahead now. Peruvian Wharf. They take gravel. Millwall Wharf, non-operative at the moment. Freight Express. They deal in specialist metals. Now you can see the two private docks I told you about. That's Scotland Dock. It's the bigger of the two. Proper lock entrance, outer basin and inner basin. It used to handle quite big craft, but of course any vessel of any size now is containerised and offloads at Thames mouth. The smaller one – we're coming up to the entrance – is Gun Dock. It's only got a single gate so you can only use it at high tide."

Every glanced at the two docks. There was a small coaster in Scotland Dock. Gun Dock seemed to be empty. He was certain, in his own mind, that the opposition would not risk a dockside disembarkation with all the formalities and chances of detection. No. It would be a sidling-up to a wharf with a party waiting on the crane and a lorry in attendance. It need take no more than a few minutes. And if he could read the riddle of Arthur Drayling and the boys, he could be waiting for them. No mistakes this time.

He knew, though he had pushed it into the back of his mind, that his feelings were coloured by guilt. If his men had done their job properly at Cuckmere Haven, Liam would not have got away and his stepson would still be alive. He wondered whether the strength of his feelings was apparent. He hoped not. Reggie Mowatt might have guessed. He had a considerable respect for the shrewdness of that stout, soft-spoken man.

They were past the Royals now, swinging up towards Barking Creek.

"Not much on either bank in this stretch. On the south it's

the Arsenal, or what's left of it, and the Thamesmead development area. On the north it's the Gas Light and Coke Company. Plenty of wharfs and jetties, but specialised equipment for handling coke and coal and that brings us to Barking Creek."

"Looks the sort of place a ship might tuck itself away in."

"If it was careful about the tide, certainly. And it's navigable for some way up. Again, one long road leading up through the Eastbury Level, to the Barking bypass. I'd notch that up as a possibility. Nothing much more between here and Erith."

"Then let's turn round," said Every. "I'd like another look at Universal, Breakspeare and Suffolk."

Back in headquarters' office, with charts and gazetteers spread over the table, they went over the ground once more.

"If you'd like my personal opinion," said Groener, "I think there are three sorts of wharf you can rule out. First there's the ones that operate under what you might call the public eye. No one in their senses is going to land a dicey cargo at Nile Street Stairs or the Steamboat Pier."

"Right," said Every. He took a blue pencil and drew a line through two and then, after thought, two more of the names on the sheet in front of him.

"Then you've got quite a few firms who are much too big and respectable to play in with a fiddle like this one."

"You know them. You'd better mark my card for me."

The blue pencil came into operation again. This time more than a dozen names disappeared.

"The last point isn't as definite as the other two," said Groener. "But I think it's sound none the less. Quite a few of these wharfs have got specialised equipment. Bucket hoists and mechanical shovels for dealing with coal or coke or gravel. I don't say they couldn't be diverted to take an ordinary load. Suppose your man has a pull with the managing director, or even with the crane boss and says, 'Just as a favour, I'd like you to land this consignment for me.' All right, maybe he'd do it. But it's the sort of thing that'd get talked about. Which is the last thing your man would want, I guess."

"I agree," said Every. "Take them out."

"Particularly," said Groener with a smile, "when, so I'm told, you've got a couple of politicos working along the south bank."

"Politicos? Oh, you mean Special Branch men. That's what you call them, is it? How did you hear about them?"

"There's not much happens on this river or either side of it that we don't hear about, sooner or later," said Groener.

"So that's the form, Micky," said Bearstead.

He was in the CID office at District and was talking to Detective Chief Superintendent Michaelson, a teddy-bear of a man, known through the length and breadth of south east London as Micky. He was a notable police officer and would, in the general view, have been one, or even two, grades higher if he had not, on one occasion, spoken his opinion of Haydn-Smith's German wife when she had tried to interfere in a police operation.

"Most of this information came from Groener, at Thames Division."

"You can bank on any information he gives you."

"Added to and cross-checked by two of our men."

"I see."

Michaelson did not add that he had heard his own boss, Commander Tancred, describe them as 'two cowboys who ought never to have been allowed off the leash'.

"Between us we've narrowed it down to four probables and two possibles. Three of the four probables are in your district. They all back on the Bugsby and the Greenwich Marshes and are all served by a single road, running south towards Woolwich. The other probable and the two possibles are on the north bank in 'K' District."

"Let's have the names of our candidates."

"Taking them from up-river, the first one is Universal Wharf. That's almost on the tip of Blackwall Point. Next is Breakspeare, which is just below the South Metropolitan Gas Works. Then the Suffolk Wharf, said to belong to one of the co-operatives, but no one quite knows which. The bull point about all of them is that they lie just below the western entrance to the Victoria Dock Tidal Basin. That means a ship could continue, as long as possible, on its stated route. If it arrived at that point after dusk, when the factories on the north bank had shut down, there'd be no one to notice if it stopped for a few minutes before it carried on, into the Royals, as per schedule."

Michaelson had his own chart spread in front of him. He

said, "It sounds very feasible, Bruno. Much better, certainly, than trying to offload in the middle of Woolwich or Plumstead. What about the owners?"

"That's what our men have been busy on. They've unearthed a few facts. Nothing specific against Blaikmores, who run the Breakspeare, except that they seem to do most of their transport work after dark."

"Curious," agreed Michaelson, "since they'd have to pay their drivers night rates."

"So I thought. The only odd thing about Suffolk is that no one seems to know who it does belong to. Everyone who is asked says someone else. Universal is the pick of the bunch. It's run by two brothers called Roberts. One of our men recognised them. He says that their real name is Rodzinsky. If he's right, they've both got form. Nothing recent. Their last convictions were seven or eight years ago, in connection with a protection racket they were running in Stepney."

"To mount a permanent watch on those three places you'd need eighteen men. If you were asking us to do it here at District, we'd have to immobilise the bulk of our Direct Support Units. Which wouldn't be a popular idea. If you want our CID personnel it's even worse. Do you realise, we're so short-handed, we can only afford to have two CID men on night duty for the whole District? People who natter about over-manning ought to look at the statistics instead of shooting their mouths off. Did you know that we have fewer policemen per head of the population than any country except Iceland?"

Bearstead couldn't help grinning. Michaelson normally looked like a teddy-bear; now he was giving a performance as a ruffled teddy-bear. He said, "It's a hard life, Micky. Sometimes I wonder how you manage to survive."

He knew the difficulties. The 1980 changes had abolished the separate CID chain of command up to Central. CID Chief Inspectors at Division now reported through their own Divisional Commander. This had left Michaelson at District out on a limb. No one reported to him at all. He was a colonel without a regiment. He knew that CID officers still went to him for help and advice, but this was a personal equation, the result of the esteem in which Micky was held. True, this made him available to take charge, in an emergency, of any major incident squad set up at District level, as had been done in the Southwark and

New Cross riots. In each case Micky's handling of the police had reduced what might have been a major disaster to an unpleasant, but controllable crisis.

"I suppose," said Michaelson tentatively, "that it's no use suggesting that Special Branch might handle the whole thing." When Bearstead said nothing, he added, "Stupid suggestion. You've got worse man-power problems than we have."

Bearstead said, "The people who are really equipped to do a job like that are the SAS. Every would jump at it."

"And think what a stink it would raise. Army doing routine police work for them."

"There's no percentage in chasing shadows," agreed Bearstead. "It's clear that if this job's going to be done properly it will have to be a straight uniformed job done through the Reynolds Road Division."

"And equally clear," said Michaelson, "that Brace won't immobilise eighteen of his men without getting a clearance from Tancred here. And he won't give it without going right up to Central."

"Which means bringing in Haydn-Smith, who'll block it if he can."

Michaelson did not feel called upon to make any comment on this. He had got into trouble for criticising the Assistant Commissioner's wife and had no desire to compound the offence.

He said, "One thing's been puzzling me a lot. Everyone seems set on the idea that when this cargo of explosive is landed it's coming to this neck of the woods. Not one of the Midland or Northern ports or Scotland, but right here, in the heart of the metropolis. I'm sure there's some reason for this odd notion, but no one's explained it to me."

Bearstead hesitated, but not for long. He knew that Michaelson was totally discreet and he needed his help. He said, "All right, Micky. For your ears alone," and repeated what he had told Anthony Leone, only more shortly, since, in this case, much of the background could be omitted.

"So the key to this is Olaf Firn."

"That's right. You've got to appreciate what an important figure he is. He would only have taken on this particular assignment if he thought it was vital and needed very tactful handling."

"You say he was posing as a journalist."

"That's right. His paper, he said, was interested in a report about racial tension. A perfectly trivial matter, incidentally, involving two boys having a scrap in the street."

"Has anyone asked the Paki kids what he said to them?"

"The Probation Officer asked, but they wouldn't tell him anything. However, in the end, they did let slip a few hints, which their father passed on. It seems Firn was really interested in the idea of further trouble occurring between them and the white crowd. Juvenile gang warfare, he called it. And naturally that appealed to them. All boys like the macho implication of being called a gang."

"Not only boys," said Michaelson. He sat in silence for nearly a minute. Bearstead waited patiently.

"I expect you've thought of this," he said at last. "Stop me if you have. This cargo, if it's four hundred pounds of explosive and is hidden in some crafty way among slabs of marble or statues or ironwork, would total up to something like half a ton in weight."

"Or more."

"And therefore you're arguing that it would need some sort of crane to sling it ashore and put it into a truck."

"Right."

"But suppose it isn't planned like that at all. Suppose the explosive is split up into a number of smaller packets. A strong boy could easily carry a load of fifty or sixty pounds for a short distance. There are any number of places on Greenwich and Plumstead Marshes with tracks running close to the bank and footpaths leading down to the river's edge. So all they've got to do is get a lorry as close as they can and the boys act as porters for the rest of the way."

"It's an idea, Micky," said Bearstead, "but I hope to God you're not right. If you are, we're not going to need eighteen policemen. We're going to need a couple of hundred."

13

Charndon Lane, Barons Court, runs south from Margravine Gardens. There are only six houses in it, all built about a hundred years ago; small and unpretentious, but with a sort of period charm. Estate Agents, with justification, describe the area as 'select and sought after'. It is certainly quiet and very peaceful.

Some alarm had been experienced by the other five house-holders when the sixth property changed hands and they read the brass plate which appeared beside the front door: 'Albert Featherstone – Music Teacher'; but their fears were set at rest. Mr. Featherstone was considerate of his neighbours' feelings. The practice room at the back of the house, he explained, would be sound-proofed as far as possible and in any event there would be no playing before ten o'clock in the morning or after six o'clock at night. Moreover he kept his word, even when his popularity, growing steadily in the three years he had been there, was making it difficult to fit in pupils.

Mostly they were of the female sex, of all ages from schoolgirls to middle-aged matrons. This is not to suggest that Mr. Featherstone was a Don Juan. There was nothing of the romantic music master about Albert. He was fat, middle-aged and jolly. When he laughed, which he did frequently, his small black eyes twinkled. He had a faint, but attractive, Irish brogue which he attributed, when anyone noticed it, to his grand-mother, a colleen from Connemara.

What people remarked on, more than his brogue, was his versatility. He seemed to be a master of all instruments from the decorous piano and violin, which the ladies preferred, to the saxophone, the drums and the electric guitars of the young male learners. If a stranger was seen approaching the house the likely question in an observer's mind was, what new instrument now?

"I tell them," said Mr. Featherstone, one of whose many

other names was Sean, "that the only instrument I haven't tried is the bagpipes. And if my grandmother, bless her old heart, had been a Scotswoman I might have added that to my repertoire."

"You're too old," said Liam, "and too fat. You need more puff for bagpipes than for blowing up balloons for a children's party."

"You heard about that, did you?" Mr. Featherstone chuckled. The previous Christmas he had given a party for the local children in the YMCA hut, supplying the decorations and food out of his own pocket. This had increased his growing popularity and had, incidentally, brought him four new pupils.

"You're a great lad," said Liam. "No doubt about that." They were sitting in the sound-proof practice room and he saw no reason to lower his voice. "Does it keep you awake at night to think that the children you were playing host to might be out shopping this Christmas and get blown higher than any of your balloons?"

"The only thing that keeps me awake at night," said Mr. Featherstone, "is wondering whether you're going to be able to deliver. For if you don't," and his black eyes twinkled, "it may be you we'll be counting the pieces of, my darling boy."

"Nothing is certain in this life except death," said Liam. "And the only reason I'm still alive is that I'm more careful than the people who want to kill me. This time I'm doubling my precautions and the only thing that worries me is that both lots turn on one man."

"That's the Arthur Drayling you've spoken of?"

"Correct. And he's a right study for a psychiatrist, I can tell you. To start with he's a – what's the name? Not a sadist, the other thing."

"A masochist."

"That's the very word. I spotted it as soon as I met him. Mind you, I expected he might be. It's the opposite side of the coin to his games with little boys."

"Does that make it easier for you?"

"Certainly. To start with I thought I was going to have to rely on that photograph I got hold of. And that might have been dangerous. Threats wear thin after a time. A level-headed man starts counting the cost and sometimes the sum doesn't come out as you'd wish it to. Not so with my Arthur. He's in such a

133

state now that he's panting for orders. He'd crawl across the carpet with a dog-collar and lead in his mouth if I told him to."

"Your knowledge of the underside of human nature is a perpetual source of amazement to me. Incidentally, I have to warn you that the postal route is off."

"Why, did something go wrong?"

Mr. Featherstone went across to a filing cabinet in the corner of the room, unlocked it and brought out two neatly wrapped and taped packages, each of them the size of a pound slab of chocolate. They were addressed to Alfred Taylor at 301A Brazil Street, marked, 'To await collection'.

"That's an accommodation address we've used once or twice before. Our man picked up these two. Luckily he's got eyes in the back of his head. The next time he went, there were two cars parked in the street which hadn't been there before. He walked straight past the shop and was glad he'd done so. There were Flying Squad men in both cars."

"I always thought the postal route was too dangerous," said Liam. "It leads straight back to the sender of the parcel, which is bad. And straight on to the receiver, which is worse. Anyway, to bring in the quantities we're dealing in would need hundreds of parcels. None the less – " he opened the violin case he had been carrying, "some of this may come in very handy."

"I suppose it's no use me asking what you've got in mind?"

"No secrets between friends. I'm thinking of a surprise for Colonel Every."

"The SAS man?"

"That's the one I was speaking of. Do you know him?"

"I don't know him," said Mr. Featherstone slowly, "but I heard something about him. Through our friends in Belgium. You remember when the Cuckmere Haven landing went wrong?"

"Yes," said Liam. He said it flatly, but there was an edge to his voice which warned his listener that he was probing a sore spot.

"And you remember the man you put the finger on. The one who called himself Dirk?"

"Yes."

"Do you know who he was?"

"I know he was working for either French or British

Intelligence. Our Belgian friends didn't think it necessary to enquire into his family history before they killed him."

"They should have done. They'd have found out that he was Every's stepson."

"Is that a fact?"

Whilst Mr. Featherstone was talking, Liam had got to his feet and now he stood quite still. There was an odd change in his eyes; a smoky film had spread over them, almost as though he had put on misted contact lenses. Mr. Featherstone was not a man who was easily alarmed, but the change disturbed him. He said, "You were talking just now about being careful. I think this is a case in which you'll have to be very careful indeed, in view of what I've told you."

"Makes it a bit personal, doesn't it?" said Liam.

Michaelson had come up to Great Peter Street by arrangement, to call on Bearstead. Bad news, he thought, was better delivered personally. He found the Chief Superintendent in his office with Commander Salwyn, whom he had never met, but knew as head of the Anti-Terrorist Squad. He said, "Please don't go, sir. This affects you, too. It's about the arrangements we were hoping to make to have six points on the river watched."

Salwyn said, "I've been told about that. It seems a sound plan."

"Three of them are on the north bank, in 'K' District. Rowlands offered straight away to co-operate. Tancred didn't feel able to do that without referring the matter to Area, who ducked it and passed it up to Central. We've now had categorical instructions that neither of the Districts is to use more than two men per site. They can do an eight hour spell each, but this leaves the period from eight p.m. to four a.m. unwatched. And the permission is only given for one week. After that the matter will be reconsidered."

Bearstead said, "And this came from the Assistant Commissioner?"

"Not in his name, but clearly on his authority."

There was a moment of silence, broken by Salwyn who said, picking his words carefully, "If there is a massive outbreak of IRA activity this winter the chief blame will fall on me. When I took on my present job, I realised the risks entailed and was

135

prepared to accept them, provided they were reasonable. But this seems to me to be unreasonable. You are asking the Met to employ thirty-six men for a few weeks. Possibly less. They offer you twelve men for one week."

There was a further silence.

Salwyn continued, in the same level voice, "I haven't followed all the arguments, but it does seem to me that a properly mounted guard, particularly on the three south bank points of entry, might prevent this explosive coming into the country and catch the IRA operatives involved. Perhaps even some of the more important ones now in this country, whose cover we have been unable to penetrate. It would be an important intelligence breakthrough. If the Met feel unable to oblige us, could we tackle it in another way? It would be a strain on our limited resources, but I could offer the services of say ten men. What about you, Bruno?"

Bearstead, who had evidently been thinking on the same lines and making mental calculations, said, "I can match that and improve on it. For a limited period I could find sixteen – maybe eighteen men."

"Then if we concentrated on what you call the four probables we'd be able, between us, to put a full team of six on to each. With perhaps a few men to spare to keep an eye on the possibles."

"And do the whole thing," said Michaelson, "without troubling Central at all."

"I'm afraid not," said Salwyn. "As matters stand at the moment I couldn't use any of my men without the sanction of the Assistant Commissioner."

The three men looked at each other.

"I suppose you could always ask him," said Bearstead at last.

Anthony Leone had been elected to the Social Club in Camlet Road. In the end it had not been Drummer who had proposed him, as he once offered to do, but Mr. Nabbs who knew him from frequent encounters in the Magistrates' Court. Crispin Locke had agreed to second him. Drummer had considered opposing Anthony's candidature. Latterly he had not found him sympathetic about the troubles of his son. But in the end discretion had prevailed. He might not like the Probation Officer, but there was no point in demonstrating open hositility.

136

So Anthony had paid his entrance fee and his first year's subscription and had been admitted to the freemasonry of the club bar. He had not found the conversation sparkling, but some of the personalities had interested him. In France, he reflected, they would have been dismissed, offensively by the intellectuals, derisively by the working class, as petit bourgeois. Here they had no such clear label or status. Some were old enough to have fought in the war and preferred to foregather with others of the same vintage and discuss a conflict which was fading rapidly into the past.

"Chiefly," said Nabbs, "because their children won't allow them to talk about it at home."

Drummer would normally have taken up the cudgels on behalf of the soldiers. Now he had something more exciting to discuss.

"I got on to them through Arthur Drayling," he said. "They're extremely rare and very valuable."

"What are?" said Locke.

"Carassius Auratus Leoninus Indicus," said Drummer proudly. "You're a scholar. You'll understand what that means."

"Not too difficult. Lion-heads from India, I take it."

"Right. Although in fact they don't come from India. Only from the north of Pakistan, as perhaps you knew."

"The only thing I know about goldfish," said Mr. Biffen, a thin sad mortician, "is that my children buy them and they die two weeks later."

"That's because you don't look after them properly, Biff. It's no good keeping them in a bowl. You need a tank with a constant flow of fresh water coming through it."

"How are you going to get them over from Pakistan then? Difficult job to keep a tank full of fresh water in an aeroplane I should have thought."

"Arthur explained that. They come over in a special refrigerator – fish can live for months inside a block of ice."

In a company in which little escaped comment it was noticed that Drummer, who had previously always referred to 'Mr. Drayling', now called him Arthur. Their association must have ripened.

"You'll have to pay for the fish and the freight in advance, I imagine," said Nabbs. "I hope the chap who is supplying them is reliable."

"Perfectly reliable. He's a well-known accountant in the City. It's one of his clients in Pakistan who is selling the fish."

Anything, Bearstead had said. Anything at all however far-fetched or trivial.

Here was a well-known accountant who had, apparently, some connection with Pakistan and now some connection with Arthur Drayling. The thread was thin. Ludicrously thin. But he had given his word. The worst that could happen would be that he would be laughed at.

There was a telephone kiosk tucked away down the lane behind the club. Better than using the club telephone, he thought, which was in the hall and very much under the public eye and ear.

He dialled the number he had been given and a courteous voice said, simply, "Yes?"

"I'm Anthony Leone, from Plumstead."

"Yes?"

How can I put it, he thought, without sounding too stupid.

"Chief Superintendent Bearstead asked me to let you know if I heard of any possible connection between a man here called Drayling and two gangs of boys. It isn't the boys, actually, but the father of two of them, a man called Abel Drummer. Drayling has clearly become friendly lately with Drummer and another man who has been described as a well-known City accountant." He explained about the goldfish. By the time he had finished, it sounded sillier than it had before.

The voice said, "Thank you, Mr. Leone. I will pass your message on."

"Bumf," said Colonel Every. "That's what soldiering is about today. Nothing but bumf."

His desk was covered with his morning mail, official-looking envelopes, most of them marked OHMS, none of them promising any excitement. He had not yet tackled them as there was a more important matter to be dealt with.

Captain Musgrave, standing in front of his desk, had been explaining that Sergeant Whitaker and Lance Corporal Abrahams had been in trouble. Ever since his unhappy encounter with Liam, Whitaker had been in an odd mood: gloomy some of the time; over-excited at others. Musgrave, who kept a fatherly eye on all of his men, sensed what the trouble was. Sergeant Whitaker was spoiling for a fight.

It had not been difficult to find one. Soldiers who wore the beige beret and the coveted winged dagger were apt to be picked on by self-appointed champions from other units. A procedure had been evolved to deal with this. SAS men tended to stick to their own bars and to go there together. Good-humoured banter and the weight of numbers could usually defuse the situation. The trouble was that when an SAS man fought he could not forget the techniques he had been taught. On this occasion, provoked by a gunner with two tough-looking friends, Whitaker had sailed straight in. Abrahams had gone in to help him. The result had been one gunner with a broken jaw, one with suspected rupture of the spleen and the third unscathed only because he had taken evasive action. He had bolted from the bar and had run into a military police patrol.

"Damn," said Every. "Damn and damn. This'll have to go up to Brigade."

"I don't think Abrahams was really to blame, sir. It was three to one. He had to go in to help."

"I've no doubt Whitaker was the one who started it. He's been asking for trouble for some time."

"If they get insulted in a pub, you can't expect them to walk off and ignore it."

"I expect them to behave like adults, not like schoolboys. And I *don't* expect them to half kill drunken squaddies. All right, David, I'll take it from here. Don't go. There's probably something in all this bumf that I can unload on to you."

He started ripping open the envelopes, with a running commentary on their contents.

"Army Council Instruction 1804/86. Something to do with not wearing gumboots in the street. You can have that one. Returning of damaged items to store. That should have gone to 'Q'. Why the hell is everything, however stupid and unimportant, always marked 'Urgent' and always sent to me?"

"You've been in the Army long enough to know the answer to that," said Musgrave soothingly. "However, I admit it does seem odd – " he had picked up a bulky envelope and was examining it, "if this collection of documents really *is* urgent – that it would appear, unless I am reading the postmark incorrectly, to have been posted two months ago."

"Put it down, very carefully please," said Every. "Right. Now slide it across the desk." He made a path for it by sweeping the other papers aside. As he did this, Musgrave noticed the missing fingers of his right hand. He said, "Do you think – ?"

"We'll find out," said Every. He chose an envelope of the same size and filled it with papers until it was the same shape as the other. Then he put them both, in turn, on to the letter scales.

"Four ounces heavier," he said. "Lucky you spotted the postmark, David. Our friend must have got hold of this old envelope somehow. He faked the address, but he couldn't change the postmark. Or hoped it wouldn't be spotted." He pulled the telephone across and started to dial.

"Then you know who sent it?"

"I've a fair idea. Home Office Explosives? Could I speak to Professor Meiklejohn? Thank you. Yes, I'll hang on."

"When you look at it closely you can see that the original label's been removed. Probably steamed off. And a new one stuck on."

"He's an ingenious beast. Oh, Ian? Colonel Every here. I hope I haven't interrupted some vital experiment."

"Ludo. Nice to hear from you. What you've interrupted is something I've been working on for a fortnight and have just decided is totally pointless. Tell me what I can do for you."

"I've a suspect packet here. Arrived this morning. I imagine it's quite safe until you start to open it, but on the whole I think I'd better bring it up myself. Be with you in about an hour and a half."

"I'll count the minutes," said the Professor politely.

14

The Prime Minister looked at the neatly typed list which showed her engagements for that morning. She was in her private room at the House. This was convenient for interviews which might attract public interest, since it could be approached from a door at the back of the Members' Library and her visitors could sit there inconspicuously until the moment came for them to be summoned. This avoided the scrutiny of public eyes and television cameras in Downing Street.

The first two interviews that morning were about money. Brigadier Pike looked after the constituency agents. He was always wanting money for them. Most of the constituencies were better off than Central Office. They could afford to pay their own agents. The second was Dr. Lovibond, who was in charge of the Central Office staff and maintained that they were underpaid. Perhaps they were. She herself was underpaid. Leading industrialists earned four times her salary.

Her third visitor was different. Deputy Assistant Commissioner Elfe had not come round from Great Peter Street to talk about money. This was something more important than money. It was the security of the realm.

She liked and approved of Elfe and she had a shrewd idea of what he was going to say. It was an inter-departmental argument which had been rumbling on for some months. One advantage of dealing with Elfe was that he always came straight to the point. On this occasion it took him no more than two minutes to outline the difficulty which had arisen.

"Not easy, Assistant Commissioner," she said. "I fully appreciate the possibilities. I wouldn't welcome an outburst of terrorism at Christmas time, any more than you would. I'm sure you understand that."

Elfe said, "Yes," and waited.

"But if I were to take any personal step in the matter it would amount to my interfering directly in the running of the Metropolitan Police, by countermanding an order given by one of the heads of that force."

"There *is* another possible solution," said Elfe. "As you know it's not a new idea and logically there's much to be said for it. It would simply be a matter of internal reorganisation. The directive would have to come from the Home Secretary, of course. But it would be a matter within the normal scope of his office." He explained what was in his mind.

The Prime Minister thought about it. It would be a slap in the face for Haydn-Smith and she tried not to allow herself to

141

be influenced by the fact that she disliked him and disliked his German wife even more.

She said, "I'll have a word with the Home Secretary this evening. I'll let you have an answer tomorrow."

Professor Meiklejohn of the Home Office Explosives Experimental Unit at Woolwich was a man who considered that care was more important than speed. This was, possibly, why he was still alive and in one piece.

It was forty-eight hours before he telephoned Colonel Every.

He said, "I'll let you have a report in writing in due course. This is just to let you know that you were right to be careful with that particular packet."

"I didn't want to lose another finger."

"Another finger! You would probably have lost your life and your office into the bargain."

"As bad as that?"

"Four ounces of compacted torpex can do a lot of damage. It's incendiary as well as explosive, you know."

"Then I can tell the Squadron Commander who was standing on the other side of my desk that his powers of observation saved his own life."

Professor Meiklejohn considered this. He was a man who distrusted extravagant statements.

He said, "If he was on the other side of the desk it might not have killed him. It would have damaged him badly and almost certainly blinded him. The trigger was ingenious. A small spring was held under tension by the flap of the envelope. Did you notice, incidentally, that the flap had been reinforced with a strip of adhesive tape?"

"I don't think I did, no."

"Points like that are important."

"I'll try to do better next time," said Every apologetically.

"I can't tell you a great deal about the explosive until I've had time to study it further. From its composition I should say that it was of European manufacture, not English and certainly not American."

"Belgian, do you think? From AMG Brussels."

"Possibly. It could equally well be French or German. One thing I did notice. It seems to have been in contact, at one time, with chocolate. Not a usual ingredient of explosives in my experience."

"I think that's easily accounted for," said Every. "It probably came across with or in a slab of chocolate. We know they've been experimenting with the postal route. In fact we located one of their accommodation addresses the other day and had it staked out. If they use it again it might give us a real lead."

"I trust so. I shall be able to give you more accurate details when we've finished the chromatographic work. Meanwhile, I can only advise you to be very careful."

Every thanked the Professor. He promised to be very careful.

Previously, when Haydn-Smith had wanted to have a word with the head of his Anti-Terrorist Squad, he had either telephoned him or dropped into his office. When, on this occasion, he sent a formal note, from his secretary to Commander Salwyn's secretary, requesting his presence at eleven o'clock that morning, it did not need a very skilful reader of the omens to detect that trouble was brewing.

Salwyn was sorry. Up to that point, his relations with the Assistant Commissioner had been reasonably friendly. He had been allowed to run his own department without much interference and had achieved, he thought, a modest degree of success in an unquestionably tough assignment. Also he was one of the few senior officers who approved of Haydn-Smith. It would be an exaggeration to say that he liked him. Haydn-Smith was not a man who invited affection from his subordinates; but he respected the competence with which he did his work.

When he went in, the Assistant Commissioner had a letter in front of him and Salwyn, reading the address upside down, saw that it came from the private office of the Home Secretary. Since it was dated that day, it must have been sent round by hand and was therefore important.

Haydn-Smith said, "I have been given a preliminary notification that C13 is to come under the jurisdiction of the Special Branch. I thought it right that you should be informed. Also that I should let you know that the change is contrary to my known views."

His voice was flat, almost conversational. Salwyn realised that he was in a cold fury. He said, "I see, sir."

143

"I don't suppose you have any idea why our masters have seen fit to make this change?"

Careful, boy, thought Salwyn. Very careful. Easy to provoke an explosion.

He said, "I believe there has been a feeling, sir, for some time that such a change might be logical. Administratively logical, I mean."

"Explain that."

"Well, sir, my branch often has to work closely with Special Branch. Guarding of VIPs for instance. That's almost always a joint job. Then, most of my men came to me from Special Branch originally."

"And that seems to you to be an adequate reason why they should return to it."

"I'm afraid it's all a bit above me, sir. I'm just a plain bobby who does what he's told."

Haydn-Smith thought about this, tapping his desk with his pencil. He knew very well that it was not Salwyn who was responsible for the change. He knew, since such matters are difficult to conceal, that Elfe had been to see the Prime Minister.

"All right," he said, "it's done and I suppose we have to live with it. There'll be a lot of administrative details to work out. Change of accommodation and new pay arrangements. 'A' branch will see to all that. I'll have a word with Mortimer this afternoon."

"Right, sir," said Salwyn. He half rose from his chair.

"Before you go, there are two things I want to make clear. First, an idea seems to be gaining currency that anyone can call on the SAS to help in police operations."

"I have used them myself on three occasions, sir. Each time with your consent."

"Certainly. And each time, before I agreed, I applied to the Ministry of Defence through General Usher. In other words we observed the proper procedure. However, I'm not sure that Special Branch has always been so scrupulous. So you might warn your new masters that the General is getting more than a little restless and that if any further attempt is made to use the SAS as a private police force, without his consent, he is prepared to – well, he is prepared to get unpleasant about it."

"I quite understand, sir."

"Good, then one other thing. The administrative moves can be set on foot now, but the change does not become effective until the end of next month."

"The end of December?" said Salwyn, thoughtfully.

"Midnight on December 31st and until that time any orders which I have given remain in force."

"Of course, sir."

"I am making the point because I understand that there was some dissatisfaction about a restriction I placed recently on members of the uniform branches in 'R' and 'K' Districts being detached from routine duty and used on some special supervision job. I am not suggesting, of course, that it was this dissatisfaction which led to such a radical change as the one we are now faced with."

It's exactly what you are suggesting, thought Salwyn. And it's gall and wormwood to you.

He said, "I think that's very unlikely, sir. The Prime Minister must have made her mind up on policy grounds, wouldn't you think?"

"He *was* in a filthy temper," said Salwyn, "and what made it worse was that he guessed that he'd precipitated the change himself by being so bloody obstructive about letting us have a few of his bobbies."

"At least he realised that he'd brought it on his own head," said Every.

"Gratifying," said Mowatt, "but it doesn't solve our immediate problem."

The three had met, at Mowatt's suggestion, in his office overlooking St James's Park station. All of them realised that their affairs had reached crisis point. If the IRA were allowed to succeed in their bloody programme for Christmas, the results could be dramatic. Dissatisfaction with the Anti-Terrorist Branch could even lead to the taking-over of its duties by the Army. If, on the other hand, they disregarded General Usher's warning and threw the SAS uninvited, into the battle, this would give its enemies in the Ministry of Defence a weapon which would enable them to emasculate their Counter-Revolutionary Warfare Team and neutralise the advantages which had been gained by their dramatic success in the Iranian Embassy siege.

145

Mowatt was the most level-headed of the three. He had seen a lot of in-fighting and departmental jealousy; he had also experienced unexpected helpfulness and co-operation. So much depended on personalities. He said, "The really awkward thing is the timing of the change. Haydn-Smith is sticking to it, I suppose."

"Midnight on December 31st. Not a minute earlier."

"And I take it he realises that the danger period is December?"

"I'm not sure he's convinced that there *is* a danger period. At that conference his general line was that the whole thing was a fantasy dreamed up by the security services."

There was a pause. Then Every said, "You know, there is a way round this." He was studying the map which he had brought with him. "What we have to cover, is a limited part of the East End of London, on either side of the river, for a limited period. Say six weeks at the outside."

The other two nodded.

"A good deal of it is still open country. Greenwich Marshes and Plumstead Marshes on the south bank. Plaistow Marshes, Eastbury Level and Dagenham Marshes on the north. What's to prevent the SAS setting up a training exercise in that area? The object of the exercise would be – let me see – to practise stopping suspected characters from leaving London by the river route."

"Operation Cork-in-Bottle," said Salwyn. "I believe you've got something there, Ludo."

"We could set up a temporary camp on each bank – "

"Just for the purpose of the exercise."

"Of course. Patrols are sent out from those camps to various points on the river and on the main roads, communications established, both by wireless and by line, and co-operation with the Thames Division could be practised."

"Hold your horses," said Mowatt. "Aren't you going to run into trouble if you involve any part of the police?"

"I don't see why. After all, it's only a training exercise. Not for real."

Every said, "I think Superintendent Groener would be willing to co-operate. And to keep the whole thing at a fairly informal level. You know I had a day down the river with him. When we were talking afterwards it transpired that he knew one of my Squadron Commanders, David Musgrave. It seems they were both at Michael Williamson's school, at the Oval. In the course of a difference of opinion David knocked out one of his teeth and he gave David a black eye."

"Sounds like the basis of a real solid friendship," agreed Salwyn.

"I'll get out a written order. I'll make it a Squadron show and put David in charge. If we do it that way we shan't have to bring Brigade in on it. Then, if something should happen while we're carrying out this piece of training, well it's just a lucky chance that our chaps should have been in the neighbourhood and able to lend the police a hand if the party gets rough. You follow me?"

"I follow you entirely," said Mowatt.

Later, when Salwyn had departed, he said, "I suppose you realise that what you're erecting is a fairly thin screen between you and trouble."

"Thinnish," agreed Every.

"Bad trouble."

"Possibly."

"If Haydn-Smith or the General heard about this and felt vindictive they could raise a stink which might blow you right out of the Army."

"Then I shall take all possible steps to see that they don't hear about it. And let me tell you this, Reggie. If I had to weigh the chances of wrecking my career in the Army against the chance of a settlement with Liam, you might be surprised if I told you which side the scales would come down."

"Other people might be surprised," said Mowatt sadly. "Not me."

The ripples caused by Haydn-Smith's directive had already spread in many directions: to Great Peter Street, to the House of Commons, to Petty France. Now they reached Reynolds Road Police Station and caused an unexpected reaction from Chief Superintendent Brace.

The manner in which the news had reached him had, admittedly, been unfortunate. He had been discussing the morning personnel slate with his second in command, Superintendent Wynn-Thomas, when the telephone call had come from Tancred at District. Tancred had said, "As you probably

147

know, there was an idea, at one time, that you'd have to detail eighteen of your men for a supervision job. You'll be glad to hear that it's now reduced to six. I'm sending round the details this morning. Something to do with suspected IRA activities. You'll be able to manage six easily enough."

When Brace had put down the receiver, with calculated deliberation, he said, "You heard that, Tommo? District is of the opinion that we can spare – that we can easily spare – six men on detachment."

Wynn-Thomas, who had been listening on an extension, said, "IRA? That's not our job, surely."

"Whether it's our job or not, we've got to do it." He looked at the list on his desk. "Easy," he said bitterly. "Would you describe it as easy?"

"We are a bit pressed in other directions just at this moment. Eight on the sick list. Five with 'flu. One suspected malaria. Johnson, a broken wrist. He collected that trying to stop a punch-up at closing time. Swindlehurst, broken leg."

"What was he trying to stop? A football match?"

"Got it jumping out of a squad car when it was going rather fast."

"Silly young ass."

"Then we've got twelve on leave. And another twelve going next week. It's always heavy in the month before Christmas." He was about to add that he could have done with a spot of leave himself, but the glint in Brace's eye warned him that this might not be the best moment. He said, "Then we've got four away on technical courses and there are the special attachments, at the Observatory and the docks."

"That's something I've never understood. Why do *we* have to operate this explosive detector? It takes one man almost permanently off his routine work. Surely it's something the PLA boys ought to be handling?"

"It's a job we could do without," agreed Wynn-Thomas.

"And talking of specialist jobs, that reminds me." He grabbed the internal telephone. "Is Sergeant Ames in the building? Good. Then send him up."

Sergeant Ames had had some of his hair cut off, but he still managed to look more like an undergraduate than a police officer. Realising that he had not been called up for commendation he stood sloppily to attention in front of Brace's desk.

"Did you see a report from the brigade about a fire at Azam Kahn's garage, Sergeant?"

"Yes, sir. I think I did."

"What did you do about it?"

"Do, sir?"

"That was my question."

"I don't think any official complaint was made, sir. At least, if it was made, I wasn't instructed to take any action about it."

"Do I understand then, that until you receive actual instructions, you don't feel obliged to do your job?"

"Well – no – sir. Not exactly."

"You were made Community Liaison Officer to keep an eye on minority groups in this division. With particular reference to West Indian and Asian groups."

"Yes, sir."

"You get a report that premises belonging to a gang of Pakistani youths have been set on fire. No question of accident. The report's quite clear about that. It was a deliberate piece of arson."

"Yes, sir."

"Also you know, if you've kept your eyes and ears open, that the leader of a rival gang of white boys has been going about looking as though he'd run into two lamp posts at once. Well?"

"I did hear about that."

"And you didn't possibly connect the two things?"

"It seemed to me that the fire might have been in revenge for the assault, but – "

When Sergeant Ames paused, Brace said, in his smoothest voice, "But what, Sergeant?"

"Well, sir, as we'd had no official complaint about either incident, I thought it might be premature to take any step in the matter."

"That's what you thought is it? Then let me tell you what I think." Brace's voice was rising with each word. Mezzo-piano at the start. Fortississimo at the finish. "I think you should hoist yourself off your backside and get out into the street and find out what's happening. Keep an eye on these Asians. That's what you're paid for. Right?"

"Right, sir," said Sergeant Ames unhappily and ambled out.

"That man gets on my tits," said Brace. "He's so wet he lays his own dust."

"I did wonder," said Wynn-Thomas, "if we are in for black-and-white trouble, whether it mightn't be a sound idea to give someone else Sergeant Ames' job. It's an important assignment."

"Now I suppose you're going to tell me that I can *easily* find someone."

"Nothing's easy when you're under-staffed and over worked," said Wynn-Thomas pacifically.

'B' Squadron Orders
Training Operation 'Cork-in-Bottle'

1 All four troops will be engaged in this operation which will commence p.m. on November 14th and continue for an initial period of fourteen days.
2 Area of operation. Troops 1 and 3: OS map Essex No. 138, squares 041/043. Troops 2 and 4: OS map Greater London No. 142, squares 001/002.
3 The objects of the exercise are to practise:
(a) Continuous observation over a defined area.
(b) Signals co-ordination, both inter-sub-unit and with other forces.
    Appendix A for frequencies and call signs.
(c) Digging-in and concealment of observation points.
(d) Laying of land-line to OPs.
(e) Setting up, digging-in and camouflage of temporary Troop HQs in the field.
(f) Movement after dark.
4 Narrative. Two suspect Redland agents, arrested in London, subsequently effected an escape and are believed to be hidden by sympathisers in the dockland area. Intelligence sources have suggested that an attempt will be made to evacuate these agents down river in some form of river craft and to have them picked up by ocean-going craft in the area Gravesend/ Tilbury. The Squadron will take up Observation Points selected by the Squadron Commander and observe and report on all movements of craft. Should the police find it necessary to stop and/or search any craft, Squadron personnel are to be so positioned that they can assist them if called upon to do so.
5 Administration. Rations for three days will be carried by troops. 'Q' will organise delivery of further rations to Troop HQs as required. Establishment of HQs and OPs and all movement to and from them will take place after dark.

6 Troop Commanders to hand in copies of their own orders (preliminary reconnaissance; start-time of main body; routes; transport; signal nets) to Squadron Commander by 09.00 hours tomorrow.

7 Important Note. In view of the possibility (see paragraph 4) of the existence of persons sympathetic to the agents, the greatest possible care will be taken to avoid civilian personnel having any sight of SAS activities. The exercise will be adjudged a success if it can take place without drawing the attention of the public to the operation or, if such attention cannot be avoided, by keeping it to a minimum.

D. Musgrave OC 'B' Squadron.

15

PC Rackham was not happy.

He was a normally courageous young man, but the cold of the November evening, the lack of companionship and the fact that his watch seemed to be operating a private go-slow, had combined to reduce his spirits to a very low point indeed.

It had not been so bad when the two factories on the north bank, opposite his post, had been in operation with workmen moving about, and there had been an exciting moment when a tug, towing two barges, had nearly overshot the entrance to the tidal basin of the Victoria Dock.

A good deal of language, which PC Rackham had appreciated, had floated across the broad waters of the Thames. These had been grey and placid when he had come on duty at four o'clock, but the tide was running out and the east wind, which had freshened as dusk fell, was now blowing directly upstream, cutting off the edges of the waves and crowning each one with a white cap.

He was squatting in a hide which his relief, PC Hind, who was something of a handyman, had constructed at the top of the concrete steps leading to the downstream end of the Universal Wharf. The hide was well dug in and had a rainproof cover, but it was small for a big man like Rackham. Its furnishing was functional; a bench to sit on and a plank to rest his elbows on. A pair of night-glasses hung from a nail and he had a scribbling-board, with a built-in light, on which to note his observations.

His instructions were simple. He would be alerted on his personal radio when any ship passed Customs at Gravesend and came upstream. He would watch for its arrival and follow it through his own zone of observation. If it continued on upstream or entered the Victoria Dock he took no action. If it approached the Universal Wharf he was to inform Reynolds Road Police Station. The main set there was netted to Gravesend and Woolwich radios as well as to the Information Room at Scotland Yard. If he needed help, his relief was available at Reynolds Road Police Station, but resting.

And a bloody sight warmer than I am, thought Rackham, looking for the third time in ten minutes at his wrist-watch. The minute-hand had crawled down to a quarter past seven. His spell ended at eight o'clock, when he would climb out, retrieve his bicycle which was hidden in some bushes at the top of the rise and pedal back to hand in his report and go home.

This report, pinned to the scribbling-board, was blank, So far, in the five days of his watch, there had been nothing to write in it and he was beginning to wonder whether Universal was used at all. Once, tiring of inactivity, he had made a cautious inspection. The wharf was a double construction, in the form of an H. The rear part, built solidly into the river bank, contained the single crane and crane-housing. It was joined by a narrow walkway to the outer section which stood in deeper water. The only sign of use was a set of fresh tyre marks in the mud beside the metalled track which ran back across the marsh to Blackwall Lane.

What seemed like half an hour later he looked at his watch again. Twenty past seven. Or might it, at a pinch, be called twenty-one past? He was debating this point when it ceased to be important.

Someone was in the crane-housing and was using a torch. Or were his eyes playing tricks? He picked up the night-glasses and focused them. No question, there was someone there.

His instructions had been specific. He was to let control know if any ship approached or anchored at the wharf. He had been notified that the *SS Beatrice*, Lorraine Line, four hundred tons, with a cargo of oranges and grapefruit, had left Gravesend Customs at ten minutes to five. If it was making six knots against the current it could be up with him shortly. But did activity on the wharf warrant a report? Chief Superintendent Brace was a stickler for precision in the carrying out of orders.

All the same, something odd was going on. The man at the crane must have arrived on foot or by bicycle and crept on to the wharf without attracting attention. Suspicious, certainly.

The silence was broken by the cough of an engine and a rattling of gear. Now he could see the arm of the crane swinging out against the evening sky. Common sense prevailed. He pressed the transmit button on his radio. The response was a single high-pitched shriek, strong enough to drown any attempt at speech. Either the set had broken down, or someone was using an interrupter to block his wavelength. There was no time to think this out, because a ship was approaching the wharf. First he saw the port-side and masthead lights, then the loom of the ship itself. It was roughly the right size for the *Beatrice*.

He heard the engines go into reverse as she sidled up to the outer wharf edge. There was a second man down there now. Where had he come from? He was dealing with the warps, first the forward one, then as the boat swung in, the rear one. He had evidently done this before, for the whole operation was carried out without any shouting of orders.

Rackham pressed the transmit button again and only succeeded in deafening himself. He wondered what the hell he should do. It would take him twenty minutes at least to reach the nearest telephone. By that time the cargo could be landed and the ship on its way again. If he went down and tried to interfere he could guess exactly what would happen. There were half a dozen men on the after deck now. They were busy dragging nets full of boxes into position under the arm of the crane.

When in doubt, use your head, not your legs.

The important point was the cargo. The ship could not escape. No doubt some sort of vehicle would be coming to pick up the boxes which were being swung ashore. As soon as these were unloaded the ship would push off as quickly as possible. He was sure of that. Then the odds would be reduced and he might be able to intervene to some effect.

Back at Reynolds Road the senior of the two officers on the

console was getting worried too. More experienced than Rackham he realised immediately what was happening. He sent his number two to extract Hind, at the double, from the canteen. There was no time to lose. The importance of the listening posts had been stressed in Station Orders. When Hind arrived, he said, "Some bugger's jamming the p.r. at Universal. I guess your chum's in trouble. Better take one of the pandas and get down quick."

But more than one man was needed. A rescue party would have to be organised. Difficult at any time, doubly so at that hour, when the evening relief had gone out, leaving the station almost empty. When Hind had departed, he thought about it for a long moment. Then he made up his mind, grabbed the telephone and dialled a number.

Two netfuls were ashore now. About forty boxes, Rackham calculated. The crane had been swung in, the warps cast off and the ship was backing away.

Now the crane driver had come down and was helping the second man stack the boxes at the far end of the wharf. The whole operation had taken less than ten minutes. How often had it happened before, Rackham wondered.

Time to be moving. He wriggled out of the hide and started down the steps. If he could knock one of the men out quickly he reckoned he could handle the other all right.

Then he heard the lorry coming. It had been driving, without lights, down the approach road. Now it skidded to a halt and started to back up towards the pile of boxes.

Rackham stood for a moment, watching it. The driver got out, followed by another man. The odds had lengthened uncomfortably. But he had no intention of backing down. He stumped on to the wharf, his footsteps echoing on the woodwork and bellowed out, "Hold it."

Any doubts he may have had were set at rest by the actions of the four men. At the sound of his approach they had not turned. Their hands had gone into their pockets and by the time they swung round he saw that their faces were covered by stocking masks.

Three of them stood by the lorry. The fourth, a thick-set man who walked with a slight limp, advanced along the planking towards Rackham.

"Well now," he said pleasantly. "It's the boys in blue. No, not the boys – just one little blue boy, right?"

The other men had continued packing the boxes into the back of the lorry. They worked neatly and without hurry.

"I told you to stop that," said Rackham.

"But are you in any position to give orders?" said the thick-set man. "That's the point, isn't it? And don't pretend you've been sending for reinforcements. That toy radio of yours has been jammed for the last ten minutes, hasn't it?"

"Never mind about my radio. And never mind about who's coming to help me. I'm here and I'm ordering you to stop handling that cargo."

"And if we don't take a blind bit of notice – "

"Then I shall have to take you in charge."

The others had suspended loading to listen to this dialogue and Rackham's final effort produced a laugh.

"What, all of us?" said one of them.

"On your bike, copper."

Rackham slid the truncheon out of its loop. He had an idea that if he could knock out the thick-set man, who was clearly the leader, the others might give in. He had no time to test this theory. The thick-set man shot him. The .38 bullet hit him below his collar-bone on the right-hand side, broke two ribs and lodged under his shoulder blade. The impact knocked him off his feet.

The man who had shot him took no further notice of him. "Sling that stuff in. Don't fuck about with it." There was a sharper edge to his voice. "We've got no fucking time to waste."

"Not a fucking moment," agreed Captain Musgrave pleasantly.

The four men swung round. It was impossible to say how it had happened, but there were now a lot of men there. Twenty at least, dressed in combat jackets without unit signs on them and carrying machine pistols in the easy way of men who knew how to use them.

In the face of such a force, opposition was going to be not only useless, but dangerous.

"On to the wharf all of you and sit down. That's good boys. Quite comfortable? Then you can take off your girlfriends' stockings."

There was a moment of hesitation. Three of the men looked

155

at the fourth. Musgrave said, "You saw this man shoot the policeman, Duffy?"

"Certainly did."

"Then it would be a fair exchange if you shot him in the ankle."

The masks came off in a hurry.

"Well, I'm not surprised *he* was wearing one, are you Duffy?"

"If I had a face like that I'd keep it under cover," agreed Duffy.

"Suppose we have a look at the fruit."

One of his men broke open a case and handed Musgrave a grapefruit. He dug into it with his clasp knife and felt inside for what he was sure he would find there. It was a thimble-sized plastic container, which he opened carefully. When he dipped in the tip of his little finger, it came out with a few grains of white powder on it. Musgrave tasted it and spat.

"Not exactly what we were looking for," he said, "but interesting all the same."

The man beside him said something and Musgrave swung round.

"I think we've got visitors."

It was Michaelson at District, who had responded to the summons from Reynolds Road. He had turned out the two Immediate Response Units in their carriers, and had come with the leading one himself. They had turned off the highway and were approaching at break-neck speed down the single approach road. Sandwiched between them, in imminent fear of being overrun, was the panda car at last extracted by Detective Hind from a suspicious Transport Sergeant.

The thick-set man, who went under the name of Roberts and whose real name was Rodzinsky, observed these further reinforcements without enthusiasm. Then he noticed something else.

The strangers had vanished, so quickly and so quietly that it was hard to believe they had ever been there. His mind worked fast. There was little hope of escaping. The one road out was blocked and if they took to the open they would soon be hunted down by one or other lot of opponents. The nearest carrier was still a hundred yards away. If they worked quickly they might destroy the evidence.

"Throw the stuff into the river," he said.

The other three men gaped at him.

"And be bloody quick about it."

He jumped up, took one of the crates and slung it. He had misjudged the weight of the crate. It cleared the inner wharf, hit the outer one and split, spilling oranges over the planks.

The others grasped, at last, what he meant, jumped up and seized a crate each, but they had reacted too slowly. Only half a dozen had been disposed of when the police were on top of them. The fight was brief. No one enjoyed himself more than Michaelson. In a matter of minutes the four men were sitting where they had been before, only now they were handcuffed.

"First thing," said Michaelson, tucking back his shirt which had been torn out of his trousers in the struggle, "is look after this poor chap. Who is he?"

"Rackham, sir," said Hind.

"He did a good job. If he hadn't held them up for a few minutes they'd have had all that stuff in the river. Get on the air and whistle up a doctor and an ambulance. Now let's see what we've got."

16

"It was a split-second decision," said Colonel Every. "When Musgrave realised that the cargo was drugs, not explosives, and saw the police coming up at a gallop, he realised that the time had come to make himself scarce. Even if the men got away, they couldn't take the stuff with them. And he knew how tricky the situation was."

"A split-second decision," agreed Bearstead. "But unquestionably a correct one. And I'm glad it was Micky here who came to the rescue. He knows the form."

Michaelson, in whose office this discussion took place, said, "If you mean that I'm in a position to head off awkward questions, don't worry. There's someone much keener to do it than me. That's friend Brace. You realise that the whole thing is a terrific scoop for him? The narcotics boys are over the moon. They haven't finished weighing and counting yet, but it was a massive consignment and you needn't think he's going to allow any part of the credit to be diverted from his boys to mysterious civilians. Incidentally, he's put Rackham in for a police medal."

"Well deserved," said Every. "How is the boy?"

"He had a rotten forty-eight hours after they got the bullet out. A lot of fever and the after-effects of shock. No one's allowed to talk to him at the moment."

"And by the time they do talk to him," said Every, "the whole thing will have faded into illusion."

Bearstead said, "Rodzinsky and his friends might talk, but no one's going to pay much attention to any ghost stories they dream up. I think you've had a clear run, Colonel. In fact, what you might call a first-class dress-rehearsal. Even Brace has been converted. He was livid when he heard that the smugglers had succeeded in blocking his boy's wireless set and he's busy laying a land-line to each of his watching posts. So one way and another it came out rather well."

"The only thing is," said Michaelson, "if the IRA hear about this scoop, might they postpone their own operation? It'd be awkward if they did, because the sort of arrangement we've set up can't be kept up for long. I imagine you'll have to call in your men soon, Colonel. They can't sit about on the marsh for ever pretending to play at soldiers."

"No," said Every. He spoke with the conviction of a man who could read the future. "They've got a plan and a timetable and they'll stick to it, to the day and the hour. They'll come all right. And unless something unforeseen occurs – " he placed one finger of his crippled hand on the wood of Michaelson's desk, "this time, pray God, we'll be waiting for them."

When Anthony came into the clubroom he could hear Abel Drummer, who was dominating the conversation at the bar.

"A most interesting man," he said.

"Who's interesting?" asked Nabbs, inserting himself into the group.

"I don't see why I should be expected to repeat everything I say. However, as it happens, I was discussing a friend of Arthur Drayling, who I've now been privileged to meet."

"The goldfish man."

"Mr. Patel is an expert on other things than goldfish."

"Foreigner, I take it."

"Mr. Patel is from Pakistan, but he speaks excellent English. Better than many of your boys."

"All right," said Locke. "Don't start getting at the poor old schoolmaster. What does Mr. Patel know about that makes him so remarkable?"

"He's an ophiologist."

"Come again?"

"Which means, as you should know, that he has made a study of snakes. He is obtaining two or three different species for me to sell."

This really did create a sensation.

"Cobras?" said Mr. Biffen.

"Who are you planning to murder?" said Seligman.

"The snake," said Drummer, "is much maligned and misunderstood."

"Tell that to Adam and Eve."

"If you were cognisant of the elementary facts of natural history," said Drummer overriding all interruptions, "you would know that only the Viperidae are poisonous. And of the Colubridae, which comprise more than three-quarters of all snakes, the majority are non-poisonous."

"Snakes can hypnotise you," said Nabbs.

"Only if you're a bird," said Seligman.

Anthony missed the remainder of this fascinating discussion. He had already headed for the telephone kiosk.

Having introduced himself, he said, "The man I told you about last time, the one who's got so friendly with Drayling, has now latched on to Drummer. You know about him?"

"Yes. We know the names of everyone involved. Please continue."

"Well he seems to be passing himself off as a Pakistani, who calls himself Patel, though I thought that was actually an Indian more than a Pakistani name. However, his new line is snakes. He's going to supply Drummer with some for his shop. Harmless ones, of course."

He repeated what he could remember of the conversation at

159

the club, but got badly bogged down with the Viperidae and Colubridae. The man at the other end listened patiently and then said, exactly as he had before, "Thank you, Mr. Leone. I will pass your message on to the Superintendent. He will be very grateful."

Didn't seem very interested, thought Anthony and wondered if what he was doing was worthwhile. He did not, of course, know that the whole conversation was taped and that a transcript of the tape went to three different authorities.

"What we done," said Len Lofthouse, "was OK. But me, I don't reckon it was enough."

"It was OK," agreed Andy Connors. "But it didn't settle the bill. People are still talking about those shiners of yours, Ted, aren't they?"

"Yes," said Ted shortly. Like all generals he disliked talk of past defeats.

"Of course, when we spread it round that five of them set on you it got you a lot of sympathy – "

But the general feeling was clear. What was wanted was not sympathy, but action. Decisive and dramatic action. Action that would wipe the slate clean for once and all.

Len said, "Why don't we just get after them? Five to five this time. Not five to one. Salim may be a useful scrapper, but the other four are daisies."

He was the biggest and strongest of all the boys and was hot for a fight.

"Hold it a moment," said Andy. "I don't say I'm not keen on a rumble, but if we do anything in public old Norrie will be down on us like a ton of bricks. Ted in particular."

"Simple," said Len. "We don't do it in public. All we got to do is find out where they've holed up and pay 'em a visit one evening. We can find that out, surely."

"We don't have to find out. We know," said Ted.

"How come?"

"Tell them, Boy."

Robin said, "It wasn't so difficult. I hung round the street outside the garage and followed them. They're using an old stable, up that lane beyond the hockey ground. Next night I went again, when they weren't there, and got right in. It's quite a place. Mostly brick and slate. It wouldn't be easy to

160

break up, or burn. Not unless you used a lot of petrol and even then it mightn't go. It's damp, see. And a lot of damp stuff round it."

"The only way, I suppose," said Andy, "would be to blow it up."

He stopped, as though frightened to say more. He could see that the others were fired by the idea. Decisive, dramatic, violent. No question about that.

Then Norman Younger spoke for the first time. He had a piece of information to pass on and he had been playing with it, much as he played with a football, tapping it from foot to foot, working out, in split seconds, whether the moment had come to pass it or whether it would be better to keep it to himself a little longer, weighing advantage against danger.

He said, "I was having a word with Liz Frazer last night."

"Sure it was only a word?" said Len. Norman, the celebrity, had a stable of willing girlfriends.

"What she said was, that she'd been talking to Marlene Davies and Marlene had told her something in confidence, but she seemed quite happy to pass it on to me."

"Quickest way of spreading news," said Robin, "is to tell it to a girl in strict confidence."

"Go on, Norm," said Ted.

"It was something Shah Kahn had told her."

"Also in confidence."

"I expect so. Anyway Shah said that Tim Sunley – that's her particular boyfriend – was on the sapper guard at the Arsenal and had promised to get hold of some explosive for them from one of the old bunkers out on the river bank. He said he could nick the key when it was his turn for sentry and put it back afterwards. Easy, he said."

There was a moment of silence. Norman knew that, by speaking, he had settled the matter as decisively as when he lured the goalkeeper out and shot between unguarded posts.

"If that's their little idea," said Ted, "there's only one thing for it, isn't there?"

Three heads nodded eagerly. Only Norman kept silent. He was faithful to the band out of personal friendship with Andy, but being the most successful, was the least keen on trouble.

"How'd we get the stuff?" said Len.

"Boy lifts it for us. Plenty of it where he works."

Robin looked doubtful. He said, "It's pretty well looked after."

"If Sunley can get it from a locked ammunition shed surely you can get hold of a bit from the company store. What is it, anyway?"

"What we mostly use is PE 808. That's open-cast gelignite."

"Is it difficult to use?"

"Not really. I mean, it isn't dangerous to handle or anything like that. It's soft sort of stuff, like plasticine. You wedge it into a crack in the rock face, shove in a detonator and push off."

"Could you get hold of a detonator?"

"That wouldn't be so difficult. They keep them in a cupboard in the basement. I could slip down and get a few of those easy enough."

"If you can do that we're home and dry," said Len.

He could already see the stable going up in a glorious technicolour cloud.

"We're half way there," said Ted. "No more than that. Just think it out. We're the first people who are going to be blamed. That's obvious, isn't it? Then what we've got to do is to be somewhere else, where everyone can see us, when the bomb goes up."

Norman said, "We have a Supporters' Club party at the ground on Friday. Beer and bangers. I could get you all in on that. It doesn't pack up much short of midnight."

Ted was thinking this out. He said, "Friday would be ideal. It's a sort of wog holy day and they wouldn't be likely to be there in the evening. If they were, we'd have to put it off. We're not out to kill anyone."

Emphatic agreement to this.

"Then all we've got to do is go along and fix it around seven o'clock, with a time-fuse to set it off at ten o'clock."

"A time-fuse?" said Robin. "We don't use anything like that. What we do is we wire the detonator to an ordinary car battery and press the tit when we're ready."

"Then we'll have to make our own time-fuse. All we need's a clock."

"How do you fix it?"

This produced a further moment of silence. It was clear that everyone had a vague idea – something they'd read in books – but nothing specific.

162

"Your father's a sapper, Andy," said Robin. "Could you get him to tell you how to do it?"

"He'd have a fit."

"Even if you told him we weren't going to hurt anyone. Just blow something up."

"Even then."

It was curious that an idea seemed to be forming in everyone's mind at the same time. Four heads were turned towards Ted, who nodded as though in answer to a question that had not been asked.

"Dad would help," he said. "He'd have done it for Tiger alone. But now he's so mad – well – he'll help all right. He was a sapper himself – only Territorial – but I remember him telling me they did a course on time-fuses and things like that – "

"Mister Lee-own?"

Anthony, who was on his way to the club, swung round. A woman on the other side of the street was signalling to him and now came across, dodging through the evening traffic of the High Street. He recognised her as someone he had seen before, but he was unable to attach a name to her.

She said, "I am sorry, reely I am. But I felt I had to have a word with you. You were so kind to little Debbie that time."

Now he could place her. She must be Sergeant Montgomery's wife. Deborah was her five-year-old daughter. He had encountered her, lost, but not altogether unhappy about it, in the British Home Stores some weeks ago, had got her name and address out of her and restored her to her mother.

"It's not right, I know – stopping you in the street like this. If it hadn't been so important I'd never have dared do it. I expect you're in a terrible hurry, too."

"Not really," said Anthony. "If it's important and you think I can help, let's have a word."

They were outside the Eagle and Child. It would be almost empty at that hour. He led the way in, settled Mrs. Montgomery at a corner table, ordered a gin and lime for her and a beer for himself and sat down. They were the only people in the bar.

"Now," he said, "what's it all about?"

Having been brought to the point, Mrs. Montgomery seemed to be finding it hard to begin. Then she said, "It's Ted – that's my husband. You know him."

"We all know Monty."

The use of his nickname seemed to encourage her.

"What I wanted to say was that there's something wrong with him. These last few weeks. He's been almost out of his mind. I don't mind him hitting me, but he's started hitting the children. He's never done that before."

Now Anthony really was startled. He knew Sergeant Montgomery, on duty, as the best sort of policeman. Steady, not wildly intelligent, but experienced and reliable. He said, "What in the world has got into him?"

Mrs. Montgomery looked at him, for a moment, quite steadily. Then she said, "You're not a policeman, Mr. Lee-owny, are you? Not exactly."

"I'm no sort of policeman at all."

"If I was to tell you something which – something you'd have to take some official action about if you was a policeman – would you promise not to say anything about it?"

How often and in how many different ways had this question been put to him? A sobbing girl, a defiant boy. If I tell you, promise you won't let it go any further –

He said, as he always did, "I should have to be guided by my conscience. If it's nothing to do with my probation work, I'd probably have no need to say anything to anyone. But I can't make promises in advance."

Mrs. Montgomery thought about this. She was no fool, as Anthony realised, and she understood exactly what he meant. But the desire for advice was stronger than discretion. The story came tumbling out.

"You mean," said Anthony, "that Mr. Drayling's been lending him money to bet with on the dogs and now he can't pay him back."

"He couldn't, not possibly. Lately it's been all losses. He won't tell me what it adds up to, but it must be hundreds of pounds."

"Suppose your husband stopped. Suppose he said, 'No more bets. I'll pay you back what I owe you as quickly as I can. A few pounds a week.'"

"That's what I told him. But he said he couldn't do it. Because if he did, Mr. Drayling would report him to the Superintendent and he'd be out. No question. He's been twenty years in the force. It'd break his heart."

Anthony put the next question cautiously. He said, "Is there something Drayling wants him to do in exchange for letting him off the debt?"

"There must be. I'm sure of it. It might be that he wants Ted to keep him out of trouble. He's soft on children, in a nasty sort of way. I know that because of something he said to young Ron. Ron didn't understand it, but when he told me about it I understood all right. Well, suppose he went too far with some kid and got into trouble, it'd be useful to have Ted to get him out of it."

"I see," said Anthony. He was not altogether surprised to learn about this side of Drayling's character.

He said, "The only way to tackle it is to try to scare Drayling. If he's making threats, that's blackmail. He can be put away for it. And the court leans over backwards to protect the person who's being blackmailed."

All the same, he thought, not much use Sergeant Montgomery trying to hide his identity as 'Mr. X'.

What an unpleasant person Drayling was. He had heard rumours about him before. Apparently none of his own circle had suspected anything, but Anthony lived in two worlds and it was from the underworld that the hints had come. Nothing definite, just a smell. It was very possible that Mrs. Montgomery was right. It would undoubtedly be useful to a man like Drayling to have a police ally handy. He seemed to remember that Monty had some job connected with the Observatory. He had been on his way there when the trouble first broke out. And Drayling's place was alongside the Observatory.

Moreover, what he did would have cost Drayling very little. A double-chancer! One of Anthony's earliest charges, a precociously evil imp of sixteen, had explained it to him. You got a mug in debt to you and took him to the races. There weren't often more than two dogs with a chance. You put him on one and backed the other yourself. If the mug won, his money came back to you in part repayment of his debt. If you won, this would more than pay for the mug's stake.

Just the sort of game to appeal to a man like Drayling. But nothing in it was connected, even remotely, with the two gangs of boys, or with plans to land explosive on the banks of the Thames.

By the time Anthony reached this conclusion he had arrived

at the corner of Wick Lane and Camlet Road. Common sense had scored a victory over conscience. He had taken two paces past the telephone box and towards the entrance to the Social Club when it happened.

A moment of blinding light, a great flash of flame swallowed by a wash of blackness. The sound and the shock wave hit him together. Sight and thought were suspended. Then he saw the orange and crimson glow of fire and started in a stumbling run, unhurt, but dazed, down Wick Lane.

When he reached the shack he saw that the explosion had blown a hole in the roof and the flames were being sucked up through it. The old woodwork of the building was already well alight. A fire alarm was hoo-hahing in the distance. He thought, they'll never get the engine down this lane. If anything was to be done it had to be done quickly.

He remembered, from the time he had visited the boys, that there were two rooms. An outer room, little more than a hall. A single room behind that.

He tore open the front door. The blast that came out was heat, not flame. The seat of the fire was in the inner room. He stumbled and almost fell over the body on the floor. This was one job which he could do. He grabbed at a coat, felt for the collar and hauled the body out into the lane. There was light enough for him to see that it was Boy Drummer. Blood was pumping from a crack in his head and darkening his light hair. So he, at least, was alive. And that meant that he had to go back.

The heat in the outer room was greater than before, but just tolerable. He noticed, with surprise, that there was very little smoke and wondered about this until he realised that he had only stopped to think because he was afraid. He opened the inner door.

He was looking into a furnace. The heat was appalling. He could see four bodies sprawled on the floor. The nearest was lying face downwards. He grabbed at the coat collar and cried out. The cloth he had hold of was already smouldering.

He tore the silk scarf from his neck, wrapped it round his right hand and bent down again to pull. This one was heavier than young Drummer. As he pulled the body rolled over on to its back and at that moment a beam fell from the ceiling with a crash, landing across two of the other bodies. As the flames

166

jumped up he saw that the boy he was trying to move was Len Lofthouse and that he was dead. The explosion had destroyed him.

With a stab of panic he realised that his own coat was on fire. No time to do anything about that. Get out and get out quick. He turned and stumbled towards the door. It had slammed shut. He kicked at it savagely and stupidly. Then he stopped, for a moment, to think. Bloody fool. Turn the handle. That's how you open a door.

It was lucky his scarf was still round his hand because the metal handle was almost red hot. He turned it, the door swung open, he fell through and rolled. In the seconds of delay his trouser legs had caught fire. The agony was so intolerable that he opened his mouth to scream and inhaled a gulp of hot air. Then he started to crawl towards the outer door. His head was swimming. Only the stark realisation that if he stopped he was finished kept him moving. As he reached the street door he saw that it was open and that there were men in the lane.

Someone, Crispin Locke he thought, shouted out. A coat was thrown over him, wrapping him round. He screamed again. Then merciful blackness swallowed him.

Part Two

Dispersal

17

Anthony was in a private room in the Woolwich Hospital. His first five days had been spent in the Burns Unit. He had little memory of them and was anxious to forget them. Periods of pain when his flayed arms and legs were being dressed; periods of relief and drowsiness as the morphine injections took effect.

During that time his only visitor had been Sandra. He had an impression of her face as she looked down at him for the few seconds allowed. She had been trying so hard to smile that it had made him smile too and this had seemed to please the nurse who was with her. After that he had hauled himself up slowly, day by day, out of the darkness, into the kindly light. Now he was beginning to get used to the fact that his body belonged to him; was not just a lay figure to be washed in warm saline and painted with mercuro-fluorescene.

"I wanted them to take a colour photograph," said Sandra. "You looked just like a Red Indian."

"Photographs be blowed," said Anthony. "What I want is to get up."

"In a day or two Nurse Williams said. *If* you behave yourself."

"I refuse to behave myself. I want to know what's happened. What are the police doing? Have they found out what caused the explosion? Is Boy Drummer alive?"

"You're not to worry about anything until you're better."

"It worries me much more being treated like an idiot child."

"There, you see. You've worked yourself into a state. I shouldn't be surprised if your temperature hadn't gone up several points. Just wait till I tell Nurse Williams."

At the door she relented sufficiently to say, "Boy's still unconscious. But the doctors are pretty sure they can save him."

On the tenth day he had his first outside visitor. He had been allowed up that afternoon and was feeling cheerful. His cheerfulness increased when he saw who it was.

Mr. Norrie parked himself carefully on the chair beside the bed and examined Anthony.

"Well, Lion," he said, "I must say you look better than I'd been led to expect."

"I am better," said Anthony.

"Like to know what the doctor said about you? In cases of over twenty per cent burns, he told me, the chief enemy is shock. In this case they've observed practically no shock symptoms at all. Extraordinary mental resilience apparently."

"Thank you," said Anthony. "I did have nightmares to start with. But now I seem to dream about nothing but scrambled egg. Do you think that's a sign I ought to get up for breakfast?"

"Doesn't do to rush these things. All the same, we could do with you. Things are moving in a way I don't like. Don't like at all. You know Dr. Allpace?"

"The Woolwich coroner?"

"Right. And that's a very suitable name for someone who tries to exceed the speed limit. The inquest opened last Thursday – that's just a week after the fire – and if he'd been allowed to have his own way it would have closed the same day. He called only four witnesses. Just four, think of it. Summerson, the Guy's pathologist, who kept his evidence toned down so as not to upset the families. It amounted only to the undisputed fact that Edward Drummer, Andrew Connors, Norman Younger and Leonard Lofthouse had died, either as the direct result of the explosion or in the fire that followed, more probably the former, and that in either case that death had been instantaneous."

"My God, yes," said Anthony with a shudder. He was looking again into the furnace.

"Then we had the fire brigade Site Inspector. He'd been on the scene as soon as the flames were under control. He said that in his view the fire itself had been caused by petrol. There were several gallons of it stored there – illegally, incidentally – in jerricans. Apparently they were for young Robin Drummer's motorcycle. No one's been able to ask him, of course."

"How is he?"

"No change. But the medicos are hopeful that he'll pull through all right. If the blow on the head hasn't hit anything vital it doesn't signify how long he remains unconscious. The longer the better, in some ways. The only thing is, he won't remember much about the time before the explosion. And the longer he stays under the longer the gap will be. A pity, since he's the only person left who could tell us what those boys were up to. After the Site Inspector we had the ATO, Major Webster."

"ATO?"

"Ammunition Technical Officer, ex RAOC. On call to the police in matters involving explosive. Most of them are good chaps, but for some reason I didn't think this one was very convincing. He seems to have visited the place once, talked to the Fire Brigade man and ducked out as quickly as possible. When the coroner asked him whether the explosion could have been caused by dynamite or opencast gelignite – putting the idea into his head, you see – his answer was that it was quite possible, but in view of the total destruction of the site – and so on and so on. In other words, he didn't really know. The coroner then brought in a storeman from the Clipstone Sand and Gravel Works, who agreed that they used both these types of explosive. He was then asked if he could identify some detonators."

"You mean they had survived the fire?"

"Yes. They were in a glass jar, which had fused in the heat, but stayed whole long enough for the contents to be identified. You know what a detonator looks like?"

"No idea."

"It's a copper tube, about an inch and a half long, with wires coming out of one end. The wires were outside the jar and had been burnt off, but there was enough left inside the jar for identification. The storeman agreed that they were common-type detonators and could have come from Clipstones. When he'd finished the coroner spent the rest of the morning expressing sympathy for the relatives who were there."

"Which were?"

"Father Drummer, Sergeant Connors and his wife and Mrs. Younger, who's a widow. Lofthouse didn't seem to have produced any parents though there's talk of an uncle in the north. It's my opinion that if the coroner had closed the hearing before lunch he'd have got the verdict he was angling for. Boys playing with explosives they didn't understand. Accidental death. However, he gave the jury the lunch interval to consider their verdict and when they came back it was clear they were

173

unhappy. I think they realised they were being pushed and they didn't like it. I've noticed that before about juries. It's a great mistake to try to bear-lead them."

"Thank God for juries," said Anthony. "But why was he in such a hurry?"

"Because he remembered what happened after the New Cross fire."

"Yes. I see," said Anthony. He too remembered the tribulations of the unhappy coroner after that catastrophe. "So what happened?"

"The foreman, a nice little man, simply stood up and said that they weren't satisfied that the evidence so far produced enabled them to arrive at any verdict at all. Allpace made the mistake of snapping at him. The situation seemed plain enough to *him*. No need to prolong the hearing. Must consider the feelings of the bereaved. The foreman wasn't to be shifted. It turned out that he was an assistant in the Royal Arsenal Laboratory and I guess he knew more about explosions than most of the people in court. He said they wanted the opinion of a real expert – a nasty back hander at Major Webster – about what type of explosive was involved. He didn't believe that the explosive used for quarrying would act in that way. The rest of the jury were solidly behind him and Allpace had to give way. He said that, since the jury seemed incapable of understanding evidence, he would adjourn for fifteen days and see if a witness could be produced who *did* satisfy them."

"And that's where the matter stands at the moment?"

"Until this morning." Mr. Norrie produced from his pocket a folded copy of the *South East London News*. "I thought you might like to see this letter. In fact, it's been copied in *The Times*, a rare compliment to a provincial newspaper, but I guess they knew what they were doing. The Wick Lane fire is headline news in all papers."

Anthony glanced first at the name of the correspondent, Angus McCaskie, a forthright character and a noted controversialist.

As Chairman and Managing Director of the Clipstone Sand and Gravel Company I hope you will grant me the courtesy of your column to make a few points which may be of public interest.

174

Coroners, as we know, are a law unto themselves. Which is another way of saying that in their courts very little attention is paid to the normal rules of procedure and evidence.

One of the victims of the recent fire in Wick Lane – not, I am happy to learn, one of the four boys who were killed – was Robin Ernest Drummer. Robin was an employee of my firm. We use various types of explosive. On these slender grounds the Coroner, Dr. Allpace, saw fit to make certain suggestions to the jury. Indeed, 'suggestions' is too mild a word. To me they sounded more like directions. The jury were to find that Robin had abstracted explosive and detonators from my premises and in playing with them had caused the disaster referred to.

You will perhaps notice that the only witness from my firm that the Coroner saw fit to call was my storeman. I am not criticising Seward. He was asked three questions and answered them as simply as he could. But if Dr. Allpace had followed what you might have considered to be the more normal practice of calling me, as the head of the firm and the party responsible for its overall management, I could have pointed out one or two important facts to him.

Under the Control of Explosives Act 1952, and Regulations made from time to time under that Act, any premises upon which explosives are stored have to be licensed. It is a condition of the licence that the licensees prepare an accurate and up-to-date schedule of those explosives, indicating types and quantities. Moreover, they have to maintain a responsible person in charge for twenty-four hours in the day, so that the police can visit the premises at any hour of the day or night, without warning, to check those lists. Fortunately such a spot-check was made a fortnight ago. Our stores of PE 808, Nobel 704 and Slurry Explosive were all carefully checked and found to correspond with our schedules. Since we have had no cause to use any of them since, they still correspond. I need hardly add that all of them are kept in a proper store, the key to which lives in the safe in my office. It has not been suggested that Robin Drummer was, among other accomplishments, a safe-breaker.

Finally, might I say that I entirely concur with the comments of Mr. Prince, the jury foreman, a respected member of the team at the Arsenal Laboratory. The explosion had none of the characteristics of the explosives we use. The blast they give is powerful, but concentrated. As well as its commercial use I have some experience of its military use. As a young officer in 1945 I was concerned in the blowing up of submarine pens at the mouth of the River Scheldt. Incautiously used it might have blown a hole in the roof, but it would not have caused instantaneous all-round destruction, nor would an immediate fire have resulted, even if ultimately assisted by petrol.

In my view, this explosion was caused by the detonation of a fairly large quantity of cordite. Not many people or institutions have any reason to own or store cordite, so might I suggest that steps be now taken to examine any known local stocks, as carefully as mine were examined two weeks ago. We might then be a little closer to discovering the truth about this appalling tragedy which has cost four young lives.

"Well," said Anthony when he had read through this letter twice, "that's going to start something, isn't it?"

Two days later, when he was demonstrating to Nurse Williams that he was ready to be discharged by doing press-ups on the floor, he had a second unexpected visitor.

"My name's Mowatt," said the stout and placid civilian. "My friends call me Reggie. We haven't met, but I've heard your voice more than once."

"You've heard – ?"

"Or, to be strictly accurate, a tape-recording of it."

"Oh, I see. Then you're a spook."

"That graphic Americanism would be more accurately applied to MI6. I'm in Five. Home security. Just a civil servant, really."

"Then you know Chief Superintendent Bearstead."

"Bruno Bearstead? Yes. He's an old friend. And we're working together on this operation. I understand he put you in the picture."

"He told me as much as he had to if I was going to help. What he seemed to want to know was any connection between a local businessman called Arthur Drayling and some Pakistani kids and another lot who – "

He found he couldn't go on. Putting the horror into words brought it to life again. He wanted to bury it.

"The other lot who were involved in the explosion in Wick Lane," continued Mowatt smoothly. "Incidentally, I thought what you did was startlingly brave. Fire knocks the guts out of most people."

"If I'd stopped to think I wouldn't have done it."

"All right. I won't embarrass you. And a small correction. It wasn't just Drayling's connection with those two lots of boys we wanted. I'm sure Bearstead made that clear. *Anything about him at all.* His home life, his business, his character – "

"I didn't understand that my remit was as wide as that," said Anthony. "But even if I had done, I'm not sure that I could have helped very much. My acquaintance with him is confined to exchanging trivialities in the club and listening to him laying down the law about modern youth."

The way in which he said this would have deceived most people, but it did not deceive Mowatt. He was so used to listening to people telling truths, half-truths and quarter-truths that the tiny hint of uneasiness had not escaped him. It was in the tone of voice, not in the words. He does know something, he thought. And he's not telling us. And it's not going to be any use bullying him.

He said, "As long as you realise how desperately important this is. I must tell you that we've had a certain amount of luck. We've succeeded in establishing a system of watching and even given it a useful dry run. But if I was a betting man I wouldn't put our chance at more than six to four on. If we were at war, it would be different. We could put a fence round this island that I'd defy anyone to break through. But we're not at war. Or not in the old-fashioned sense of the word. And we have to spend half our time worrying about whether we're standing on someone else's toes, or upsetting the public or giving a field day to the opposition press."

"I do understand that," said Anthony. "And I'll do what I can. That's one of the reasons I want to get out of here."

When Mowatt left the hospital his chauffeur noticed that he looked pleased. He came across, but did not at once get into the car. He said, "What do you do, Sam, with someone who knows something important, but for some reason won't spill it?"

"Burn the soles of his feet."

"I'm afraid that wouldn't be practical in this case. No, we shall just have to wait and hope that his conscience does the trick. In Mr. Leone's case, his conscience is a very powerful monitor, or so I should imagine."

"Is what he knows connected with the job you're on?"

"I think so, yes."

"And it's important?"

"It could be very important."

"Then hadn't someone better keep an eye on him when he comes out?"

"Actually," said Mowatt, "that's one of the reasons I came to see him. I suppose we've got our usual tail?"

"Well, there's a man in the passenger seat of that van, parked three back. He arrived after we did and has been doing nothing much since. I suppose that's why you come out grinning all over your face, so he'll think that anything the other chap knows has been passed on to you."

"You read my mind, Sam. It occurred to me that we are more used to looking after ourselves than he is." He got into the car and shut the door. When they moved off the van pulled out and followed some distance behind. Mowatt was not worried. As head of the Irish Section of MI5 he would have been surprised if, at that juncture, he had not been kept under observation.

Crafty as a waggon-load of monkeys, thought Sam. Probably nothing in it. But when he was putting the car away he got the gun out of the door pocket, unloaded it, cleaned it carefully and reloaded it.

"Something on your mind, Sergeant Major?"

Captain Olbright, who commanded C Company of the 134th Regiment RE had known Sergeant-Major Pearce long enough to detect when he had something he wanted to tell him. The importance of the matter was indicated by the intensity of the frown on Pearce's normally good-tempered face.

"You read that piece in the local paper, sir. About checking explosives."

"We all read it."

"It was what Sergeant Alnutt said to me this morning. You know he's been in charge of the 3 Platoon guard. It was something he noticed at the time, but he didn't report it, thinking it wasn't all that important, I expect. It was between sentry changes. The way they do it – it's not exactly Brigade of

178

Guards style – the sentry on duty does his two-hour spell, then he comes in and wakes up his relief, who takes over."

Olbright nodded. This was the way most night guards worked.

"Well, sir, Alnutt happened to be awake when the change-over was being made and he saw the guard who'd come in – Sunley, that was – over at the other side of the room where the ammo shed keys are kept. The guard isn't supposed to handle the keys at all. They're kept in the guard-room for safety. So he asks Sunley what he's up to. Sunley says, 'I noticed one of the keys had fallen off. I was putting it back. Didn't mean to wake you up.' "

"How long ago was this?"

"Sunley's in 3 Platoon. They and the other two do a week on duty each. So it must have been a fortnight ago."

"So what made Alnutt bring it up now?"

"Well sir, he's not exactly a genius, but he's got a lot of common sense. And when he was turning it over in his mind afterwards, what he thought was that once a key is hung up on a hook it doesn't fall off. Really, practically speaking, the only way it could come off its hook is if somebody took it off and it looked as if that somebody must have been Tim Sunley. Well, then he reads that piece in the paper and he begins to think about it some more. And then he remembers something else. The buzz is that Sunley is friendly with a Paki girl, who's the sister of one of that lot who were in trouble for scrapping with the white lot. So, adding two and two together, he decides he'd better tell me. And I thought I'd better tell you."

Thus obeying the age-old custom, thought Olbright. If the buck looks awkward, pass it up quick. And if what Sergeant Major Pearce suspected turned out to be true, it might be very awkward indeed. Clearly the first thing to do was to check the stores.

He said, "I take it you've got the hand-over schedules?"

"Signed them myself, sir. And checked them. I wasn't going to sign blind."

"Then get hold of the keys, quietly. We don't want to start people talking. Particularly as there may be nothing in it."

"New guard doesn't mount until five o'clock. Give us plenty of time to go round."

179

"All right. I'll meet you at half past two, by the footbridge over Lower Dock Creek."

At a quarter past three they were standing outside the northernmost of the three store sheds and neither of them were looking happy.

"You're quite sure, Sergeant Major?"

"It's not difficult with this lot, sir. They're charges for the old twenty-five pounder. They're in different coloured bags so that the loader who was making up the charge knew which to put in. Blue for charge one. Blue and red for charge two and so on. I counted them myself when we took over."

"And we're four bags short."

"I'm afraid so, sir."

"This must go straight up to the CO," said Captain Olbright.

When Colonel French understood what his subordinate was telling him he, too, looked unhappy.

"We'll have to call in the MPs," he said. "I don't like it. They're apt to play a bit rough in cases like this. But I don't see any alternative, do you?"

"I'm afraid not, sir."

"What sort of chap is Sunley?"

"Well, he's young. Just average, I should have said."

"He's not a raving bolshy; I mean, the sort of type to go round blowing people up?"

"Absolutely not, sir. But, of course, that girl may have led him on."

"I suppose that's right."

18

The Military Police headquarters, known locally as the Bastille, was a square yellow brick building tucked away behind the Royal Artillery Barracks. Colonel Craik's office was on the second floor at the back overlooking an unfrequented corner of Woolwich Common. The Colonel, who had white tufted eyebrows and brick-red cheeks looked like a prosperous, but over-worked, farmer. He was within six months of retirement; a retirement not destined to last long since he was to be carried off within the year by a massive cardiac occlusion.

Tim Sunley had been interviewed, briefly, by his own CO and warned that there was a serious charge pending. He had been driven, late in the afternoon, to the police headquarters and lodged in one of the cells on the lower ground floor. Enough light filtered through the barred semi-basement window for him to examine the furnishings. A canvas cot on an iron frame; a wash-basin and a chamberpot; a varnished set of prison regulations on the wall. From the moment he had entered the building no one had spoken to him.

The cell was uncomfortably hot. When he was making up his bed with the two blankets which had been provided he had noticed a blackened stain along one side of the canvas and had wondered about it. He had heard stories of what went on in the Bastille and had half believed them. He slept badly and was woken in the middle of the night, imagining that he had heard screams. It could have been a dream. He lay awake, listening. The only sound was water running somewhere. When that stopped the silence was so intense that it seemed to press him down.

A red-cap brought him his breakfast and his midday meal. He had little appetite for either. The day passed slowly.

When the last of the daylight had gone the single electric light in the ceiling came on. Sunley looked at his watch and saw that it was half past five. This reminded him of something. It required an effort to tear his thoughts away from his own predicament. Then he remembered. He had arranged to meet Shazada at six o'clock in the old stable. He had intended to exact a full and delicious reward for what he had done for her and her brothers. The thought had been exciting him for days. Now it seemed unimportant. He was more interested in the stain on his cot than in Shazada. He was certain that it was dried blood. And he had noticed something else. There were steel slots in the metalwork of the cot. A strap passed through them would secure a man's wrists and ankles. In spite of the warmth in the cell he had started shivering. Oh God, whatever

181

they were going to do to him let them do it soon and let it not hurt too much.

There were heavy footsteps in the passage. The bolts shot back and the door opened.

It was the silent red-cap with his supper.

Shazada had reached the stable in good time. She was not happy. Something had happened. Something which involved Tim. It was hardly a rumour. No one had said anything. It was the faint cold breeze that runs before bad news.

As six o'clock became six fifteen and crept along to six thirty her fears were increased. Vague apprehension hardened into certainty. Something bad had happened. Tim had been late before, but never as late as that. She would give it another quarter of an hour.

She had noticed, on other occasions, that the stable was full of noises. The old timbers moved, overhanging branches tapped on the roof, creatures rustled in the straw. Now there were other more disturbing noises. When she had arrived before Tim she had found that, however quietly he came, she could detect his arrival at the last moment when he broke through the last screen of brambles which surrounded the tiny clear space in front of the door. Now she heard the same sounds, but with a difference. It seemed to her that someone was moving through the brambles, but was not approaching the door. More than one person.

She went across to the window and looked out. The wind was blowing the clouds across the moon. Perhaps it was the wind which had made the noise. The shadows came and went in confusing succession. One thing was certain. She had to get out.

At the door her courage almost failed her. But it was no use standing still. Better to move. The first part, through the brambles, always had to be done on hands and knees. The closeness to the wet earth gave her a sort of courage. When she scrambled to her feet and moved towards the wire fence she thought that the worst was over. Then it happened.

A flash of brilliant light lit the whole glade. In that blinding moment she saw, or thought she saw, two figures crouching under the bushes. Fear jerked her like an electric shock. She tore through the last barrier of thorns, hurled herself at the

182

fence, wriggled through leaving a strip of her anorak on the wire, and ran, sobbing, down the path towards lights and people and safety.

On the morning of the third day, Tim had just completed a rough wash under the cold tap when two red-caps he had not seen before marched in. Both were immaculate figures identically dressed and shining with offensive confidence from the toes of their polished boots to their gleaming brass cap badges. The only observable difference between them was that one, who wore a sergeant's stripes, was taller than the other. Both of them carried thick two-foot swagger sticks.

The tall one, whose face looked as though it had been carved out of red stone, jerked a hand towards the door. Sunley put on his jacket, grabbed his cap and followed them along the corridor and up the steps to the second floor.

The Sergeant knocked on the door of the room at the end of the passage, a voice bellowed, "Come in" and the three of them trooped in and formed up in front of Colonel Craik's large desk. It was bare of papers, a fact which seemed, somehow, to increase its menace.

There was a long pause. The Colonel examined Tim carefully, as though he was compiling an inventory of every item from his unpolished black boots to his uncombed blond hair. Then he turned to the Sergeant and said, in a tone of cold displeasure, "How dare you bring this man in front of me in that state?"

The Sergeant said nothing.

"Take him away and clean him up."

The Sergeant said, "Sir." The two policemen swung about as smoothly as puppets worked on the same string and stamped towards the door. Tim shambled after them. Neither of his warders seemed surprised by the Colonel's reaction.

"In here," said the Sergeant.

It was an ablutions room with a concrete floor, two wooden forms, a row of wash basins and a single shower.

"Strip."

Tim took off his battledress jacket, khaki shirt and vest.

"Everything," said the Sergeant. "Unless, that is, you want to take a shower in your trousers and boots."

"Might be the custom of his unit," said Shorty.

The showerhead was rusty and the jet of water that came out of it was icy. The Sergeant handed Tim a cake of soap of almost exactly the size and colour of the bricks out of which the building was made. He soaped himself half-heartedly, got out and dried as quickly as he could. Whilst he was dressing the Sergeant said, "Trousers only. We've got a lot of work to do on your top half."

He opened a canvas bag and produced a large nail-brush. With it he proceeded to scrub Tim's arms, shoulders and, finally, his face. Then he produced an old-fashioned cut-throat razor. Tim said, "I've got my own washing kit in the cell. Couldn't we use that?" He was afraid of razors. When the hairdresser was shaping his hair he would never allow him to use one. "Please, I'd much rather you used my stuff."

The Sergeant was stropping the razor, whistling as he did so. When he had finished he said, "You talk too much. Siddown." And when Tim hesitated, "We could handcuff you, but that mightn't be so comfortable."

Tim sat down. Shorty, who was acting as barber's assistant, had run some hot water into a basin and made a rough lather with the yellow soap which he slapped onto Tim's face and neck. Then the Sergeant, using the razor ruthlessly removed what seemed to be most of the layers of skin left by the nail brush. It was horribly painful and the tears ran out of Tim's eyes, but the menace of the razor kept him from moving.

"Hair now," said the Sergeant. His assistant produced a pair of scissors and chopped off, not unskilfully, the surplus hair above Tim's ears and down the back of his neck.

"Lovely," said the Sergeant. "Get dressed. You can clean your own boots. Why should we do all the work?" He produced two brushes and a tin of polish. "Clean 'em good. We don't want another bollocking, do we?"

Shorty agreed that one bollocking was enough.

"You get us into trouble again," said the Sergeant, "and we might get cross. When we get cross, we sometimes do things we're sorry for afterwards."

Tim polished diligently. The policemen relaxed with a cigarette.

"I wouldn't call it Guards' standard," said the Sergeant. "But it'll have to do. Mustn't keep the old man waiting."

"Not good," was Colonel Craik's verdict. "But a bit better."

Having pronounced this judgment he dismissed the two red-caps. Tim knew that they were not very far from the outside of the door. The Colonel got out of his chair and came round the desk, approaching until his face was not more than twelve inches from Tim's. Fascinated, but repelled, he could see the threads of purple in the red cheeks, the tufts of hair in the nostrils, the very faint yellow tinge which indigestion had painted round the eyes, the gold-capped teeth which showed when the Colonel opened his mouth to roar at him "Stand to attention when I'm talking to you."

Tim jerked back and stiffened.

"Didn't they teach you how to stand to attention in that mob of yours? Chest out, stomach in, shoulders back. Do you want me to have the Sergeant in to give you a lesson?"

"No, sir."

"Very well, then." The Colonel padded back to his chair. "I've got a few questions to ask you. And the quicker you answer them the quicker we'll have finished with this panto-mime. You're friends with a Pakistani girl called Shazada, aren't you?"

"I know her, sir."

"That wasn't what I asked you. Are you a particular friend of hers?"

"I – well, yes, sir. In a sort of way."

"You used to meet in that stable. Trespassing on War Office property, incidentally."

"Yes, sir."

"She'd arranged to meet you there last night. Didn't know you were otherwise engaged, perhaps."

When Tim hesitated the Colonel extracted a photograph from a drawer in his desk and laid it on the desk, turning it so that Tim could see it. He saw Shah, trapped in the flashlight, an expression of stark terror on her face. It upset him more than anything that had happened so far. There was a thick feeling in his throat, as though he was going to be sick. Words would not come out. The Colonel saved him the trouble of answering. He felt in the drawer again and pulled out a strip of blue fabric.

"Left that behind," he said, "when she was getting through the wire. All right. We know she was there. What was she doing? Not meeting some other chap, was she?"

"No, sir."

185

"It was a private meeting place. Just for the two of you?"

"Yes, sir."

"So what did you do?"

Tim stared at him.

"Screw her, boy? Roger her? For God's sake, do you want me to draw you a diagram?"

"Nothing like that, sir."

"Then for God's sake, what *did* you do?"

"We – we used to talk."

For some reason this answer seemed to please the Colonel. He relaxed in his chair and said, "Really? What did you talk about then? Stealing explosive from that shed?"

The switch was so unexpected that Tim almost jumped. This was the one thing he must never, never, admit to. The consequences were unthinkable.

He said, "Nothing like that, sir."

The Colonel got up and walked towards the window. He said, "Come here." When Tim followed him he saw that there was a cup-hook fastened to the woodwork. From it was hanging a key which he recognised.

"I want you to give me a demonstration. Show me just exactly how a key *falls* off a hook."

"I don't really see how it could, sir."

"But you told Sergeant Alnutt that it had fallen off and you were putting it back. Right?"

"I noticed it on the floor and thought it must have fallen off. It's rather a dark corner. Perhaps someone made a mistake. Thought they'd put it back, when they hadn't."

"It *is* a dark corner," agreed the Colonel. "And it's on the other side of the room from your bed isn't it? And when you came off guard your one idea would have been to get back into that bed, wouldn't it? So how did you *happen* to see a key lying on the floor in a dark corner on the other side of the room?"

Tim had no answer left.

The Colonel said, "You're lying, boy. You'd helped yourself to the key. You used it to open that explosives shed and take out four bags of cordite. Correct?"

Tim could only shake his head.

"Better admit it now. If you don't, you're simply wasting time. My time; my men's time. I don't like that, nor do they."

Tim started to say something, but the same sick feeling

186

prevented the words from coming out. The Colonel stared at him for a moment. Then he seemed to make his mind up.

"Sergeant!"

The two red-caps were instantly back in the room.

"Look after this man, will you?"

"Sir."

As they marched away, down the passage, down two flights of stairs, along the ground floor passage, towards a room at the back of the building, Tim could not keep his eyes off those thick sticks. They were going to hit him, he knew. An old soldier in his platoon, who had been in the military prison at Aldershot, had told him that they could hit you really hard, really painfully, but so cleverly that it left no mark.

"In here," said the Sergeant. Except for a table and a few chairs the room was empty. The Sergeant picked up a chair, placed it so that it faced the window and said, "Siddown. And don't get up until I say you can. Or else." He went out and Tim heard the bolt on the outside of the door being shot.

It was some time before he realised that the room was very cold. There seemed to be no heating at all. He would have liked to get up and move round to restore his circulation, but he was afraid to do it. There was a glass panel in the door and any move he made could be observed. Several times he had heard feet passing in the passage. Sometimes they stopped outside the door, before moving on.

He began to shiver. Only part of it was the cold. He had had very little sleep for two nights and had been badly frightened. As he sat there, staring out at the wilderness of grass and bushes outside the window, he was shaken by a series of uncontrollable shudders which started round his ribcage and ran down his arms and legs.

Shah had been picked up by a military policeman and a policewoman when she left the shop at the lunch interval. She had offered no resistance when they motioned her into the car. From something the man said she understood that it was to do with trespassing and causing damage to War Office property. Tim must be involved in it, she thought, and this was a sort of comfort to her.

She was taken into a building which she knew was a police headquarters and along a passage. When they stopped she saw that they were outside a door with a glass panel in it. Since she seemed to be expected to do so, she looked through the panel and saw Tim. He had his back to her and something seemed to have happened to his hair, but she knew it was him. She saw that he was shaking. Her two warders were moving along. She ran after them and grabbed the woman by the arm.

"What have they been doing to him? Can I speak to him?"

"Not now," said the woman. "Come along, we don't want any fuss, do we? The Major wants a word with you. Nothing to be afraid of."

"But I must speak to him."

"Afterwards, perhaps."

The tone in which this was said did not admit of argument. She followed them upstairs. The room they were making for was the one next to the Colonel's on the second floor. A pleasant-looking grey-haired man got up from behind the desk, came across, said, "Miss Shazada, isn't it? Come in and sit down. No need for you two to stay."

Shazada had made up her mind before they were out of the room. She said, "I know what you want. I'll tell you the whole thing."

"Well, that's friendly," said the grey-haired Major.

"It wasn't Tim's – I mean Sunley's fault. It was mine."

"Let's go slowly. Then I can make a few notes."

It didn't take very long. Twenty minutes later the Major was saying, "Fine, fine. I'll get something typed out and you can sign it. That can be done later. I expect you want to get back home now."

"You mean I can go?"

"Of course. I'll come down with you, then there won't be any trouble."

When they were approaching the door with the glass panel, she said, "Could I – please – have a word with Sunley?"

"It's irregular," said the Major, with a smile. "But you've been so co-operative, we might stretch a point. Five minutes only."

He unbolted the door, opened it and saw Shazada dart through. Then he rebolted it and walked slowly back to his own room. He found Colonel Craik waiting for him. "I think we shall get what we want now, sir."

The Colonel said, "Carry on, George. I leave it to you. Let

me know as soon as it's over. I've got a game of golf waiting for me and unless I'm on the course by three it'll be too dark to finish."

A short time afterwards, when Shazada had departed, the two red-caps came for Tim. They seemed, he thought, less aggressive than before. When they reached the second floor there were a number of further surprises. They did not make for Colonel Craik's office, but stopped at the door next to it, knocked and opened it without waiting for an answer. The grey-haired man, who wore the crowns of a major on his service jacket, said, "Leave him to me, Sergeant," and, when the men had stumped out, "My goodness you are cold, aren't you? Come and sit by the fire."

It was a proper fire, of coal and logs. The Major drew up two chairs to it. He said, "The central heating in this building is a disgrace. Either it roasts you or it freezes you. The latter, in your case, I guess. I expect you could do with some hot coffee."

There was a Thermos flask on the desk. The Major filled two china mugs, said, "Milk and sugar? Fine. That's how I like it." Tim found himself clasping the mug with both hands. He was still shaking.

The Major said, "Now, I've got a surprise for you." He fetched a box-shaped machine from his desk and pressed a switch. Tim found himself listening to his own voice and to Shah answering him. Short, gasping sentences, each of them interrupting the other; sentences which incriminated both of them beyond hope of contradiction.

"Should have warned you, perhaps," said the Major with a smile. "Most of the rooms in this building are bugged. This one, too. Miss Shazada was talking to me here just now. I could play what she said back to you, if you liked."

Tim shook his head. He had no intention of withholding anything. Any resistance he had left had melted in the warmth of the fire and the warmth of the coffee and the warmth of the Major's smile.

"I got most of it from the young lady, but there are still one or two pieces you can fill in."

He was an easy man to talk to. Most of his interruptions were helpful. "I imagine you'd no idea the stuff would be used to kill people. Just to give them a fright."

Tim accepted this gratefully. He said, "Salim told me, oh,

189

lots of times, that all they were going to do was make a mess of the other boys' headquarters."

"Just so. Salim would be Salim Kahn? Did he come with you when you took the powder?"

"Two of them came. Salim and his friend, Javed."

"And I imagine Miss Shazada does very much what her elder brother tells her, doesn't she?"

"She's very fond of him," agreed Tim.

He was now experiencing great difficulty in keeping awake. When it was finished the Major said, "You haven't been charged and if you and Miss Shazada go on being as helpful as you have been, there's no reason you should be. It's clear now where the real blame lies. We think it would be a good thing if you were out of the way for a few weeks and we're arranging to have you posted to the RE Holding Depot at York. You're to go there straight away. When you get there you may be subject to some restrictions. Not allowed outside the camp area. But you're not under arrest."

When Tim had gone he opened the door which communicated with Colonel Craik's office. The Colonel, who had been listening in, said, "Good enough, I think, George. One copy to Tancred at District and one to the Director. I might just be able to get in nine holes if I hurry. These things always take longer than you think they're going to."

Chief Superintendent Brace had been summoned to Commander Tancred's office at District. There he was presented with a copy of the report received that morning from the office of the Director of Public Prosecutions. He had seen such documents before, usually signed by subordinates. This one was signed by the Director himself.

"I have read the statements made by Sapper Timothy Sunley and the girl Shazada Kahn with the comments of Lieutenant Colonel Craik CMP which accompanied these statements. On the assumption that Sunley and Kahn are prepared, subject to suitable indemnities, to give evidence in any proceedings which may follow, I consider that the five Pakistani youths, Salim Kahn, Rahim Kahn, Javed Rahman, Rameez Rahman and Saghir Abbas should be charged with conspiracy to steal government property. There will be separate charges against Salim and Javed of actual stealing and

190

against the other three of receiving property knowing it to have been stolen. Since you will be charging them there will be no question of interrogation, nor do I consider that further interrogation is necessary. They should be invited to consult solicitors and will no doubt be granted legal aid. It is, of course, likely that there will be a further and more serious charge to follow, but this will depend on evidence, not yet available, to connect the stealing of cordite with the explosion and fire in Wick Lane. There are a number of points which need clarification. How did the youths obtain detonators and what sort of timing device was employed? If it was the normal one, based on a clock, it might be possible to prove the purchase of one. Also, in view of some of the evidence given at the inquest we shall clearly need further technical advice on the question of the explosive used. Major Webster must be asked to consider this further. I am assuming that the enmity between these youths and the five youths involved in the explosion will be easy to prove."

This was the end of the first paragraph. Brace could visualise the Director pausing at this point and taking a deep breath before he penned the final paragraph.

"If it appears that a charge should be brought in connection with the explosion and fire, then this will clearly result in interracial tension. There are political aspects of this which are outside the scope of my present report, but, for a start, I consider that the police should oppose any grant of bail, if only for the protection of the five Pakistanis."

There was a long silence when Brace had read the report and laid it back on Tancred's desk as gently as if it was itself explosive. Both policemen were looking down a long, dark tunnel and seeing no light at the end of it. Then Tancred said, "Some background please. What do these youths do with themselves all day?"

"Salim Kahn is an apprentice workman with Petter & Co., the electrical people. Javed Rahman has a job with Quarrels."

"Airguns and survival knives. I've seen their window. In Camlet Road, isn't it?"

"Right. Rameez Rahman helps his father. He's a locksmith, with a small shop in the Pakistani quarter. Corner of Rixen Road."

Tancred was following this on a street plan. He said, "And the other two?"

191

"Unemployed."

"They'll be the most difficult. You'll have to have a man watch each of them. I take it they live at home."

"Yes."

"You'll have to pick up all five of them together. Early evening will be the best time. Three cars. One for the Kahn house, one for the two Rahman's and one for Abbas. As soon as they've been charged let me know."

That was on Thursday. On Friday Rahim Kahn came home, as he usually did, to lunch. That he was unemployed was not for want of trying. He had spent the morning in the public library reading the periodicals and making notes of possible jobs. He had already applied for more than fifty.

He said to his father, who also came home from the garage for his midday meal, "I'm getting worried."

"What about?" said Azam Kahn absentmindedly. He was thinking about a lorry that had been brought in that morning with its gear box in a mess.

"Well, first there was that business about Shah. Did we ever discover what happened that afternoon – when the Military Police took her off?"

Azam removed his thoughts from gear boxes. He said, "No. She hasn't told me a thing. Except to say that it was a routine enquiry and she was able to tell them what they wanted."

"Everyone's now saying that it was something to do with Tim Sunley. The boy she was keen on."

"If you really want to know, why not ask Tim?"

"Can't. He's disappeared. They say he's been posted away."

Azam thought about this. Soldiers got posted away without much warning. He said, "So what's the worry?"

"It's not only Shah. It's what happened this morning."

"Well?"

"There was a policeman outside the library all the time I was there this morning."

"So?"

"And he followed me home. He's outside the house now."

19

The news of the arrest of the five Pakistanis spread with the speed of a prairie fire racing through brushwood. On Friday evening it was a rumour. By midday on Saturday it was a fact. Five boys from the Bisset Street area had blown up and killed four white boys and near enough killed a fifth. The criminals were known and had been charged with their crime.

Old supporters of capital punishment found ready listeners. What's the point of gaoling them? They'll be out in a year or two, ready to burn up a few more of our boys. The rope's the answer. Some people felt it was a pity that they couldn't be flogged first and hanged afterwards.

On that same Saturday afternoon South London had a home game. They had chosen the occasion to honour Norman Younger. The Secretary said a few appropriate words over the loudspeaker. He made a sympathetic reference to his mother, Mrs. Younger. He finished by saying, "We decided that a fitting tribute to this young man whose career has been so shockingly cut short would be to stand for a minute in silence before the game starts."

The crowd rose obediently to their feet and the two teams, which were already lined up on the ground, stood to attention.

Ghulam Sher Kahn, a middle-aged Pakistani greengrocer, did not stand up. He meant no disrespect by this. The truth, which he tried to conceal, was that he was almost stone deaf. He was sitting in the south stand, behind the goal. This stand was only half full. A man behind Ghulam shouted, "Stand up you black monkey," and another said, "Doesn't just burn our boy. Dishonours him too." He wasn't shouting, but in the sudden silence his voice was heard all over the stand. Heads turned.

Realising, at last, that something was happening Ghulam shambled to his feet. By the time he sat down again he was isolated. The people on either side of him had moved back to other seats. It was clear to him that something was wrong and that it affected him. He had no idea what it was all about.

When the game was over he decided that it would be better to let the crowd get clear. There was a stall that served teas. He bought a cup and took his time over drinking it. When he reached the exit point most people had left the ground. But not everyone. Half a dozen men were hanging about inside the gate. He realised that he had been stupid. He should have gone out with the crowd.

One of the men shouted, "There's the Paki bastard. Come on Sambo, we're waiting for you."

Ghulam saw the stone coming and dodged in time. But the sudden movement dislodged his glasses, which fell on to the asphalt. As he stooped to pick them up a second stone hit him on the side of the face. He abandoned his glasses and bolted for the exit. There were two turnstiles and an open gate beyond them. Not being able to see the gate he made for the nearer of the turnstiles. This had been set for entry and when he pushed frantically against it, it refused to move. He tried to scramble across the top. When he was halfway over a stick landed across his back. Then another one, much harder.

A voice, which tried to be authoritative, said, "Now then lads, stop that." It was Sergeant Ames, the long-haired Community Liaison Officer.

"Naff off, Charlie. This is one of the bastards who burned our kids. We're just teaching him a little lesson. Leave him to us."

"You can't do that." The Sergeant was already speaking into his bat phone. This was noticed. One of the men said, "More bluebottles here soon. Better be moving." And, giving Ghulam a final lash, "This time you were lucky. Maybe next time you won't be. Think about it."

The Sergeant found Ghulam's glasses, which were not broken, and handed them back to him. He said, "You'd better come along with me to the Station. You'll want to make a charge."

"No," said Ghulam. "No, I want no trouble. I only wish to return to my house."

"I'd better go with you, then," said Sergeant Ames sadly. He would have to make a report. No doubt Brace would have something scathing to say. As usual.

That same afternoon, Anthony was just finishing his tea

when the telephone rang. It was Azam Kahn. He said, "Mr. Leeown. I would so much like a word with you. Might I come to your house?"

Anthony thought about this. Then he said, "It would be better if I came to you."

"Can you do that?"

"I'm not a cripple. And I'd like the exercise. Expect me in about an hour's time."

His own house was in Old Mill Road, south of Wynns Common. A short walk up the east side of the common brought him out into Plumstead High Street, which was full of folk doing their last-minute weekend shopping. The contrast when he crossed the High Street into the Pakistani quarter was unpleasant. It was a place of empty streets and silence. It had never occurred to him before what a segregated area it was: a triangle of small houses, bounded on the south by the High Street and on the north by the railway.

There were a few small shops. Most of these were not only shut, but shuttered.

The Kahn house was at the north end of Bisset Street. There was a light in the ground-floor window. When Anthony knocked on the door he noticed, with a stab of alarm, that the letter-box had been blocked with a metal sheet. There were footsteps in the hall. Anthony identified himself, bolts were shot back, a chain was lifted and he was allowed inside.

"What's all this barricading in aid of?" said Anthony crossly. People who overreacted always irritated him. "Are you getting ready for a siege or something?"

"There will be trouble," said Azam. He spoke resignedly. Trouble was nothing new in his life. "You did not hear what happened at the football ground this afternoon?"

"No."

When Azam had told him, Anthony said, "You always get a few roughs at soccer matches. They don't need much excuse to start throwing their weight around."

"Ghulam had done nothing. The attack was not on him. It was on us, as a people. It will get worse, no doubt. Then it will die down again. It was not of that I wished to speak, but of my own boys and their friends."

"I heard they'd been charged. They'll be brought up on Monday, but that won't be more than a formality."

195

"Even so, I should wish them to have help."

"Of course."

"I spoke to Mr. Nabbs. He is the only lawyer I know. He said that he could not help me. He will be representing the police."

"Not for long. They'll be bringing in heavier metal soon. All the same, difficult for him."

And even if he could have acted, thought Anthony, it was most unlikely that he would have agreed to do so. He was not a defender of unpopular causes.

He said, "I could probably get you someone."

"If you could."

"It might not be easy. Solicitors don't work at weekends. But I'll have a try."

He walked home thoughtfully through the silent streets. What he was refusing to believe was that the scenes he had witnessed in Abbottabad were going to be re-enacted in south east London. Men being dragged from their houses and torn into pieces, or soaked in petrol and burned alive. Not only men. Women and small children, too. Impossible. Azam had magnified a single incident into a jehad.

When he got home Sandra said, "So what did he want?"

Anthony told her, but he said nothing of the uncomfortable thoughts at the back of his mind.

"What are you going to do about it?"

"I thought of asking Dan Sullivan."

"Yes. He'd help if he could."

Dan Sullivan, who was one of the middle-rank partners in the very large firm of City solicitors, (still known as Macintyres, though the original Macintyre had long been in his grave) was at home and listened patiently to Anthony.

"It's the Wick Lane fire, I suppose," he said cautiously. "I'd have to have a word with my senior partner before I allowed us to get involved in that. Luckily we're both members of the same golf club. I'll talk to him tomorrow and ring you back."

His senior partner, Sir Wilfred Paternoster, had white curly hair and a deceptive look of innocent benevolence. He was feeling cheerful because he had done well in the morning four-ball match and had lunched well. He and Dan Sullivan sat together on the balcony of the Sunningdale clubhouse watching the afternoon players strolling towards the first tee.

"This chap Leone," he said, "would you call him a reliable type?"

"Totally reliable, I should say."

"How did you come to know him?"

"Over one Ron Perkins."

"Come again."

"It would not perhaps be reasonable," said Sullivan with a smile, "to assume that the senior partner of a firm as large as ours – "

"Too large, in my view. But go on."

"Should know the name of all his employees. Particularly of employees as humble as post-room boys. Perkins was in trouble over some discrepancies in the postage stamp account. He lives in Plumstead and Leone was asked to help. He weighed in and persuaded everyone that what had happened was an honest mistake."

"And is Perkins still with us?"

"Oh, certainly. He tells me he's very interested in the law."

"I expect he'll be asking for a partnership soon," said Sir Wilfred gloomily. But he wasn't thinking about Ron Perkins. He was thinking about the Wick Lane disaster. He often talked about one thing when he was thinking about something quite different. He said, "All right, Dan, go ahead. You'll have to get Counsel involved as soon as possible. A strong Junior to start with. I was impressed by the work Eric Lording did for us in the Westlake business. And he's in a first class chambers, so we'll have a choice of good leaders when the time comes."

"Fine," said Sullivan. Choice of Counsel could safely be left to his senior partner who had a dearly bought knowledge of their strengths and weaknesses.

"It'll be a legal aid case, of course."

"I'll apply for an emergency certificate on Monday."

"One advantage of legal aid," said Sir Wilfred, rising heavily to his feet and preparing to renew his assault on the golf course, "is that your client has got to do what he's told."

The residents in Charndon Lane, Barons Court, looking out of their windows that Sunday afternoon would have noted two visitors to Mr. Featherstone's house. One of them they had seen before, a nondescript man carrying a violin case. The other was new. He was a small man, not a dwarf, but certainly no more than five foot high, if as much. It was noted that he walked with a limp, dragging his left leg. A new pupil, they imagined.

When the three men were safely installed in the sound-proof music room, Sean said, "I thought it was time that I made you two known to each other."

The small man had not offered to shake hands. Nor did he smile. He said, "Who's your friend, Professor?"

"Murphy. Pat Murphy."

"And why did you think Mr. Murphy and I ought to know each other?"

"You've been given my name," said Liam. "Wouldn't it be fair if you told me yours?"

The small man inspected him. He seemed puzzled by what he saw, but in some way reassured. He said, in a more friendly tone of voice, "You can take your pick. Jimmy Taylor or Jack Walker or Tommy Tucker. They're as genuine as Pat Murphy."

Sean said, "Then let's stick to Jimmy and Pat. Pat is interested in what's going on in south east London. The Wick Lane fire and its repercussions. I imagined that you and your – er – organisation would be interested in it too."

"Certainly."

"Your organisation being – ?" said Liam smoothly.

The little man smiled for the first time. "I'll tell you something for free," he said. "When you're doing work like mine it's a great mistake to give it a name. Once people have got hold of your name, they've got something to shout at. They can nail you to the tree. That's the mistake Militant made. As long as they were a movement without a name, they were effective. Now they're sitting ducks."

Liam, listening intently, knew the sort of man he had to deal with.

He said, "Agreed, it's sense not to publish your name. But you must call yourselves something, among yourselves I mean. A sort of by-name. Might it be Triple F, Fascists for Freedom. Or perhaps HJF. That's Houses Jobs and Families, isn't it?"

"Your friend seems to know a great deal."

"Oh, he's very well-informed," said Sean. "It occurred to both of us that what was happening in Plumstead was ready-made for your organisation. Only the National Front seem to have got ahead of you. I'm told they've billed a meeting

198

in Plumstead Victory Club for this Thursday. Abel Drummer has promised to speak."

This calculated insult had the desired effect. The little man drew himself up. Almost everything he said was platform-built, ready for delivery to the faithful.

"The National Front," he said, "is exactly what its name implies. A front. Everything in front and nothing behind." (Pause for applause, thought Sean.) "They publish a newspaper and they use up a lot of chalk, which might more usefully be employed in schools, putting NF on other people's walls. Also, as you have noticed, they hold meetings. Public meetings. But what do they actually *do*? Tell me that."

"Tell me what you think they ought to do, Jimmy."

"What we do. Recruit. At the school gates and in the factory canteens. Sound out and enrol real supporters. Young men, who are prepared to go to the limit."

"And young women?"

"Women can be useful, but mainly we need fighters, wholehearted fighters, who will operate without too much regard to what may happen to them. If my men had been at that football ground the Pakistani would not have escaped with bruises."

"I imagine not."

"To control the masses you must first control the street."

Liam recognised the quotation from *Mein Kampf*. He was beginning to be extremely interested. He said, "You are a professional organisation and you will not therefore be offended if I mention money."

"Did not Lenin say, 'Ideas can be planted in the soil of men's minds, but they are matured by a judicious application of gold'?"

"And very well put, too. Now I've been considering an idea. It's connected with the man my friend mentioned. Abel Drummer."

"The father of two of the boys involved."

"Yes. I made his acquaintance some time ago and have cultivated him very carefully for reasons of my own. An interesting man. Heavily biased, but basically honest. An uncomfortable combination, you'll admit, Jimmy."

The little man had got up and was moving round the room, apparently to relieve the pain in his left leg.

199

Liam said, "It's an idea that would cost money. Not much. But a certain amount. I could arrange a donation for you of £5,000."

"How would it come?"

"In cash, of course. A gift from an anonymous friend."

"And what would you expect in exchange?"

"Let me explain. These public conflagrations which are set off by such incidents as the Wick Lane disaster have a habit of burning fiercely to start with, but dying down for want of fresh fuel. Public support and enthusiasm is easy to arouse, but difficult to maintain. You agree, Jimmy?"

"Correct."

"So what is needed is a stimulant, or, better, a series of stimulants, applied at the right moment. Let me tell you the sort of things I had in mind."

Liam spoke for ten minutes. Mr. Taylor, alias Walker, alias Tucker, who spent most of his own working day talking, was, for once, content to listen. He recognised a superior professional.

20

When Mr. Norrie came into court on Monday morning he could sense that he was in for trouble.

It was not only the crowding of the public and the press benches: that was expected. Everyone wanted to catch a glimpse of the Wick Lane murderers and the crowd outside the court had been even greater than inside. No. It was the conduct of those who had managed to get in. A number of youngish men had forced their way to the front and were now collected immediately behind the dock. They had listened impassively whilst the morning's work began, and Mr. Norrie dealt with his normal stream of drunks, prostitutes and motorists. This was not what they had come for.

There was a stir of interest and a ripple ran through the crowd when the gaoler said, "Bring up Salim Kahn, Rahim

Kahn, Javed Rahman, Rameez Rahman and Saghir Abbas."
The boys filed in. Salim seemed to be as controlled and resolute
as when he had stood in the same dock a month before. The
others looked terrified.

"The charge," said Mr. Combs, the Clerk, "is conspiracy to
steal government property – "

Before he could get any further a red-haired man, in the
centre of the group behind the dock, shouted out, "You got it
wrong, chum. The charge is murder." This was followed by a
concerted shout. Norrie rapped his gavel on the desk for some
seconds, before the shouting subsided, apparently at some
signal.

"If there is any more disturbance," he said, "I shall have the
court cleared."

"Just you try it," said a thin man next to the redhead.

"Come on, what are we waiting for?"

"Bring the bastards outside and string 'em up."

The attack was so unexpected that it very nearly succeeded.
Sergeant Blascoe, who was posted at the end of the dock,
was pushed aside and two men grabbed Saghir Abbas who
succeeded in kicking one of them on the knee. Other men had
got hold of Javed and Rameez by the hair and were trying
to pull them over the rail at the back of the dock. Salim
came to their assistance. He hit one of the men hard, in the
throat.

Then the police reinforcements that Brace had stationed in
the corridor surged in. For a moment everyone seemed to be
fighting: policemen, spectators, pressmen and the prisoners.

Norrie, who had kept his seat and his head, noticed
something. The small knot of men who had started the riot were
now edging out of it and had nearly reached the door. With
their withdrawal the impetus of the fight was slackening and it
was clear that the police, now further reinforced, would soon
have the court clear. He shouted to Sergeant Montgomery,
"Grab hold of that red-haired man. I want him back here."

A few minutes later the body of the court was empty. Two
policemen reappeared, escorting the red-haired man. He was
offering no resistance and looked puzzled.

"Bring him up here," said Norrie. "I want your name and
address."

"You've got no right. I've done nothing."

201

"Concealing your identity and your address when questioned by a magistrate or policeman is an offence. I'll have you held in custody until you produce it."

The man appeared to be thinking about this. Then he said, "Ernest Simpson. 3 Hornsey Lane Gardens, N6."

"Evidence of identity."

The red-headed man fumbled in his pocket and finally produced a banker's card and a driving licence. It seemed possible that he really was Mr. Simpson.

Norrie said, "You're a long way from home, Mr. Simpson. What brings you down here?"

"I read the papers."

"And that's the only reason?"

"I didn't need a reason. This is a free country."

Norrie was puzzled by the accent, which seemed to be deliberately flat and classless. All the same, an educated man.

"Well, Mr. Simpson," he said, "you'll be charged with a breach of the peace, obstruction of the police and the much more serious offence of attempting to obstruct the course of justice. When we've verified your address you may go." He then turned to the Clerk. "Continue reading the charge against these five accused, if you please, Mr. Combs."

The proceedings which followed were very brief. Nabbs, looking ruffled, applied for an adjournment. Dan Sullivan, who seemed to have enjoyed his unusual morning in the sticks said that the defence had no objection. Mr. Norrie said, "In view of what happened this morning, you will understand me if I say that we want no unnecessary delays in this case. I'll adjourn it for fourteen days. Can the prosecution be ready in that time?"

"I'm sure they'll do their best," said Mr. Nabbs.

"The defence also," said Sullivan.

When Eric Lording arrived at the Brixton Remand Centre the warder, who knew him, let him straight in and took him down to the Interview Room.

"Normally," he said, "that is, usually, you get half an hour for an interview, but seeing there are five of them we could stretch a point and call it an hour."

"I doubt if I shall need as long as that," said Lording with a smile.

When he went in the young policeman, who had been

standing by the window, went out, shutting the heavy door behind him. What Lording saw was five boys dressed in the scruffy everyday clothes of youth.

What they saw was a man dressed in a neat black coat, a white shirt and well creased pin-striped trousers. The only splash of colour was the tie he was wearing, dark blue with light blue diagonal stripes.

Lording sat down at the table, opened his notebook and said, "Right. Now let's get to know each other."

After five minutes he had identified them against the names in the charge sheet and was clear that the tall, solemn one, Salim Kahn, was the leader. He addressed most of his remarks to him. He said, "Your father has instructed the firm of Macintyres – " A pause for reaction, but the name clearly meant nothing to them. "Well, they're a big outfit in the City. I believe he got in touch with them through your Probation Officer, Mr. Leone – " yes, they knew about him, "And I, in turn, was instructed to handle your defence. At the start, that is. Later on there'll be a leader involved."

"A leader?" said Salim. "You mean a QC? Why do we need all that?"

"It's early days to say what you're going to need. But there are one or two things I have to make as plain to you as I can, now, right at the start."

Five pairs of eyes centred on him.

"What you're charged with is being concerned with taking four bags of cordite from an army store. There are two quite different ways that this could be looked at. One way would be to call it a fairly innocent prank. You meant to cause an explosion – Guy Fawkes plus, you might call it – and give the other boys you'd been feuding with a bad fright."

Four heads nodded emphatically. Salim, he noted, remained impassive.

"The alternative version is much more serious and could lead to charges of arson and possibly murder." He paused to give the words their full effect. "But whichever path the prosecution takes, it seems to me that it would be useless, indeed possibly dangerous, to deny that you took the cordite. The soldier concerned, Sapper Sunley, has made a statement about this. We could suggest that he was bullied by the Military Police; I expect you remember that case in Cyprus.

But if we try to shake his evidence and fail, the impression will be that you've got something to hide. And that will lead people to believe that you had got more serious plans for using the stuff. You follow me?"

They all nodded, but Lording realised that only Salim was following him properly, and that he had possibly worked it out for himself already.

"Then before I ask you any questions, let me make one further point. If you tell me anything but the truth, you're tying my hands behind my back."

"There is no cause for anything but the truth," said Salim. "I persuaded Sunley to steal the explosive."

"You. Not your sister?"

"My sister had nothing to do with it. It was I who persuaded him."

Lie number one, thought Lording. But understandable.

"What you said about its use is true. We intended no harm to any person. That was the object of the time-fuse."

"Explain about that."

"It was not difficult. This book explained it. You needed a clock. A cheap alarm clock was best."

"You had one?"

"No. We stole it. From a shop in the High Street. That seemed the safest way. We removed the minute hand and bored a hole in the face of the clock beside the number eight. One wire from a battery was sticking out through this hole. The other was fastened to the central pin behind the minute hand. The opposite ends of the wires would go to a detonator. None of that was difficult to me. I work in an electrical firm."

"What about the detonator?"

"That was more difficult. It is a small copper tube, you understand, with a primary charge at one end and a plug at the other."

"You got this out of a book, too?"

"Yes. From an engineering manual. It was the most difficult part. The book spoke of a match head inside the detonator. It did not explain what it was, but I concluded it was stuff which would heat up when the wires were connected. After some experiments I produced one which I thought would work."

"You thought?" said Lording sharply. "Explain, please. You mean you never tried it?"

"We had no opportunity. When we heard of the explosion we took everything, that same night: the bags of powder, the clock and the detonator and dropped them in the river."

Lording sat staring at him, for a long moment, in silence.

"Well," said Brace, "did you recognise any of the men who attacked – what was his name – Ghulam Kahn?"

"Oh yes, sir," said Sergeant Ames. "They were local characters. I recognised almost all of them."

"Then why haven't they been charged?"

"Ghulam refused to make a complaint."

"A citizen doesn't have to complain. You saw a crime being committed, didn't you?"

"Yes, sir. But – "

"But what?"

"I had a word with Ghulam as we were going home. He said that if we started any proceedings, he would deny that any attack had taken place."

"Deny it?"

"Yes, sir. He'd say I'd made the whole thing up."

"He must have been scared stiff," said Wynn-Thomas.

"Oh, he was sir. What he said was, he was sure there was bad trouble coming and he didn't want to be, what he called, a target."

"Pity it had to be Ames," said Brace, after Sergeant Ames had shambled out. "We've got officers on this force would have gone for the nearest trouble maker, no matter what the odds were. Then we should, at least, have had a charge of assaulting the police."

"It takes all sorts to make a police force. When Ghulam talked about trouble I suppose he was thinking of this meeting."

"No doubt," said Brace. He had picked up a sheet of paper from his desk. "Kind of them to send us a copy." The heading was in scarlet letters, 'The Wick Lane Massacre Action Committee'. It announced that a public meeting would be held at 6 pm on Thursday November 27th at the Victory Club in Berridge Road.

"You realise why they chose that particular title," said Wynn-Thomas. "It was the name of the committee the West Indians formed after the New Cross fire. Now the boot's on the other foot. You see the idea?"

"I can see they're asking for trouble," said Brace. "And I'm proceeding on that assumption. I've applied to District for help. They're sending us thirty men and three vans. All leave will be stopped here, as from tonight. Will you get out the necessary order?"

"Will do," said Wynn-Thomas. It was one of the moments when he was glad Brace was in charge, not him. He added, "I almost forgot to tell you. We've had one bit of luck. Lampeter – he owns that shop in the High Street that sells Army Surplus stuff and things of that sort. He says there was a group of boys in there about a fortnight ago, fooling round near the door. He thought they were up to no good and chased them out. When he was checking stock later he discovered that a clock was missing. One of the cheap tinny alarm clocks. There's so much shop-lifting and this particular item was so unimportant that he didn't think it was worth reporting."

"Being overinsured also," suggested Brace.

"Maybe so. Anyway, when he read the report of the inquest and the suggestion of some timing device, he started to put two and two together and came along."

"Did he recognise the boys?"

"Not all of them. But the two Rahmans definitely. He knows their father who's a locksmith and does work for him."

"And he won't be scared to give evidence – like Ghulam?"

"You've got this wrong," said Wynn-Thomas. "He'll be absolutely delighted to give evidence. He's on the popular side, this time."

On Wednesday morning Anthony was in a second-class carriage, sitting beside Azam Kahn, who had summoned him urgently by telephone.

"Salim is a sensible boy," he said. "Very level-headed. He does not take wild or extravagant views. I was allowed to speak to him, you understand, yesterday evening."

"And you say he didn't approve of Mr. Lording?"

"He recognises that he is an experienced and skilful advocate. What he said was, he is not really on our side. That was why he wished us to see him, so that we could form our own opinion."

"Does Mr. Sullivan know that I am coming too?"

"Yes. He does not object."

206

The train they were in was a stopping one. Up to that point the carriage had been empty. Now it started to fill up. People got in, people got out. Irritatingly it was never empty again. When they arrived at Charing Cross Anthony said, "Our appointment isn't until eleven. We've got plenty of time. Why don't we walk?" Azam agreed at once. Clearly he had something on his mind.

They made their way down Villiers Street and out on to the Embankment. The pavement on the riverside was clear. When they reached Temple station they still had twenty minutes in hand and sat down, overlooking the river. The tide was making, pushing the grey waters upstream towards Westminster Bridge. For a full minute Azam sat staring ahead of him. Then he said, "I have a question to ask you, Mr. Lee-own."

"Shoot," said Anthony.

"Do you think that violence should be met by violence?"

"No, I don't. Violence, counter-violence, more violence."

Azam thought about this.

"You remember, when I first spoke to you, I said that some years ago there had been much in the papers about the sport of Paki-bashing. And that it had stopped. I understand that one reason for this is that the people who were being hit were prepared to hit back."

"Self-defence. Certainly. But not counter-attack."

"You think that would be wrong?"

"Not wrong. Injudicious. And now will you tell me why you asked me?"

"I have been approached by a number of our people. They wish to set up an organisation."

"You already have one. The Community Relations Council."

"An organisation prepared to fight. Not just to talk."

"I've told you my answer to that. There are times and places where a militant organisation might be necessary. But not in this country, not now. You have the protection of the law. That should be sufficient."

"And do you think that the law extends into the back streets and housing estates of London?"

"Yes," said Anthony shortly. "I do." He certainly hoped so. The alternatives were uncomfortable.

Nothing more was said as they walked up Essex Street and climbed the steps that led to the Middle Temple.

When they reached the building to which they had been directed Anthony stopped to check the names painted inside the entrance hall.

"Can this be right?" said Azam. "It seems to be the residence of a number of noblemen."

The list was headed by Lord Winterhouse and Lord St George. Below them were four knights and three names prefaced by the word Judge. Below that again more than twenty names. Eric Lording was about two-thirds of the way down the list.

"I think the top two must be Law Lords," said Anthony. "The 'Sirs' will be High Court Judges. The 'Judges' are people who function in the Crown Courts. Come on. They can't eat us."

The Clerk, who had the bearing and presence of a family butler, seemed pleased to see them. Dan Sullivan was already there, talking to one of the Junior Clerks. They were led up a flight of polished stairs, along a carpeted passage hung with framed legal caricatures, to one of the rooms at the end. The Clerk went in first. There was a murmur of voices and he came out, followed by two beautifully dressed young men.

"Just clearing the decks for you," said Lording. "Please sit down." And when they had found seats, "As I think you know I saw my five clients last night. What they told me disturbed me. Very considerably. They admit that they took the explosive. That was sensible, as I told them. There is no point in contesting the evidence of Sunley on that point unless we are sure we can shake it. They then went further. It seems that they had made all the necessary preparations to explode the cordite. They had succeeded in manufacturing a detonator and had constructed a time-fuse out of a clock which they stole from a shop in the High Street."

"Stole?" said Sullivan. "They admit that?"

"Yes. What they actually said was that stealing seemed the safest way."

"And now that they have told you," said Azam, "will you have to tell the prosecution?"

"Certainly not. I shall say nothing about it. But it may be awkward if your son was asked about it when he gives evidence."

208

Sullivan said, "Have you decided to call him?"

"We shall have to, if we are to run either of the defences which are open to us. But I have not yet told you the really disturbing information which I received. It seems – " Lording was speaking more slowly now, "that when they heard of the explosion in Wick Lane they immediately threw all the stolen cordite, and the other items, into the river."

Sullivan said, "Christ!" under his breath.

"You see the vital importance of this, of course. Four pounds of cordite are known to have been stolen. If we could have produced them, the more serious case would have fallen to the ground. If we can't, then the situation, as I see it, is simply this. The Army has reported – it is in the newspapers – that all their other stores of explosive have been checked and found correct. Private firms that handle explosive cannot give such a blanket clearance, but there is no reason to suppose that they do not take the sort of precautions that the Clipstone Chairman mentioned in his letter. So – if the explosive was not this stolen cordite – *where did it come from?*"

There was a long silence. Then Sullivan said, "You mentioned possible defences."

"Two lines are open to us. The first is to deny that this explosion was caused by cordite. I thought that the evidence of Major Webster was not very convincing. First he thought it was open-cast gelignite. Now he thinks it might be cordite. To run that line we should want a top-class scientific expert prepared to give evidence."

"Might not be easy to find," said Sullivan.

"I agree. The more hopeful line, in my view, is to persuade the court that the disaster was accidental. That the accused had no intention of harming anyone. I found their statements convincing on that point. And that is why we shall have to put at least one of them in the box."

"And if you get home on that, you reduce the charge to theft and arson?"

"I am afraid that is unavoidable."

Azam said, suddenly and angrily, "Do you think that my boys and their friends murdered the white boys?"

"That is a question you must never ask Counsel," said Lording. "His job is to present the best case on behalf of his clients. His own belief in innocence or guilt is immaterial."

209

After Azam had stalked out, followed by Anthony, Sullivan said, "I've heard you give that little homily on Counsel's duty before, but I've rarely heard it go down so badly."

"It's difficult for a layman to understand the rigid rules which constrain members of the Bar."

"Difficult for solicitors too, sometimes. But now that we are off the record, tell me, what *do* you think happened?"

"I think that the Pakistanis did construct an explosive device. I think they managed to conceal it in the headquarters of their opponents. I am fairly certain they did not intend it to go off until much later that night, when the place would be empty. By their account it was set on an eight hour delay. They weren't experts. They made a mistake and the thing went off prematurely. That's the only explanation that accords with the facts."

Sullivan said, "I'm afraid you're right."

Until they were clear of the Temple Azam said nothing. He seemed to be trying to bring his feelings under control. Then he said, "So you see, I was right."

Anthony said nothing.

"They are not on our side. They are against us. All the lords and knights and the young gentlemen. They use us, to dress themselves in smart suits and carpet their floors and polish their staircases."

By this time they had reached the seat they had used before and Anthony sat down on it forcing Azam to follow suit.

He said, "Believe me, I hold no brief for the young barristers of today. As soon as they get into a large chambers, and are fed a little pap by the clerk, they think they know it all. Then they discover that they don't know quite everything and it is a shock to their self-esteem. After that, they may improve. Many of them will never be worth the money they charge, but I've known some good ones, in the middle ranks."

"They are no good to us. How can we fight with an ally who does not believe in our case? Who will take the first opportunity to plead guilty and pocket his fee."

In his job Anthony had run up against a lot of young barristers; almost all of them supported by Legal Aid; a few of them doing the work properly, many of them not troubling even to go through the motions.

He said, "What do you suggest?"

"We can have no more to do with Mr. Lording."

"If you reject Counsel chosen by Macintyres I doubt if they can continue to act for you."

"I am sorry about that. I spoke to your friend, Mr. Sullivan. I think he is a good man. But if Mr. Lording is the price of Macintyres we must reject them both."

"And then – ?"

"I will speak to Mr. Diwaker. He will act for us."

Anthony knew Qadir Diwaker, a remarkable man who had been called to the Bar in Bombay and had then qualified as a solicitor in London. He had seen him in action, in defence of Indian and Pakistani defendants. His knowledge of the law was wide, his manner was abrasive and he was disliked by all the magistrates of south London.

He said, "If you switch at this hour and without having very sound reasons for it, you may jeopardise your Legal Aid Certificate."

"I shall not seek Legal Aid."

"Diwaker is expensive."

"We have all the money that is necessary. I spoke at once to my brother, Akbar, in Islamabad. He manages the fortune of his grandmother, who is the head of the family. She has instructed the National Bank of Pakistan in Finsbury Circus to open a credit for me of £5,000 and has offered security for a further £5,000 if it should be necessary.

A passing steamer whistled, disturbing a flock of pigeons which wheeled up into the air and scattered. Somehow that seemed to Anthony to be a more fitting comment than any he could think of.

21

When Anthony got to the Victory Club on Thursday evening the National Front stewards were already turning people away from the door.

"Sorry, mate. House full half an hour ago. We'll be relaying the speeches to the courtyard if you like to go round the back."

Anthony was moving round to the back happy to be out of the crowd. His arms were well-protected, but he was nervous of people bumping him. One of the stewards spotted him. "Can't keep *you* out, sir. Not after what you did for young Drummer. Come along. We'll manage to squeeze you in somehow." Anthony followed him reluctantly.

The club had been constructed to hold an audience of five hundred. There were at least six hundred people there already, mostly men. All classes were represented, from a group of dock and railway workers at the back, who looked as if they expected trouble and would welcome it, to Crispin Locke and his wife sitting with Seligman in the front row looking apprehensive.

The steward said, "They'll expect you on the platform, sir," and ushered him through the crowd which filled the gangway.

The platform was as full as the hall. There were two rows of chairs, all occupied and a fringe of people standing behind the chairs. Anthony hid himself among them. He could see Abel Drummer in the front row. Arthur Drayling, who was sitting immediately behind him, said something. As Drummer turned his head to answer Anthony saw his face and was shocked. He seemed to have aged ten years.

The President of the local branch of the National Front was chairing the meeting. He was an enormously fat man. Anthony recognised him from his single appearance in court on a charge of obstructing the police and using language whereby a breach of the peace might have been caused.

"No difficulty about the first charge," Sandra had said. "He could obstruct three policemen by simply standing on the pavement."

He now rose to his feet, adjusted the microphone with the practised care of an old hand and said, "Friends, may I have silence."

When silence of a sort had been obtained, he said, "Our first duty, a duty in which I am sure you will wish to join me, is to express our heartfelt sympathy for the parents and loved ones of the four boys who have been – murdered."

He made a slight pause before the last word. It sent an almost visible shock wave through the audience. The sound which greeted it was hard to describe. Halfway between a purr and a growl, thought Anthony.

"What we must ask ourselves is whether sympathy is enough. Whether we should not be doing something – something more tangible. Sympathy will not bring these youngsters to life again. Should we not, by deeds as well as words, see to it that such a bestial outrage can never be repeated here? Or if we cannot prevent a repetition of it, then let us make such an example of those responsible for it that anyone who may be anxious to imitate them will think twice."

More a growl than a purr this time.

"You may say that the law is taking care of the five animals directly responsible. Very well. Our first task is to see that the law does not shrink from exacting a full penalty. But there may be others just as guilty. Others of their race and colour who supported them and helped them. It is to them that we have to demonstrate our feelings."

The Chairman glanced down at the paper in his hand. He said, "As to that, I shall have some proposals to put to you. But first I will call upon one of the principal sufferers to say a few words to us. Our friend, Abel Drummer."

The applause was thunderous and sustained. Anthony looked at Drummer. He must have known that he would be expected to speak, but he seemed unable or unwilling to move. Drayling leaned over and said something to him. He climbed slowly to his feet and the microphone was moved across. He mumbled, "I don't know what to say. One of my boys is dead. The other, by a miracle, is still alive."

A round of applause, directed at Anthony, which seemed to give Drummer time to collect his wits.

"I'm thinking of the other boys, too. And their parents. These boys were killed more than a fortnight ago. I've been told that they can't be given a decent Christian burial until the police have finished their enquiries."

"They'd better get a move on then," said a big red-faced man.

"So we shall have to wait," said Drummer lamely. "That's really all I've got to say."

The Chairman was glancing at his paper when a small man, who had been sitting next to Drummer, relieved him of the microphone. The Chairman looked surprised. This was evidently someone who was not on his list, but it was clear

213

that a number of people recognised him and there was a strong shout of welcome, mainly from the back of the hall.

"Friends. Our Chairman has told us that we can safely leave these animals to the law. It's a pity they can't be strung up, but at least they can be put away for life. *If* the law does what we expect. I say 'if'. In the ordinary way we could have trusted British justice to defend the rights of British people. But I have heard some news which makes me wonder whether this will happen."

He had the attention of the hall now, no question.

"Previously their case was in the hands of a well-known firm of solicitors and of reputable barristers. They would, no doubt, have conducted the case strenuously – but honestly and fairly. However, it seems that they were *too* honest for the prisoners. So – they have dismissed their respectable British lawyers and intend to employ" – pause – "a dirty shyster of their own colour."

No one liked this. Anthony could feel the tension mounting. He wondered how on earth the small man got the news so quickly. Some typist or secretary in Diwaker's office – ?

"We all know how a tricky lawyer can bamboozle the court. But he can't bamboozle us. We shall know what to do."

A roar of applause. Even Seligman and Locke, Anthony saw, were joining in. He felt slightly sick. He pushed his way out of the crowd at the back of the stage, found an emergency exit with a panic bar, eased it open and stepped out. It was quite dark now. There was a sizeable crowd in the courtyard at the back of the building. He noticed two CID men. He imagined that they were recording the speeches. But he was not thinking about them. He was thinking about Drummer.

There was something very odd there and he felt that it could be important. Drummer was by nature, a bluff outspoken patriot, with a personal reason to dislike all Indians on account of his father's wounding and death and these five in particular who had shamed and then killed his eldest boy and killed his dog. Now was his chance to get his own back. He would have anticipated a rip-roaring speech. Instead, Drummer had been nervous and almost non-committal.

When he got home, he put the point to Sandra who considered it carefully and said, "Perhaps he's got a guilty conscience."

214

Anthony could make no sense of this. It was only later that he realised that he had been presented with a key to the whole matter. One key. The other was to be handed to him ten days later.

"Well, that didn't go off too badly," said Brace.

"No bloodshed," agreed Wynn-Thomas. "One gathers from the speeches that they're saving their main efforts for the committal proceedings. If Norrie should find no case, I gather the idea is to pull down this building and lynch the prisoners."

"I don't see Norrie finding no case. On the evidence he's bound to commit. All I want to do is to get them up to the Bailey and out of my hair."

"Incidentally, you'll be glad to know that we've located the detonator."

"You have?"

"I went round with Major Webster to Petter's, where Salim worked. They were very co-operative. Salim's locker hadn't been touched. What we found in it wasn't actually a detonator, but the sort of component parts that might have been left behind in making one. Several lengths of thin copper tube, cut to one and a half inch lengths, some lengths of flex and a piece of neoprene. That's the stuff they use to block one end of the plug."

"Excellent. One more escape-hole shut. Has Webster made anything more out of the scene of the explosion?"

"He's examined it again, but I don't think there's much to find."

"We'll have to keep a man permanently on guard there," said Brace gloomily. "Until the proceedings are over, anyway. If we don't, half the kids in the neighbourhood will be helping themselves to souvenirs. As if we weren't short-handed enough already."

"Talking of which, have you considered what we're going to do if there's real trouble? Are you going to call in the Blue Berets?"

"It won't be my decision, thank the Lord," said Brace. "If real trouble blows up it will be controlled by District. Ten to one they'll put Micky in charge. He's had a lot of experience of that sort of thing. Personally, I hope he says no to D11. We don't want a lot of gunmen mixed up in this. They usually do more harm than good. Weight of numbers and treading on toes is the British recipe for crowd control. Anyway – we've got nine days. Tempers can cool a lot in nine days."

But any hope that tempers might cool was to be quickly destroyed.

On the Friday evening Abel Drummer was walking home from work. His shortest way was along Camlet Road and then down a side-turning to his house in Pardoe Street. As he turned into the side-road three men jumped him. He had very little time to defend himself. One of them caught each arm. The other one hit him, first in the stomach, then quite deliberately in the face.

The man who was hitting him had a stocking mask over his head. He was wearing leather gloves and there must have been rings on his fingers under the gloves, because the blows, though not hard, tore the skin of Abel's face. When the man behind him let go of his arms he fell forward on to the pavement. The third man said, "That's a little present for the white filth, with the compliments of the black filth." Then they were gone. The whole episode had not lasted more than thirty seconds.

Abel was sitting on the pavement trying not to be sick when a patrolling policeman turned the corner and spotted him.

"I wouldn't have brought you up here from Hereford," said Mowatt, "if the news hadn't been important."

"You haven't brought me up," said Every. "Your message was relayed to me in Wapping. I'm planning to be there for the next fortnight. More of that anon. First tell me your important news."

He could see that Mowatt was pleased.

"We got it from an Insurance Agent in Brussels. It cost £500 to ease his conscience at passing on confidential information, so it had better be accurate. Here it is. The Lorraine Line ship *Marie Louise* has been chartered by private interests for a single trip. Loading at Het Zoute, offloading London River. And the chartering has been done through Dr. Bernard's bank, Bernstorf Frères."

"Yes," said Every. "That is good. Very good."

"I'm assuming that the *Marie-Louise* will have a legitimate cargo as well as the items we're interested in."

"If it's got a legitimate cargo, it will ostensibly be making for one of the regular offloading points. Your informant couldn't be a little more definite about that, I suppose?"

"Apparently not. It did strike him that 'London River' was rather vague, but since it didn't affect the premium he didn't pursue the matter. Is it important?"

"It could be helpful. So many of the docks are closed now that there are really only three possibilities. Gun Dock or Scotland Dock. Or the Royals. If we knew they were heading for one of the two private docks, we could take the watchers off the up-river posts and double the down-river ones."

"I'll see if I can find out. But we don't want the alarm bells to start ringing."

"No. Leave it alone. We should be able to deal with *Marie-Louise* wherever she's heading."

"How are your men organised?"

"We've got two troop headquarters on the south bank. 'A' Troop south of Blackwall Point, 'C' Troop near the southern outfall, 'B' and 'D' Troops at corresponding points on the north bank. To cover their zones of observation they've got a line of dug-in one man posts. Each post is relieved every twenty-four hours, after dark, of course. The men then come in and join the stand-by party at troop headquarters. And we've got line communications from post to post and post to head-quarters."

Mowatt thought about it. It seemed reasonably effective. As good as could be contrived under existing restrictions.

"The real difficulty, Musgrave found, was having to control both banks. That's why I'm moving in. I'm going to take charge of the north bank. Since I shall be on the move most of the time I've arranged with Groener, at Thames Division, that one set in my car will be on the police net, the other on the squadron net."

"Sounds fine."

Every said, "It sounds all right, Reggie, but do you realise that those drug runners landed *forty* crates in eight minutes? Sometimes, when I can't get to sleep, I see a ship sliding up to a lonely wharf, in the dusk, slinging a single crate ashore, straight on to a lorry. Best time so far, forty seconds."

Mowatt laughed. He said, "And your nearest man, who's spotted all this, what's he doing? Scratching his head and wondering if he ought to tell someone about it?"

"Not quite. But everyone will have to move like greased lightning. *That drug landing was not more than four hundred yards from 'A' Troop headquarters* and even then we'd have been too late to stop their lorry if that policeman hadn't held them up."

"When I was in the Army," said Mowatt, "we were taught that, when it came to the crunch, nothing is ever as bad or as good as you think it's going to be."

He hoped that Every wasn't losing his nerve. That would be the final catastrophe. He added, "There's one other thing, when I was talking to my boss about this, it seems the Home Office is a bit worried about Webster."

"The explosives officer? Good chap, I thought. Wasn't he the man who tackled the Westminster Bridge bomb? The one that nearly evacuated Scotland Yard *and* the House of Commons."

"That's the man. There's no question about his courage. But he's not reckoned to be so hot on the theoretical side. And something else. He's been having bad wife trouble."

"Takes a man's mind off his job," agreed Every. "What did they want you to do about it?"

"They think we ought to bring in a top boffin."

"No problem. I'll have a word with Professor Meiklejohn. He knows more about explosives than most people."

"You realise," said Mowatt, "that if he does unearth anything, it'll have to be given to both sides."

"Why not? It's nothing to do with us. Either the Pakis blew the Brits up, or the Brits made a mistake and blew themselves up. It doesn't affect our problem."

"I suppose not," said Mowatt thoughtfully.

"Of all the bloody stupid things to do," said Anthony.

"What do you mean, Mr. Lee-own?"

"I warned you. Violence breeds violence."

"What are you talking about?"

"You know damn well what I'm talking about. The attack on Abel Drummer."

"That was nothing to do with our people. Nothing at all."

"Who then?"

"We have discussed the matter. We conclude that it was organised by the men who are inciting the crowd to violence."

"You're certain that none of your people had a hand in it?"

"Quite certain. We are a close community. Such a thing

218

could not be concealed. What we have done is to organise some patrols. People use their own cars. They are not intended to fight. They report trouble before it goes too far."

Anthony thought about it. It was true that Drummer had not been able to swear to the colour of his attackers. Two of the men had been behind him. The one in front was masked. The only real evidence was what they had said.

"Also," said Azam, "I understand that the damage is not severe."

This was true. Drummer had been discharged by the hospital with a bruised and cut face.

When he reported this to Mr. Norrie, the magistrate said, "It could have been a put-up job, Lion. Just to stir the pot. Not that it needed much stirring. The committal proceedings on the 9th are going to be a real dog's dinner. I see the Crown has briefed Leopold. We don't often see a QC at committal. They must be taking it seriously."

"Won't the boys simply plead 'Not Guilty' and reserve their defence for the Bailey?"

"That's what I'd hoped. And their original advisers would have done. Not Diwaker. He'll go the whole way. An old-style committal. No restrictions on reporting. And you realise that you'll have to give evidence."

"Why?"

"Because you know more about these two lots of boys than anyone else."

"What happens if I refuse?"

"You'll be subpoenaed."

"I'd prefer to be subpoenaed. Then people can see that anything I do say is said unwillingly."

"No one's going to attack *you*," said Mr. Norrie sourly. "You're the local hero."

Qadir Diwaker, solicitor and Counsel (Bar of India) had his office, which was also his house, in the High Street opposite West Heath Police Station. It is possible that he had chosen it with an eye to the safety of this arrangement. More probably it was a coincidence. Qadir had a number of faults, but he was not a coward.

He was well-known to the West Heath police officers, having, at one time or another, insulted most of them in court.

When Sergeant Darling, who was on the desk in reception, saw him coming he said, "Here's our little brown brother."

"I'm not in," said Chief Inspector Watrous. He departed through a door at the rear of the office as Diwaker came in at the front and said, "Good morning, Sergeant. I require to see the Superintendent."

"Not in, I'm afraid, sir."

"Then the Chief Inspector."

"He's out, too. Why not try me?"

"I have a serious complaint to make. Last night my yard was entered and my car was covered with offensive words."

"Sorry to hear that, sir. What words?"

"Such words as I would not dirty my tongue to repeat. You may see them for yourself."

The Sergeant signalled to one of the telephone operators to take his place on the desk and accompanied Diwaker back to the yard behind his house where his car was standing.

"Well, well," he said. "Someone's done a job on that, no question."

"I am not asking for your comments, Sergeant. I am asking for your assistance."

"What would you like us to do, sir?"

"I should have thought that a Sergeant would not have had to ask such a stupid question. First – to discover the perpetrators of this outrage and charge them. Then I want your assurance that it will not be repeated."

"There hardly seems room for much more."

It was a solid job, carried out in yellow paint. Such words as were legible were certainly insulting.

"You take this matter very lightly, Sergeant."

"Oh no, sir. Not at all. We'll certainly do our best."

"And what will your best consist of?"

"Well, sir. It would help if you could let us have some idea of why anyone should want to do a thing like this."

"I know very well why it was done and so do you. It is because I have undertaken to defend those unfortunate Pakistani boys."

"I see, sir. I suppose that was bound to stir up trouble."

"Oh, why?"

"Well, after all, they did blow up five white kids."

"You are presuming them guilty, Sergeant?"

220

"Oh no, sir. Not at all. I know very little about it."

"I advise you, for your own good, not to repeat what you just said to me."

When Sergeant Darling reported this to Watrous, the Chief Inspector said, "Bloody little toad. I suppose we'd better tell the man on the beat to keep an eye on his house. Can't do more than that. We've just had an urgent request from Reynolds Road for help with crowd control."

22

Since the attack, Abel Drummer had walked to his shop every morning without undue apprehension. But he had made a point of shutting up early so that he reached his own house before dark. This meant a long evening at home.

Since his wife's death he had usually had his dinner at the club, an arrangement which had suited his sons who had liked to have the evening free for their own devices. Now he was driven to eating whatever his daily woman, an unimaginative caterer, had left out for him. After that, there was nothing to do but sit in front of the electric fire – and think.

His thoughts refused to run straight.

This was disconcerting, since he was a man who, until recent events had overtaken him, had lived all his life by clear rules. Some things were right, other things were wrong. Now everything was misty and uncertain.

The only person he could have discussed matters with was Arthur Drayling. He hesitated to make any approach. There was a question he wanted to ask him, but it was a question to which he dreaded the answer so much that it was almost better to leave it unasked.

It could be expressed in bleakly simple words.

Was it possible that he had been responsible for the death of one of his sons and the wounding of the other? True, Robin, his favourite, was not dead and the doctors were hopeful that he would pull through. But the longer he remained unconscious, they said, the greater would be the gap in his memory. It might extend for days before the tragedy. There was no solution to be expected from that source.

The trial might clear up the horrible uncertainty. It could be that his hands were clean, that the responsibility lay with the Pakistanis. If so, they must pay the heaviest possible penalty. But suppose, unbelievably, unthinkably, it was not them. Then might not he himself be a murderer, in thought if not in deed?

If that should be the answer, one way of escape did remain. It was in the locked cupboard in his bedroom. The double-barrelled sporting rifle which had belonged to his father. Since his death he had used it, once or twice, for pigeon shooting and there was an almost full box of ammunition. The gun between his knees. The barrel under his chin. Finish.

He was able to face this stark possibility without any great apprehension. For he had lost everything. First his wife. Then one, or maybe both, of his sons. And his dog, Tiger, who had been his only close companion. And if what he feared was true he would lose his good name as well. So what was left? A long succession of lonely evenings.

Was there, indeed, any point in waiting for the answer? He had only to walk upstairs and unlock the cupboard. The key was on his ring. In a few minutes it would be over, his difficulties disposed of and his problems solved.

In the end, what stopped him was a memory.

He had been ten years old when his father had come back from the war, a helpless cripple. The doctors had done their best. They had taken off the arm and the leg neatly enough and had patched him up, but they had not been able to do anything about the twisted ligaments and the tortured nerve ends. His father had sat, in that same chair he was in now, night after night, postponing as long as possible the moment of going to bed. Knowing that he would get little sleep, fearing the agony.

And the gun had been there, all the time, in the cupboard. If his father had used it, no one would have blamed him. But he had not done so. Because he was a man of courage. Because to have done so would have been to admit defeat.

His mind made up, Abel went upstairs, passed the cupboard

222

without a second glance, undressed and got into bed. Oddly enough, he fell asleep almost at once and slept soundly.

On the following night Azam Kahn's garage was burned to the ground.

Fearing trouble he had installed a night-watchman, a retired policeman, said to be reliable. According to his own account, this man had taken the precaution of locking himself in the office. In the early hours of the morning someone had broken a pane of glass in the door and shouted through it, "Better move, or you'll be the Guy Fawkes on the bonfire." He could smell the petrol which was being splashed around and had quickly unlocked the door and come out.

Three men had grabbed him, had bundled him into a car, driven him out on to the marshes and dumped him. They were hooded and he was unable to identify them.

There was some dispute about what happened next. The helpful Mr. Foulkes, owner of the newspaper shop opposite, had been the first to spot the fire. He had immediately telephoned the fire brigade. He was a methodical man and had noted that the time, by the clock in his bedroom was five minutes before three.

The fire station was less than half a mile away, at the far end of Reynolds Road. They maintained that they had received the call at five past three. It was certain that they had not arrived until nearly a quarter past three. By that time the flames had such a firm hold that there was little they could do for the garage itself, and they had turned their hoses on to the neighbouring buildings to prevent the fire from spreading.

A story was told – it is far from certain who started it – that after the brigade had turned out with its usual speed and efficiency an argument had developed between the driver of the fire engine and the Captain. The driver had said that, speaking personally, he was in no hurry to help the father of the Paki murderers. Some of the brigade had supported him. It had taken ten minutes to sort this out. Long enough, said people, smiling as they listened to the story, to be quite sure that the garage burned down properly.

The Rahman shop was two along from the corner where Bannockburn Road ran south into Plumstead High Street. It

223

was still called 'Abdul Rahman, Locksmith', although Abdul had long been dead. It was run by Tahira, his widow, and Gulmar, her son, the father of Jay and Ram. The four of them lived above the shop. Standing almost outside the Pakistani triangle it seemed an obvious target and Gulmar had, some time before, installed shutters across the shop window. Now he had added to the locks and bolts on the front door and had blocked the letter-slot. He was not unduly worried about his own safety, being something of a fighter.

On that Wednesday evening he was returning home from a visit to his suppliers in Woolwich. As he turned the corner a man, sitting in the window-seat of the public house opposite the end of the road, took a torch from his pocket and flashed it twice. Two groups of men started to move. One lot, who had been standing talking in the High Street, sauntered forward. A second lot, in Bannockburn Road, moved towards the main road. Gulmar was trapped between them.

He saw the group ahead of him, realised it would take too long to get Tahira to unshackle the front door, swung round and ran for the High Street and the bright lights. The first group was already blocking that escape route. As he hesitated he was set on from behind. He swung his shoulders, putting one man down, was tripped and went forward on to his knees. Then his attackers started to use their boots. The first kick landed in his ribs. He wriggled round and grabbed the nearest leg. As he tugged at it, someone stamped on his hand, forcing him to loose his hold. The next kick hit him full in the face. As he rolled over in an effort to protect himself, the next one landed, with paralysing power, in the small of his back.

At that moment a car, which had been cruising slowly along Blaydon Road, turned the corner and flicked on its headlights. Then its horn began to sound, long – short, long – short. Street doors opened and men came running. They were mostly young Pakistanis, some were no more than boys.

The attackers were all armed with heavy sticks or clubs. They swung them savagely. A young Pakistani took a blow on his arm and heard the bone crack. For a moment the assault wavered. Then Tahira, who had got her door open at last, ran into the road and started to scream. A shrill note, not a signal for retreat, a call to battle. More Pakistanis joined the fight. They had had time to arm themselves with a variety of weapons.

A blow from a furnace rake broke open the head of one of the attackers. It was the signal for flight.

The crowd, which had now grown, chased the attackers towards the end of the road. One of them left a trail of blood on the pavement. This excited the pack, in full cry after a wounded quarry. But at that point where the side-road entered the High Street they halted, without any order given. They had reached the frontier. Beyond was enemy territory, not to be carelessly penetrated. They stood in silence and watched the men hurrying off. Two of them seemed to be supporting a third. One of the others was hobbling.

By now, Tahira had taken charge. She allowed no one to touch Gulmar, who lay crumpled in the gutter. "If there are bones broken," she said, "you will do more harm than good."

Someone had telephoned the hospital, also the police.

On Friday morning there was a council of war at Reynolds Road Police Station. The meeting was in Brace's room. Commander Tancred was there with Superintendent Michaelson, whose appointment had been confirmed the night before. He was to co-ordinate all police activities in 'R' District.

Brace said, "The score last night was one broken arm, three cracked ribs and – Gulmar Rahman."

"I've spoken to Braithwaite, the surgeon who's in charge of his case," said Tancred. "There's a suspected fracture of the spine and a depressed wound in the skull. Other injuries, too. But those are the worst. One thing Braithwaite said was that it didn't look to him like a mindless piece of brutality. He was kicked four times, each time where it would do most damage."

"They were professionals," agreed Brace, "and they weren't locals. They were none of them masked. The people who came to Rahman's rescue got a good look at them and they all swear they haven't seen any of them before."

The thought that the villains had come from outside his manor seemed to cheer him a little.

"I fancy that's the shape of it," said Michaelson. "What we're up against is a smallish organisation of professional trouble-makers who've got a crowd of ordinary citizens worked up to boiling point."

"It's their opportunity," agreed Tancred, "and they're getting their teeth into it. They've been holding meetings all over the place: in pubs, in parks, on street corners. Clever stuff, too. What they're plugging is, 'Watch the lawyers'. If Norrie does what's expected and commits the Pakistanis, the row may go rumbling on, but the sting will be out of it."

"I don't understand it," said Michaelson suddenly. "And I don't like it."

The others looked at him. They knew that he had more experience than them in these matters.

Tancred said, "What's worrying you, Micky?"

"I've got an odd feeling about it. That we're being deliberately challenged. They've chosen the time and they've chosen the place. It's altogether too cold-blooded for my liking. Someone's pulling the strings. Don't you feel that?"

"Maybe," said Tancred. "But surely it makes your job that much easier, Micky? They're asking for a show-down next Monday. Fine. They shall have it."

Brace nodded his approval.

"I'm not averse to a show-down," said Michaelson. "It's just that I don't like having the lines laid down for me by the other side. All right maybe I'm imagining things. Let's have a look at the map. We shall have to pack Reynolds Road on either side of the court-house and right up to the station forecourt. And we'll have to put a cordon round all three sides of the Paki-triangle."

He marked the map with a heavy blue pencil.

"That means diverting traffic," said Brace.

"Certainly. Pedestrian traffic only on the High Street. All cars turn off there – " He drew a line. "Down Berridge Road, along the north of Plumstead Common and back up the old Mill Road. They should be clear of trouble by then. To do the job properly I reckon we shall need a minimum of eight hundred men. I'm drawing on all ten south London districts and the PLA are lending us a contingent of the docks' police. Everyone's willing to help, but – " he turned to Brace, "It's going to make them even more willing, if they see you putting all your men into it."

Brace looked surprised. He said, "We're doing our stint, all right. We've got everyone back from leave. Anyone who can hobble will be out of hospital. And we've cancelled any special assignments for the time being. It'll be a hundred per cent turn-out for us. I can assure you."

"Fine. And don't let's assume that nothing's going to happen

226

until Monday. If there's any trouble stamp on it and stamp hard."

Brace nodded again. It was the sort of instruction he appreciated.

Friday night was quiet.

On Saturday morning PC Gurney, on guard outside the burnt-out building in Wick Lane, was accosted by an elderly gentleman who seemed to wish to examine the site.

"Sorry, sir," he said. "Strict instructions. No one's allowed inside."

"Quite right, Officer," said the old man. "Quite right. Mustn't have a lot of people messing about. Could destroy valuable evidence. But as it happens I have got authority to make an inspection."

"Authority from Superintendent Brace, sir?"

"Well, no."

"Then I'm afraid – "

"An even higher authority." The old man had opened a battered brown attaché-case, fumbled round in it and fished out a sheet of official-looking paper. PC Gurney saw that it was headed 'Office of the Home Secretary' and that it directed 'All whom it might concern to give every assistance to Professor Ian Meiklejohn', whose name was followed by a number of initials which meant nothing to Gurney, but certainly looked impressive. He said, "If you don't mind, sir, I'd better just have a word with the Station." He spoke into his personal radio and was put, almost at once, on to Brace.

"I suppose you can read," said Brace. "It says you're to give the Professor every assistance."

"Yessir."

"THEN DO IT."

Brace had been called out on two false alarms the night before and was not feeling happy.

"Was that your Superintendent? He sounds rather a violent man."

PC Gurney did not feel called on to comment on this. He said, "It's all right for you to go in, sir."

"Splendid," said Professor Meiklejohn. He picked his way, over the charred beams and littered fragments in the outer room, into the inner room which had been the seat of the explosion. Gurney followed him.

"Anything I can do, sir?"

"Yes. Chase those boys away."

A moment before the lane had been empty. Now three small boys had their chins on the front wall. Like sparrows, thought Gurney. Come from nowhere. He chivvied them away and turned his attention to what the Professor was doing.

He seemed to be particularly interested in an area in the middle of the tiled floor. He had taken a torch from his case and placed it on the ground so that it shone across the floor. Now he was taking photographs, using one of the smallest cameras Gurney had ever seen.

This was explicable conduct. The next move was less so. From the case had come what looked like a miniature battery-powered, vacuum cleaner. The Professor passed this in a sweeping circle round the central area in which he seemed to be interested. For these operations he had been on his hands and knees. Now he creaked to his feet and pottered across to the wall. This, built of stout breeze blocks and plaster-coated, had withstood the force of the explosion and the subsequent fire better than the roof. What the Professor seemed to be doing was collecting pieces of plaster. When the bag on the cleaner was full he detached it, labelled it with a felt-tipped pen and stowed it away in his case. Then he took out an empty bag and turned his attention to the opposite wall.

Gurney was fascinated. He felt certain there was something helpful he ought to be doing. Before he could offer, Professor Meiklejohn looked up and said, "Instead of breathing down my neck, Officer, would you very kindly get those boys to hell out of it."

There were five of them now.

Saturday night tried Brace hard.

He had been sleeping, uncomfortably, on a camp-bed in his office. Another false alarm, set off by a nervous shopkeeper in the High Street, had dragged him from his first sleep. When the real alarm came, at two o'clock on Sunday morning, it took him a few moments to work his way back to reality. Then he said, "That sounds like business. Get after the bastards and get after them hard."

A group of men had slipped into the Pakistani quarter by crossing allotments on the east side of Bannockburn Road.

Since few of the houses had garages, cars and vans were normally parked in the road. The wreckers, some two dozen of them, attended to each vehicle as they came to it. If it was small enough they heaved it over on to its side, pulled off the petrol cap and set it alight. If it was too heavy to deal with in this way they attacked it with sledge-hammers. First breaking the glass, then cracking open the bonnet and smashing the engine.

The police at Reynolds Road were alerted by the fires even before the telephone began to scream for help. They sprinted towards the holocaust. Wynn-Thomas, who was in charge at that time, issued his orders. First, each exit from the area on to the High Street was to be blocked. As soon as the blocking parties were in position an assault party would go in and drive the wreckers towards the stops.

This was a perfectly sound plan. Unfortunately it had been foreseen by the opposition. As soon as their scouts warned them of the police arrival they knocked off and made for the railway. This was no obstacle. Once they were over it, they scattered in different directions across the marshes.

The police, beating through the streets and clearing the way for the fire-tenders that were following them, encountered no opposition. The episode was started and finished inside ten minutes.

Brace met Wynn-Thomas at the far end of Bisset Street. They stood for some minutes, in silence, surveying the battlefield. The firemen, armed with chemical extinguishers, were putting out the last of the fires, whilst the owners of the vehicles searched cautiously to see what they could salvage.

"Another professional job," said Wynn-Thomas. "Quick in, quick out. No genuine feeling about it."

"What do you think's behind it?" said Brace. He had known his second-in-command long enough to ask his opinion.

Wynn-Thomas said, "Personally I'd be inclined to class all the things that have happened so far as what theatrical folk call 'ticklers'. That's to say, preliminary performances put on to excite the public and make sure that they roll up for the real first night."

"The first night being tomorrow."

"Correct."

"Well, we shall be in the front row of the stalls," said Brace. He didn't sound displeased at the idea.

229

23

By five o'clock that Monday morning the crowds were already collecting.

At seven o'clock the police started to divert the traffic. At nine o'clock, as the crowd grew even larger, further diversions were organised.

Two hundred yards of the pavement on either side of the court had been lined by a row of linked steel barriers. It was impossible to prevent people from using the pavement. There were owners of houses and shops who needed access. What the police had to do was to keep them moving. The first trouble occurred when a group of men, walking down the barricaded stretch of pavement, decided to stop directly opposite the court entrance.

No amount of 'Move along there, please', had any effect. A dozen policemen came down the pavement to try more direct action. The group was well organised. They linked arms and stood their ground. More policemen arrived. A van drove up and after a struggle the men were hustled into it. There were casualties on both sides. Everyone who was in a position to see what was happening bellowed abuse.

A small man had managed to secure a second-storey window-seat opposite the court-house. He shouted down, through a loud hailer, "Leave them alone. It's a free country. We've a right to see what's going on. Why are you trying to stop us? What are you hiding?"

The crowd roared its appreciation.

Michaelson said, "Awkward, him being on private premises, but if he goes on we shall have to have him out."

He had set up his own command post in the yard alongside the court building: two massive six-tonners, parked side by side. One was a communications vehicle which was in touch by radio and by line with the subsidiary posts which had been set up, one at each end of Reynolds Road and one at each of the traffic diversion points in Plumstead High Street. The other was a Public Order Surveillance vehicle, borrowed from the Home Office. It contained two television cameras and a 35 mm photographic system mounted on a periscope and backed up by a pair of video monitors.

"You can reckon that the media will be there in force," Michaelson said. "Most of the photographs they print are slanted. We've found it's useful to have a few unslanted ones to put alongside them."

At half past nine the people concerned in the court hearing started to arrive. This gave a fresh opportunity for the crowd to express its feelings. The five Pakistani boys escaped notice. They were driven along Maindy Road in an unmarked van and got into the court by a side entrance. Mr. Norrie disdained concealment. He walked from his house to court. As he passed down the road between the solid ranks of police he received a good deal of advice as to how he should conduct the proceedings. It seemed to amuse him. The loudest cheers greeted Abel Drummer. The loudest abuse was reserved for Qadir Diwaker, which he took as a compliment.

When Michaelson had raised the question of admission of the public, Mr. Norrie had said, "As long as it can do so, justice should always function in public. We will admit the first thirty who turn up. That should fill the public benches comfortably, without crowding."

"Suppose they interrupt the proceedings?"

"I'll deal with that. You keep things under control outside the court, Superintendent. Leave the interior to me."

The Clerk rapped with his gavel and said, "All Stand."

Mr. Norrie entered, bowed, and took his seat. A quick glance round the room had shown him nothing unexpected. The press reservation was, of course, overflowing and two extra benches had been inserted in front of the press box. The public area at the back was full, but not uncomfortably so. Mr. Norrie recognised no one in it. He thought that they were all strangers. He had been told that the lucky ones who had got in had been queuing since four o'clock that morning.

Directing his remarks to both press and public Mr. Norrie said, "Most of you will be aware of the disgraceful scenes which occurred when I was sitting previously in this matter. I should perhaps let you know that you were all photographed as you entered the court. That is so that any trouble-makers – I trust there will be none – can be identified and dealt with. A man who took a leading part in the disturbance last time has been charged. If he is found guilty, his sentence may not be a light one."

He allowed the last words to echo, for a moment, round the totally silent court. Then he leaned forward and said, "Mr. Leopold."

Crown Counsel rose, bowed, and said, "I appear in this case for the prosecution. Mr. Rumford is with me. My learned friend, Mr. Diwaker, appears for the defence of all five of the accused. The original charge was one of theft. The theft of explosive from a locked shed in the Old Royal Arsenal grounds. My first witnesses will be dealing with this. It would, however, be idle to pretend that the matter rests there and, as you will note, additional charges have now been added of arson and conspiracy to cause grievous bodily harm, with an alternative charge of manslaughter. These matters arise not from the theft itself, but from the use to which the stolen explosive was put. Later testimony will deal with this point."

The first witnesses, the officer commanding at the depot and his sergeant storeman, roused no excitement as they proved that a certain shed had contained a certain quantity of cordite on a certain day and now contained four pounds less. Diwaker asked only one question. He said, "The shed contained nothing but cordite?" The storeman assured him that this was correct. The next witness to be summoned, from the room in which all the witnesses were detained until they had given evidence, was Sapper Sunley. It was observed that as he made his way to the stand he avoided looking at any of the prisoners.

Leopold led him skilfully into his story. How he was persuaded to purloin the key of the powder shed – (it was noticed that he was not asked *who* persuaded him. Leopold had stringent instructions on this point) – how he met Salim Kahn and Javed Rahman, how they went to the shed and he unlocked it and took out four blue bags from a box of red, white and blue bags and handed them over and how he went back and replaced the key in the guard-hut and – that was all.

232

Mr. Leopold sat down. Qadir Diwaker stood up. He said, "I have reason to believe that what this witness says is, broadly speaking, true and I have no questions to ask him."

This was the last thing the press and the public had been expecting. They looked like children deprived of a promised treat.

Leopold said, "It is the contention of the prosecution that, having obtained this explosive, the accused then used it to construct an explosive device. This consisted of the explosive itself, confined into a metal container, possibly the cylinder of a hydraulic jack, a home-made detonator and an electric firing arrangement which depended on the use of an ordinary alarm clock. You have heard how they obtained the explosive. My next witness will deal with the second and third items."

The Manager of Petters and Mr. Lampeter of the clock shop each said their piece. Diwaker questioned neither of them. He seemed to have lost interest in the whole affair.

"I shall now endeavour," said Leopold, "to show why the accused, having armed themselves with this infernal machine, chose to place it in premises used as a meeting place by Edward and Robin Drummer and three of their friends. It is a question which, in the ordinary way, should have been put to the accused. It was, I understand, intended by their original advisers that Salim Kahn should have been called. It seems that their new advisers have altered this plan."

He looked at Diwaker, who smiled politely.

"There are, however, two people who are in a position to offer direct evidence of the hostility between those groups of boys. The father of two of the victims, Mr. Abel Drummer, and the Probation Officer in charge of their case. We felt that the latter was less personally involved and would be likely to speak with less prejudice and have decided to rely on his testimony. If the learned Magistrate would like to hear Mr. Drummer also, he is in court and available."

"I must leave it entirely to you, Mr. Leopold. It is your case."

"Very well. Call Mr. Leone."

Anthony had been sitting in the witness room, empty now except for himself and Major Webster. When he had taken the oath, Leopold said, "I should like to make it clear that this

233

witness did not volunteer to give evidence. He is here in response to a subpoena. Now, Mr. Leone, I understand that the leaders of what I might call these two gangs, Salim Kahn and Edward Drummer, were on probation to you as the result of a fight in Plumstead High Street."

Not all that long ago, thought Anthony. But separated by such a chain of events that it seemed almost to be an episode of prehistory. He answered Leopold's questions carefully, keeping to facts and avoiding opinions. The dog, the one-sided boxing match, the destruction of the Pakistani headquarters. When Leopold had finished, Diwaker stood up. He seemed uncertain how to begin. Then he said, "When you made your very gallant rescue, Mr. Leone, you first penetrated into the outer lobby, where you found Robin Drummer and dragged him clear. You then went back to see whether you could do more. You remember that? What was your impression, *before* you opened the inner door?"

"My impression was that I was standing in an oven."

"The heat was intense?"

"Almost over-powering."

"Thank you. Just one other point. It was part of your duty to talk to these boys?"

"Certainly."

"And this would give you a fair idea of their characters?"

"Some idea, yes."

"Very well. We've heard from you of the sort of things they did to each other. The sort of escapades that high-spirited boys might indulge in. But answer me this question, if you will. Do you think they would plan to kill each other?"

"No," said Anthony. "I don't."

When Leopold rose to re-examine, he phrased his question very carefully. He said, "Do you not agree, however, that someone who constructs and uses the sort of machine which has been described must be held responsible for any damage that it does?"

Anthony said, angrily, "That wasn't the question I was asked. I was asked if any of these boys would plan to kill. I said 'No'. I should have put it more strongly. I think it is totally incredible."

Having got the worst of that exchange Leopold was experienced enough to leave it alone. He said, "No more questions."

234

"In that case," said Mr. Norrie, looking at the clock, "it will be a convenient time to break. We can take the technical witnesses this afternoon. In the circumstances I have arranged with the police that anyone who wants to, may lunch in the police canteen. No one will therefore need to leave this building unless they wish."

Most of the members of the press and public showed distinct signs of relief at this suggestion. Only one man, at the back of the court, seemed to want to go. He slipped out, almost unnoticed, crossed Reynolds Road, was allowed through by the police cordon and disappeared up a side-street. A few minutes later he was talking to the small man who was still at his second-storey vantage point.

"Dull as ditchwater," he said. "The opposition aren't really putting up a fight. A couple of boffins to come after lunch, then it'll all be over."

"We can't have that," said the small man. "I've promised to keep the crowd happy until half past four. Don't want them drifting off."

He turned to the boy at his side who seemed to be acting as his adjutant.

"Which do you think is the weakest of the four posts they've got manned?"

"They're none of them exactly weak. I should think the one at the west end of Plumstead High Street would be the easiest to get at."

"Right. In an hour's time then. A quick rush. Knock out a few policemen. Then out again."

The boy nodded and took himself off.

"Might as well all have lunch," said the small man. "Who's got the sandwiches?"

At two o'clock the court reassembled and Major Webster took the stand. He did not look happy, but this was possibly the result of wife trouble.

"You are Arnold Webster, formerly a Major in the Royal Army Ordnance Corps, an Ammunition Technical Officer, now attached to the Metropolitan Police?"

"Correct."

"Would you explain to the court what your job involves?"

"If there is a report of a suspect explosive device, I or one of my colleagues examines it and attempts to deal with it."

"You defuse it?"

"Not always, sir. If we decide it can be moved, we remove it to where it can do no harm and demolish it. Or we might have to clear the area and demolish it on the spot. Of course, if we can render it harmless we do so."

"And if you are called after the explosion has taken place?"

"Then we examine the location to see whether we can obtain any evidence as to what sort of device it was and, possibly, to deduce from this who had been responsible."

"And that is what you did here?"

"That is correct. It was difficult, in this case, because of the almost total destruction. But I did recover a portion of thick steel which could have been part of a hydraulic jack. I also found a heavy torch battery. It had been blown by the explosion into the far corner of the room and was comparatively undamaged. There were fragments of wire still attached to each terminal. The only other item which might have been significant was a twisted scrap of tin."

Leopold said, "These are exhibits W 1–3 in this case, sir. And can be seen by you if you wish."

"Thank you. I'll look at them afterwards."

"We have heard a suggestion, Major, that the accused may have stolen a cheap alarm clock. Could this metal have been part of it?"

"Yes. It could have been."

"Now, as to the general condition of the site. Could I ask you about that?"

"As I said, the destruction was considerable. Most of the breeze-block walls were standing, but everything else had been carried away. All the woodwork had been burned to ashes by the fire which followed the explosion."

It was clear that Major Webster had very little more to tell them.

Leopold chose his final question carefully. He said, "Speaking as an expert, is it your view that the destruction you have described could have been caused by the detonation of four pounds of compacted cordite?"

"Yes, it is."

Diwaker was on his feet. No sign, now, of lethargy. He leaned forward, resting his hands on the rail in front of him and said,

"Major Webster, you have just given us your opinion 'as an expert'. May I ask you, an expert in *what?*"

"In dealing with explosive devices and their effects."

"On the first point, we must agree. Your exploits in dealing with unexploded bombs have been amply applauded in the press."

Trying to make him lose his temper, thought Leopold. Too old a hand to fall for that, I hope.

Since this was not a question, the Major did not feel obliged to answer it. Diwaker said, "On the second point, however, the effect of explosives, what are your qualifications for dealing with that?"

"After qualifying as an ATO I spent a year at the Central Ammunition Depot at Bramley, followed by a practical course at Trawsfynydd in North Wales. I also attended the short course at the Royal Military College of Science."

"That was the six month's young officers' course?"

"Yes."

"Not the three year degree course?"

"No."

"I am not attempting, Major, to depreciate your expertise." Diwaker showed his teeth in a token smile. "Merely to indicate the precise field in which it lay. Which was the practical matter of dealing with bombs. Yes? Not theoretical considerations of the thermo-dynamic properties of explosives."

"We had to consider such points, from time to time."

"We shall find out about that," said Diwaker smoothly.

He turned over a page in the file which he had on the desk in front of him. It was a thick file, with a Cambridge blue cover. Anthony noticed that Leopold and Mr. Norrie appeared to have similar files.

"May we now turn to the evidence you gave at the inquest? It seems that your first view was that the explosion was caused by open-cast gelignite. What is that, precisely?"

"Nitro-glycerine and nitro-cotton. Possibly some ammonium nitrate as well."

"A powerful, high-density explosive."

"Yes."

"Very useful, therefore, for quarry work."

"Certainly."

"However, you later abandoned the idea of gelignite and

adopted the view that the explosive concerned might have been cordite. Can you tell us something about that?"

"Cordite is also based on nitro-glycerine. Its other constituent is largely gun cotton, with some mineral jelly."

"A considerably less powerful, less easily activated explosive?"

"To some degree, yes."

"Much safer to handle. But – " here Diwaker leaned forward a little, "very much more difficult to detonate, yes?"

"Somewhat more difficult. I couldn't go any further than that."

"Could you not perhaps, go a little further if I tell you that I shall be adducing evidence – from a ranking expert – who will tell us that a single detonator in four pounds of cordite would probably not detonate it at all. That it would blow the container to pieces and make a mess, but nothing more."

"I have given you my conclusion."

"Then may we examine the basis on which you came to that conclusion? What is the detonation speed of gelignite?"

"I don't carry all these figures in my head."

"You find the question difficult? Let us take a somewhat simpler point then. What is the direction of the explosive waves of gelignite?"

"More or less all round."

Diwaker selected a book from the pile on his desk and opened it at the place he had marked. He said, "In this work on blasting practice I see it is stated that the shock waves generated by gelignite travel mainly in a lateral direction. It is this that makes it particularly useful in quarrying. Well?"

"Mainly lateral, perhaps."

"Not all round, then?"

"I may have used the expression loosely."

"I see. You spoke loosely. Just so. Now, when you examined the site, Major, did you examine the floor underneath the spot where the explosion is presumed to have taken place and the walls on either side of it?"

"Certainly."

"There was nothing in your report about them."

"There was nothing to report."

This answer seemed to please Diwaker more than it did Leopold, who was frowning.

"Now you mentioned that the walls, being breeze-block, had largely survived. This would include the wall between the inner and the outer room?"

"Yes."

"If the explosion, as we were told, set fire to some petrol in the inner room, did it occur to you as significant that Mr. Leone, who was there within a minute, should have found the heat in the *outer* room – I use his own word – over-powering?"

"Not particularly, no."

"Major, are you not doing what no scientist should ever do, trying to fit the facts to your theory rather than the theory to the facts?"

"I don't think so."

"You really wish the court to believe that this massive explosion of force and heat was caused by four pounds of comparatively inert explosive, a home-made detonator and an alarm clock?"

"It's a possible explanation."

"Possible, Major, possible. But is it the truth? You showed us a scrap of metal. You say it could have come from an alarm clock. Could it not equally have come from a Thermos flask, a tin of beans, or a canary cage?"

Without waiting for an answer, Diwaker resumed his seat.

Leopold did not re-examine. He was reading the report in the Cambridge blue cover. Mr. Norrie said, "Is that your last witness, Mr. Leopold?"

Without looking up from his reading Leopold grunted out what sounded like agreement. Mr. Norrie said, "Very well, Mr. Diwaker."

"I have only one witness, sir. I think that when you have heard him you will agree that there is no case to go forward on the second and third charges."

As Professor Meiklejohn ambled into the court, took his stand in the witness box and adjusted his glasses, another man slipped out of the back of the court. The small man in the upstairs window listened to him with interest. He said, "That's lovely. Spread the news that the bloody lawyers may be wangling the Pakis off. Say we're planning an assault on the court."

239

His young adjutant looked doubtful. He said, "I don't think they'll fancy that. The old Bill are getting a bit rough. There've been a lot of heads broken on both sides."

"I didn't say we're going to assault the court. I said we were *planning* it. Get them massing at either end of the street." As the boy turned to go, he said, "You can spread the word, privately this time, that we start shutting up shop at half past four. Our lads should all be clear by five. Understood?"

In the court room, Diwaker had introduced his witness, rolling the alphabet of his distinctions lusciously round his tongue. Then he said, "My learned friend, Mr. Leopold, and you, sir, have a report produced by this witness. To save time, I intend to adopt it as part of his evidence."

"I can't agree to that," said Leopold.

"You feel that it would be improper?" said Mr. Norrie.

"Most improper, sir. To start with, I have hardly had time to read it. Also, as you may be aware, the Lord Chief Justice has recently laid down strict lines on the admissibility of written evidence when the writer is available as a witness. Allow me to refer you to the case of the Romford Urban District Council against Walliker – "

Professor Meiklejohn gazed mildly round the court. With his prim mouth, his scholarly half-moon glasses and his domed forehead topped with untidy grey hair, he personified the scientist of tradition; the absent-minded boffin, lost in abstract thought, blind to the realities of life. Nothing could have been further from the truth. He was a poet. A man who was delighted by the significance and the contradictions of the world.

He found the present situation enchanting. The noise of the crowd outside, rumbling and grumbling and occasionally bursting into spurts of sound, like an angry sea beating against the rocks; in the centre, a calm temple of justice, with its arguments and its precedents and its legalistic disputes.

One of the policemen touched Anthony on the arm. He said, "Is that right, you've got a St John's Ambulance certificate?"

"Yes."

"The Super wondered if you'd come along and lend a hand?"

Anthony said, "Of course." He was anxious to learn what evidence the Professor was going to produce, but Diwaker had opened a law book and it looked as though the argument about the admissibility of the report was likely to take some time.

What had been the witness room was now a first-aid centre and half a dozen of the walking wounded were sitting round smoking and waiting for damage to be attended to. From the way Sergeant Blascoe was holding his arm Anthony diagnosed a broken collar bone. The long-haired Sergeant Ames had a black eye and had lost some teeth in this, his first experience of physical combat. He was talking to Sergeant Montgomery, who had been kneed in the groin and kicked in the ribs, but had managed to remain cheerful. He said, "'Ullo, Mr. Leone. Come to patch us up?"

"Do what I can," said Anthony. "Better take your jacket and shirt off."

As he was undressing, Montgomery said, "I wish now they'd let me stick to my job up at Scotland Dock. But no such luck. It was all hands to the pumps down here. Even the PLA boys. So what I did, I went up there very early this morning, before the crowd started to thicken up, and handed over my box of tricks to Bunny Larwood – he's the Dock Superintendent."

Anthony said, almost choking, "*Are you telling me that your regular job was handling the ACID detector at Scotland Dock?*"

"That's right. It isn't all that hard to use. If a ship turns up today Bunny should be able to cope."

"And he'll be there on his own?"

"Well, he lives there, see. The point is, no one else can get to him until this crowd makes off."

"I'm sorry," said Anthony. "Someone else will have to look after you."

"Something wrong?"

He left the room without stopping to reply. Sergeant Montgomery sat staring after him. He was trying to work out why anything he had said should have upset the Probation Officer so much.

In the passage outside, Anthony ran into Wynn-Thomas. He said, trying to control his voice, "I most urgently need to telephone."

241

"Well," said Wynn-Thomas, "if it's urgent, why don't you use the Super's phone? He's not in his office at the moment."

Mowatt had decided that, on that critical afternoon, Great Peter Street would be nearer the storm centre than St James's Park. He found a badly worried Bearstead. Settling himself in a chair he said, in his placid voice, "Something wrong, Bruno?"

"To tell you the truth," said Bearstead, "I'm beginning to wonder if we're being made fools of."

"How? Why?"

"It's the old conjuror's ploy. Making the audience watch his right hand, whilst it's his left hand that's doing the dirty work. I'm beginning to wonder whether the *Marie-Louise* has got anything to do with the IRA plans at all."

"What makes you think that?"

"They're not fools. They must know that we've heard about that missing aeroplane bomb and will deduce that the explosive is coming over from Belgium."

"We've been through all that," said Mowatt patiently. "Their plan is to sling the stuff ashore at some isolated wharf and have it whisked away inland. Every's so sure about it that he's been having nightmares. He sees the ship sliding up, in the dusk, unloading in a matter of minutes – seconds even."

"Exactly," said Bearstead. "Then why is the *Marie-Louise* coming up in broad daylight?"

Mowatt stared at him.

"She cleared Customs at ten o'clock. Not the regular captain, incidentally. She'll be about half an hour below Scotland Dock at this moment and at the Royals, if that's where she's heading, by four o'clock."

Before Mowatt could say anything the green telephone, which was his direct line, rang. Bearstead listened for a moment, passing the extension to Mowatt and switching on the tape recorder.

Anthony tried to speak slowly and calmly. It took him two full minutes to get his message across. Almost before he had finished, Bearstead was dialling. He found Groener in his office. He said, "You've got a link to Colonel Every's car. Would you please call him back to your place, now. As fast as possible."

242

It took Bearstead only one minute to repeat what Anthony had taken two to tell him. There was no need to embroider it. He said, "As soon as the Colonel's on his way back, you can explain what's happened and what he's got to do. He'll have to move fast."

"I'll have a boat ready," said Groener.

"To put the matter quite simply," said Every, "we've been had. All our careful defences have been put in the wrong place."

He was sitting with Groener in the forward cabin of RDB 9, the newest of the Thames Division launches. He tried to sound calm.

"We know, now, that the *Marie-Louise* will unload at Scotland Dock." He looked at his watch. "By my reckoning they're about fifteen minutes below it at this moment. We'd always supposed, you see, that if they used a dock, any explosive they tried to land would inevitably be detected and that the police and the PLA would be able to detain the cargo. Neither of those suppositions is correct. The officer who would normally use the ACID detector at Scotland Dock is under such a heavy obligation to the assignee of the cargo that he would probably have faked the examination and let the cargo through. But the opposition weren't relying only on this. They like two strings to their bow. They have so organised things that, as it happens, there are no policemen there at all *and nothing on wheels can get near the place.*"

He demonstrated on the map spread in front of them. "There's only the one road running inland from the dock, through Plumstead Marshes, coming out at Plumstead station – where there's a milling mob that you couldn't get through with a Sherman tank."

"If no one could get through, how are they going to get the stuff out?"

"I expect they'll have thought of that," said Every grimly. "They seem to have thought of everything else."

"In that case, it might be a good idea to get to Scotland Dock first. If we can."

The boat seemed to hear him and gave a leap forward, its scarlet bow coming clear out of the water. They were headed directly downstream, keeping to the centre of the fairway.

243

"If we hit anything at this speed," said Groener, "we'll both go under." The horn snarled and a launch four hundred yards ahead which had started to turn across their bows hurriedly changed its mind.

As they swung round the butt end of the Isle of Dogs, Groener was speaking to the Woolwich Control Zone. He was asking permission to pass through the Thames Barrier without reducing speed. After a few exchanges he said, "Right. They're leaving Span B open for us and keeping everyone else clear."

When they turned up Blackwall Reach they were heading due north and the east wind picked up their bow wave and whipped it like a sheet across the windscreen. Both wipers, working overtime, could only clear it in flashes.

"It'll be better when we turn the corner. Two miles to go. Say five minutes to the dock. Is there some way we can get up to it, Angus?"

The bearded engineer, a Scotsman who had not opened his mouth so far, said, "Aye. There's a run of steps at the west side of the dock. It comes up alongside the Arsenal wall. There's a path from there to the entrance."

"What do we do when we get there?" said Groener. "We're not what you might call a massive force. Just Angus, you and me."

"Have you got guns?"

"I have. He hasn't."

"In that case, two will be as useful as three. We'll leave Angus to look after the boat and you come up with me."

"What are we going to do?"

"Play for time. 'C' Troop are not far off. They're at the Southern Outfall. I got through to them before I left the car. Their quickest way is along the river-bank, on foot. Which means that they can pick up men from the five observation posts as they come."

"It's a rough road," said Angus. "'Twill take them all of half an hour."

"Now don't start depressing us," said Groener. "I was just beginning to think we were winning."

They could see the dock. The *Marie-Louise* was coming in.

Scotland Dock had acquired its name in the nineteenth century, when it was a depot for ponies coming south from

Scotland to be sold into slavery in the Kentish coal-mines. The rings to which the animals had been fastened could still be seen. It ranked as a 'timber dock', since it possessed no cranes of its own. All the work was done by the ship's own gear.

The *Marie Louise* had already started unloading.

There were two men on the dockside, thickset men with flat expressionless faces. One had slicked down black hair. The other, who seemed to be directing operations, was bald. Tinus Meagher would have recognised both of them.

The ship's crane swung the heavy packing case off the ship and on to a trolley. Three other men came ashore and manhandled the trolley to the transit shed. Blackhair and Baldy followed it in. It was placed on the long wooden bench, and pushed along to the far end where a small bespectacled man was standing.

Baldy, who spoke good English ornamented with Flemish gutturals, said, "We ordered a lorry. It is here?"

"Yes."

"Then we will get the stuff on."

"It will have to be examined first."

"Who says?"

The words echoed round the emptiness of the shed.

"I'm the Docks Superintendent. I have the apparatus here."

"You can stuff your apparatus."

The other three men had come into the shed. One of them was the gorilla who had scared Tinus. The others looked equally formidable.

Baldy said, "There's no one within a mile of this place so don't start throwing your weight about, little man. Right?"

"Wrong," said Every.

"He and Groener had positioned themselves at the far end of the shed, with their backs to the wall where there was a stack of crates awaiting collection. He guessed that all of the men from the ship would be armed and he would only start a fire fight if he had to. Baldy, he felt certain, was one of the men who had tortured and killed his stepson. He would shoot him first. Groener might be able to knock out the black-haired man, after which they would dive down behind the packing cases and hope to hold them off until 'C' Troop arrived.

Baldy had swung round. He stared at Every and Groener for a long moment, as though summing up their potential opposition. Then he said, "Two of you? Two to five is long odds."

Every came out, perched himself on the edge of one of the packing cases and crossed his legs. Groener stayed where he was, with his legs apart and a scowl on his face. He was angry at the liberties being taken with his river and very ready to fight.

"Just what do you propose to do?" said Every.

"No time to waste. Either you stand aside or we shoot your legs off and get on with the job."

"And then?"

"We push off."

"The *Marie-Louise* won't move until we say so."

"Why not?"

"Because the lock gates are operated by electricity and the power has been cut off."

"Well, well," said Baldy. He walked across and pressed one of the wall switches. No light came on. "So it has." He was looking at Blackhair. They seemed amused, not alarmed.

"It doesn't worry you?"

"Why should it? We've finished with the ship. You can keep it. You'll find the skipper locked in his cabin. And one of the sailors, who got naughty, has got a bullet in his leg."

Of course, thought Every. He was being stupid. Arrangements to get the men home would have been part of the bargain. They'd be out of the country, by air, before anything could be done to stop them. Where the hell were 'C' Troop? Surely to God they could cover three miles in twenty-five minutes, even cross-country? That was the sort of thing they'd been trained to do. Come on, come on.

He said, "That vehicle we found outside. I gather its job is to take the stuff away. And, maybe, give you and your friends a lift to somewhere where you can catch a train."

"Correct. And before we go, we shall make quite sure that you are not in a position to interfere. That may not be so pleasant." He smiled at the black-haired man who said, "We could nail them to the table." This was in French, understood by Every and Groener, but not, fortunately, by Larwood.

Every realised that he had only one card left. He played it reluctantly, since he knew what it would provoke. He said, "No doubt the driver has been well paid and will do what you tell

246

him. There's one snag. The vehicle is immobilised. We've confiscated a vital part of it."

For the first time Baldy looked really ugly. A gun had appeared in his hand. He said, "Then you'll give it back. Now. Quickly. Which of you has it?" He turned on Larwood. "Have you got it?"

"No."

"Who has? Come on. Where would you like the first bullet? In your knee or your ankle?"

Larwood jerked his head at Every. "It's in his pocket."

"Right." He swung round on Every. "Hand it over. And what's the joke?"

Every had heard the crunch of boots outside. He said, "You mentioned that two to five was poor odds. What about five to fifteen?"

This was an underestimate. Captain Musgrave had brought eighteen men with him. He said, "Sorry we were so long, sir. Corporal English fell into a drainage ditch and had to be pulled out. What do you want done with this crowd?"

It was clear there was not going to be a fight. Baldy was a realist. The gorilla made a dash for the door at the back. A neat group from a Hechler-Koch machine pistol, which reached the door ahead of him, discouraged him. He came back.

Every said, "We'll split the party. This is Superintendent Groener of Thames Division. He'll hold these men, with your help, until reinforcements arrive. I take it a charge of threatening a port official with firearms will be enough for the moment?"

"More than enough," said Groener.

"This crate will have to be looked after. Have you got a lock-up store?"

Larwood nodded. His face was grey and covered with sweat. He said, "Sorry. Yes, there's the old In-bond Store."

"Please show these men where it is. Handle that crate carefully. And put a guard on the door, David. Next thing, I'll need six of you." He spotted Sergeant Whitaker, whose ankle had, somehow, stood up to the cross-country run. "You've been looking for a fight, Sergeant. If you'll pick five others and come with me, I'll find you one."

The vehicle outside was one of the new four-wheel-drive

Caravelle Synchros. It had steel-linked chains on all four wheels. The driver, a young West Indian, was dozing in the cab with the heating and the wireless full on. When Every opened the door, he opened his eyes.

"Come on out, Sambo. I've got new orders for you."

"I'm not Sambo," said the driver with dignity. "I'm Mr. Delroy. And who are you? First, you abstracticate a vital component of my vehicle. Now you start giving me orders."

"I thought it was time you changed sides."

The driver looked at the grim bunch behind Every and said, "OK, I've changed sides."

"Good boy. Your new orders are dead simple. Go where you were told to go. You'll have a different cargo, that's all. Jump in, chaps. I'll ride in front."

Every had never actually seen a Caravelle Synchro, but he knew that the normal drive on one set of wheels was supplemented by a drive on the other set as soon as the going became slippery. This and the chains on the wheels, warned him that they were going across country.

Half a mile down the road they swung left on to something which was certainly not a road and hardly a track. The entrance was criss-crossed with the tyre marks of some vehicle that had tried to turn into it and had either backed, or been towed out.

"This way for cows and horses," said the West Indian cheerfully. He was handling the Caravelle like a craftsman, meticulous and careless at the same time. And he was more relaxed than Every, who had his heart in his mouth every time they hit a soft place.

He said, "What happens when – Ouch. I thought we were stuck then."

"Don't you fret, Colonel. This baby, she'll skate over cobwebs."

"What happens when we hit the road?"

"What we do then is we keep right clear of all the folk what's milling around. Cross Wynns Common and Plumstead Park. Then round the outside of Woolwich Common. There's a house up at the top, with a big garden full of statoos. You know it, maybe?"

"Yes," said Every softly. "I know it. What were you to do when you got there?"

248

"Stop by the gate in the side road and sound off with my horn. Two short – one long."

"Pull up just where you were told to," said Every. "But you needn't bother about sounding your horn. We'll announce ourselves."

"I gather," said Professor Meiklejohn with a smile, "that the upshot of your deliberations is that I may not read out this report. But since I wrote it very recently and have an excellent memory, I am quite prepared to dispense with it. The first question which arose from an examination of the site was the nature of the explosive used."

"So far we have two candidates," said Diwaker. "Cordite and open-cast gelignite."

"Yes. Well, it certainly wasn't cordite. In the circumstances in which I understand it was used, it would have exploded, but it is most unlikely to have detonated. And it would not have caused anything like the damage. It would have made a mess. Nothing more. Added to which it would not have produced the immediate and intense heat which was noted."

"Then what about open-cast gelignite?"

"More plausible, certainly. But there are two things against it. It has a low-velocity detonation speed of 3,000 metres per second and its explosive wave is lateral. In this case the main force of the explosion was vertical. Imagine the device was on a table in the centre of the room. The tiles underneath were shattered and even the cement sub-base was cracked. Also, although it is a hotter explosive than cordite, I thought it unlikely that it could have generated such intense heat of its own accord."

"Did you come to a conclusion then as to what the explosive substance was?"

"Oh yes. I don't think there's much doubt about that. I took some samples of plaster from the wall on either side and submitted them to thin-layer chromatography. As I expect you know – " he turned courteously to Mr. Norrie, "this is a process which breaks down a sample into its constituent parts."

"I did know that much," said Mr. Norrie. "But go slowly, I'm trying to get this down."

"Certainly. Apart from the plaster and paint, a number of substances were present. First, cyclotrimethylene trinitramine,

249

otherwise known as Research Department Explosive, or RDX. Secondly, trinitrotoluene or TNT. Neither of these would be found in open-cast gelignite. But it was the third substance which was really interesting. Aluminium. Finely powdered aluminium. This burns at such a high temperature that it causes what is known as an exothermic reaction. The gases given off by the explosion expand and generate further heat."

"And your conclusion from this?"

"Almost certainly, the explosive was torpex."

The word hung in the air. People in court started to look at each other and then switched their eyes to the accused.

If what this old man was saying was right, and he certainly seemed to know his stuff, was it possible, was it even probable that the accused were innocent? Innocent, anyway, of the more serious charges.

Mr. Norrie said, "Is torpex obtainable in this country?"

"Only through official channels, sir. Being incendiary it is largely used for aeroplane bombs. Most of the supplies are held by factories in France and Belgium."

There was a long pause. It was observed that Diwaker was still on his feet. He said, "That is our evidence, sir, as to the type of explosive. Professor Meiklejohn has some additional points on the method of detonation which, though not strictly relevant to the charges, will I think be found of interest."

"Please," said Mr. Norrie.

"I mentioned," said the Professor, "that chromatographic analysis threw up a number of substances which were present in the explosive device. One of these I found very puzzling. It was a quantity of mercury."

Everyone was hanging on his words now. What other rabbits was this astonishing old creature going to pull out of the hat?

"A very possible explanation only occurred to me when I was extracting plaster from the wall. I found something which had been impacted into it by the force of the detonation."

"Exhibit IM5," said Diwaker.

Norrie said, "Might I see it, please?"

Exhibit IM5 was extracted from its plastic envelope and handed up. Mr. Norrie said, "This looks to me like the back-plate of a very small gold wrist-watch. What did you make of it?"

"The same as you, sir. It think it is undoubtedly part of a wrist-watch. The most likely explanation is that there was a second detonator. The main one would be in full view: the torch battery which Major Webster discovered, the alarm clock and the home-made detonator. All that stuff. The secondary one would have been concealed. It was very much smaller. A tiny wrist-watch and an equally tiny mercury battery. The sort of thing which is used in a deaf-aid."

"And what would be the object of it?"

"As to that, I can offer no firm opinion, sir. But it occurs to me that if Edward Drummer and his friends thought that the explosion would not take place for, say, eight hours, they could have intended to place the device in the headquarters of their Pakistani rivals. What they would not have known was that, in fact, it was timed, *by this secondary device*, to go off almost immediately. I can only offer this as a suggestion."

Everyone in the court, except Anthony, had their eyes on the Professor as he said this. Anthony was looking at Abel Drummer. Registered successively on his face were surprise, deep relief and blazing anger. He saw him edge his way towards the exit and shoulder his way out. No one thought of stopping him. No one except Anthony really noticed him. All the drama was with the Professor in the witness-box.

The Caravelle drew up short of the west wall of Arthur Drayling's garden and Every dismounted. They could hear the roar of the crowd some way ahead of them, but the road was deserted.

"Two of you at the back," he said. "Two round in front of the house and keep your heads down. If anyone comes out running, shoot *at once*. Understood? Sergeant Whitaker and Baylis with me."

He climbed the low garden wall and moved forward, dodging among the marble figures. His two men had spread wide on either side of him. The sky was already overcast and darkening. He thought that snow was coming.

Maybe the best way into the house would be to circle it, find the kitchen quarters and open a window. He was under no illusions as to the danger of what he was doing. Liam had killed at least three policemen in direct confrontation.

Then he saw that the front door was open. It might be a trap, but it offered an unexpected alternative. As he was thinking about this he heard two shots. He had no idea what was happening, but it was a diversion and must not be wasted. He charged through the door and down the passage. Baylis remained outside; Whitaker followed him, crouching.

Every kicked open the drawing-room door and jumped inside. The room stank of powder. Abel Drummer was still holding the shotgun. With one barrel he had killed Arthur Drayling. With the other he had blasted the man who called himself Liam and whose real name was Stefan Slowaki.

Stefan said, speaking slowly, the words bubbling out of his mouth, "Late as usual, Colonel. It took a fucking amateur to show you how to do it."

Every said nothing. The man was dying.

24

"He said, 'an amateur'," said Every to Bearstead. "And, by God, he was right. A professional would have made a cautious approach and probably got shot in the process. Drummer walked straight in and killed them both."

"Has he explained why?"

"Certainly. He was only too glad to talk. He regarded them as the murderers of his son. His boys had got wind of the Pakis stealing the army cordite and were determined to get in first. Neither side wanted to kill the other, you understand. Just to bust up their headquarters. Ted knew his father would help. What he didn't know was that for all his skite about his RE expertise, he was pretty rusty on detonators and timing devices. However, Arthur Drayling had introduced him to a man who seemed to know it all."

"Slowaki, otherwise Liam."

"Otherwise a dealer in goldfish, otherwise half a dozen other things. I know he had a supply of torpex, because he used some of it to try to blow my hand off. He built the bomb for Drummer and showed him how the alarm clock could be set to detonate it after an eight-hour interval. What he didn't mention, of course, was that there was a second device which would set it off one hour after the first one was started."

"Guessing that the boys would take it to their own headquarters and sit round admiring it while they planned to plant it on the opposition later that evening."

"Yes."

"And that it would blow them all to shreds."

"Yes. And that the Pakis would at once be suspected. Drayling had told him all about the feud. And that there would be an unholy row, which he could use very nicely, since it was bound to escalate when committal proceedings came on. All he had to do was time the arrival of the ship for that particular afternoon. He reckoned the authorities would have their hands full. He wasn't to know that they'd take away all the police from Scotland Dock. That was a piece of good luck."

"Or that Sergeant Montgomery would talk to Leone. That was bad luck."

"At the last moment," said Every, "the very last moment. I still sweat when I think of it."

"Another amateur to the rescue of the professionals," said Bearstead. "I make the final score – Gentlemen two. Players nil."

"What will they do now?" said Sandra.

Anthony said, "Norrie adjourned the hearing. He couldn't really do anything else. My guess is that the charges of arson and manslaughter will be withdrawn. Unless the Crown can find a bigger expert than Professor Meiklejohn."

"They'll have their work cut out."

"Agreed. But that leaves the admitted offence of stealing the cordite. The trouble there is that the prosecution had to give Sunley an indemnity to secure his evidence, which will make it difficult for them to get too rough with the other two concerned. They might even get away with being bound over."

"They won't get away with anything," said Sandra. "People are already beginning to say that the whole thing was a legal wangle. They'll probably be lynched."

"That's what their grandmother thinks. She's planning to take the Kahns and the Rahmans back to Pakistan."

"What will they do with Drummer?"

"Difficult. Liam was armed, so if he'd just shot him he might have pleaded self-defence. Drayling's different. The charge must be murder. It doesn't seem to worry Drummer. If there'd been a third barrel to his shot-gun I think he'd have blown his own head off."

"What a mess," said Sandra. "What a mess. What a mess. Oh, and I knew there was something I had to tell you. Simon Leibovitz has pushed off again."